ON TRACK TO MURDER

Married at sixteen to a man over thirty years her senior, ten years on Larissa Barton begins to question the decision she made, especially when she discovers that Miles is cheating on her. All the same, she is shocked when Miles is the one to ask for a divorce. After leaving him, Larissa returns to her childhood home; she must rebuild her life with new friends. But Miles is jealous of his wife's new-found happiness, and he begins to use his power and influence to meddle in the lives of the people she loves . . .

Books by Heather Graves
Published by The House of Ulverscroft:

FLYING COLOURS
RED FOR DANGER
STARSHINE BLUE
EMERALD GREEN
INDIGO NIGHTS

HEATHER GRAVES

ON TRACK TO MURDER

Complete and Unabridged

ULVERSCROFT
Leicester

First published in Great Britain in 2012 by
Robert Hale Limited
London

First Large Print Edition
published 2013
Robert Hale Limited
London

A catalogue record for this book is available
from the British Library.

ISBN 978–1–4448–1714–0

Published by
F. A. Thorpe (Publishing)
Anstey, Leicestershire

Set by Words & Graphics Ltd.
Anstey, Leicestershire
Printed and bound in Great Britain by
T. J. International Ltd., Padstow, Cornwall

This book is printed on acid-free paper

Prologue

'You listenin' to me, Riordan?' Aware that he didn't have the lad's full attention, William Willett poked the young jockey in the chest, emphasizing his words. 'Don't make me sorry I let you take this ride.'

'No, boss. I got ya.' Reluctantly, Johnnie dragged his mind back to the matter in hand, trying to ignore the mini-skirted teenagers who were hooting and waving at him, leaning over the fence. Mounting-yard groupies, his brother called them, warning him not to take too much notice of them. But these girls were pretty and Johnnie was only human; he couldn't help being flattered by their blatant attempts at flirtation. Turning his back on them, he forced himself to listen to what the trainer was saying.

'I'm not expecting a win today. Roxy's Robin is young and fairly untried. We're bringing him out today just to get used to the course and the distance — '

'But he's more than ready, boss.' Johnnie felt disappointed at the turn the conversation was taking. 'Felt like a ball o' muscle at track work. Look at him now — ears pricked, calm and interested. Crowd doesn't bother him, either.'

'An' you listen to me.' Willett glared at the lad. 'I don't want you showin' off for those girlies. Just take it easy with him today.'

'OK. I get it. Keep your hair on.'

The groom brought Roxy's Robin around for Johnnie to mount and Willett gave him a leg up into the saddle. As he did so a fat brown envelope fell out of the trainer's inside pocket, hitting the ground with a smack. Willett snatched it up but not before Johnnie had seen that it contained a very large number of banknotes.

'Wow! That's a lot of dosh even for you, boss!' The words were out before he could think better of them.

Willett glared up at him, tucking the envelope back in his jacket. 'You seen nothin' if you know what's good for you,' he growled.

'None of my business. I get it.' Daunted by the older man's grim expression, Johnnie shrugged, urging the horse to move out on to the track, happy to be leaving the disagreeable trainer behind. He knew that large amounts of money could change hands on the racecourse but it meant little to him. Still only halfway through his apprenticeship, he hadn't seen much of big money himself.

All the same, he was smart enough to know

when he had a good horse under him. After leaving the mounting yard and heading out on to the track, he tested the animal's willingness on the way to the gates. It was a hot January afternoon and most of the competition seemed to be sweating up, unhappy with the stifling weather and dancing sideways on the hard ground, not looking forward to racing. Not so Roxy's Robin, who loped along easily, tempting Johnnie to ignore the trainer's explicit instructions and think about winning. He would have to make certain he did, though; Willett would be just as mad if he managed to lose after all and take second or third place. It wasn't a major race day but this was the feature race and the money was good — they would have to be pleased with him. Wouldn't they? Surely it was too good an opportunity to miss.

Ignoring Willett's orders not to push the horse, to let him take it easy this time around and get used to the track, Johnnie decided to follow his instincts and race Roxy's Robin to win. He grinned at the barrier attendant who was leading the horse into his appointed place.

'Looking good, Johnno!' The lad smiled up at him. 'And ready to win. If he can take this one out, he'll be at short odds on his next race.'

If Johnnie had only listened he might have understood what the boss really wanted and acted differently, but his judgement was clouded by his desire to win. He could taste victory already, anticipating the roar of the crowd as he flew past the winning post, many lengths in front of everyone else.

Moments later, they were off. It was quite a large field and, instead of allowing the other runners to crowd in front and behind him as he'd been instructed, letting them box him in, Johnnie kept his horse back at the rear of the field, waiting for an opportunity to sneak through on the inside as the others tired, or else charge around them on the outside if they didn't leave him enough room. Roxy's Robin was a good horse with plenty of spring in his step and intelligent enough to have the will to win. The race wasn't long and, as most of the field dropped away from the fence, tiring and beginning to wilt in the heat, Johnnie seized the chance to come through on the inside and overtake them, a clear winner by several lengths. Although he was by no means a hot favourite, Roxy's Robin had looked good enough to be well backed and, returning to scale, Johnnie Riordan saluted the crowd, acknowledging their congratulations as he rode in to take his place in the winner's enclosure.

His triumph lasted just until Robin's trainer caught up with him. William Willett was neither smiling nor red with rage as John might have expected. Instead, he looked more like a dead man, all colour gone from his face as if he'd been drained by a vampire. White to the lips, he was breathless and looked ready to faint.

'So, Riordan. What was all that about?' he managed to gasp at last. 'Didn't you hear me? I told you not to push Robin today. What was it that you didn't understand?'

'But he felt so good, Mr Willett. Soon as I got him out there, I felt sure he could win.'

'You're not paid to think, you young fool, but to follow instructions. I suppose you realize all hell's going to break loose over this?'

'Don't see why.' Johnnie was truculent now, smarting at the lack of praise for his achievement. 'I gave you a respectable win. You an' the city gent.'

'Aw, don't speak to me about *him*.' If it were possible Willett turned a shade paler. 'Get out of my sight. An' don't be surprised if you hear more of this.'

'Sorry, boss.' The adrenaline was leaking away now and Johnnie was beginning to realize that ignoring specific instructions might have unpleasant consequences that he hadn't foreseen.

His older brother, David, was waiting for him when he reached the jockey's changing room, having finished his own rides for the day.

'Well done.' He gave Johnnie a quick, brotherly hug. 'Your first city winner. But what's up?' He caught sight of the younger lad's less than happy expression. 'You should be over the moon.'

'I was — until I saw Willett. I didn't follow his instructions so he isn't best pleased.'

'Oh?'

Briefly, Johnnie described how he had been told to keep a low profile and lose the race.

'Ah.' David's smile faded. 'Up to their old tricks, are they? Willett and his shonky pals. Holding the horse back so that next time he races he'll be at long odds. Dragging you into it this time.'

'Into what?'

David shook his head, smiling ruefully. 'Sometimes, I think you're too honest for this game, Bro. Haven't you heard of jockeys and trainers being paid by a bookie to hold up a favourite, preventing the horse from getting a clear run and winning the race?'

'I've heard of it, sure, but I didn't believe it. I thought it was just a rumour put about by disgruntled punters who'd done their dough.'

'And most of the time that's all it is. But for Willett to be that upset, you must have blown quite a hole in their future plans.'

'He did look awful. Ready to throw up or faint. An' he did say I might hear more of it.'

'Hmm.' David looked thoughtful. 'Who owns Roxy's Robin?'

'Posh city gent. Far too full of himself to speak to me. Barton — Miles Barton — that's who it is. Gives me the creeps. He doesn't look *at* you, he looks through you. It's as if he can't see people who aren't important to him.' Johnnie thought for a moment. 'And Willie lost a fat envelope when he was giving me a leg up in the mounting yard. I've never seen so much dosh. Willett shoved it away pretty fast but he knew I'd seen it.'

David's frown deepened. 'I'd say he was going to place a substantial bet — and not on Roxy's Robin. I don't like you being mixed up in this, Bro. The best thing you can do now is go home to Mum for a day or two and lie low. You've not talked to anyone else about this?'

'Haven't had the chance.' Johnnie shrugged. 'You're the first person I've seen.'

'Well, say nothing to anyone. And don't go back to Willett's stables. Not right away.'

'I'll have to, Bro. Or I'll lose my job. He's not the forgiving sort.'

'Make up an excuse then. Tell them anything. Say you've been starving to keep your weight down and it's made you sick.'

'I've got one more ride in the last and then I'll go home. Promise.'

'I dunno. I'd feel happier if you gave up the ride and came home with me. We can carry the bike in the back of the truck.'

'Nah. No need to panic. Willie's mad at me now but he'll get over it. S'only money, isn't it? An' he's loaded, anyway. Look what he spent at the sales — everyone saw, it was on TV. 'Sides, I like Stella Arkwright — she's good people. I don't want to let her down. Her daughter's a great kid, too — promised to go out with me next week.'

'OK then.' David grinned in response to his brother's twinkly smile. With his thatch of dark hair and sparkling blue eyes, Johnnie was popular with all the girls. 'But don't hang about when the race is over. I'll see you at home.'

Later, David was to remember this conversation and wish he had made Johnnie give away that last race.

★   ★   ★

Although it was still breathtakingly hot, a thunderstorm threatened and by the time the

8

last race of the day was run, only a small number of people remained on the course. Johnnie brought in a winner for Stella Arkwright, even more easily than he had steered Roxy's Robin to victory, and he was pleased that he hadn't allowed any sense of panic to make him give up the race.

By the time he got back to the jockeys' changing room he had a raging thirst and was disappointed to see that someone had already stolen the bottle of iced water he had left in the communal fridge, saving it for after the race.

'Did you see who took it?' he asked an older man who was already dressed and ready to leave.

'No, mate,' the man said. 'But I've got this bottle of Gatorade I don't need. You can have that if you like.'

'Thanks, you're a life saver.' Johnnie unscrewed the bottle and swallowed most of the yellow liquid in several gulps before pulling a face. 'Don't want to sound ungrateful but I'm not sure I like this stuff. Has a funny aftertaste.'

The man nodded. 'Know what you mean. But sports drinks are better than water on a hot day like this — replace some of the salts you've sweated out.'

'Thanks, anyway.' Johnnie saluted the man

on his way to the showers. 'Cheers.'

Less than a minute later he began to feel dizzy and had just enough time to realize that the drink had been spiked before he began to pass out. He hadn't even made it to the showers.

★ ★ ★

He awoke some time later in a confined space where it was totally dark. His first instinct was to gag but he managed to breathe deeply, suppressing it when he realized that duct tape was spread firmly over his mouth to prevent him from crying out. If he were to vomit now, he could easily choke. He writhed underneath the tape and tried to dislodge it, but to no avail. Someone had taken the trouble to dress him in his everyday clothes but he was trussed like a chicken, with hands and feet tightly bound. It didn't take him long to register that he was riding in the boot of a car, being bumped along an uneven country road.

Effectively silenced by the duct tape, he still wanted to make a protest to let his captors know he was conscious and alive. He rolled on to his back and kicked at the lid of the boot that was restraining him. It was an effort but at last there was a response.

'Stow it, will ya,' said a gruff voice. 'There'll be all hell to pay if you put a ding in the boot of the boss's car.'

All hell to pay. That's what Willett had said to him when he won that race and it provided him with his first clue concerning his captors. But that was ridiculous, surely? His own boss wouldn't arrange for him to be kidnapped, would he? Unless he was carrying out someone else's orders? His heart lurched and stepped up its beat as he wondered what fate might await him at the end of this journey. For the first time that afternoon Johnnie Riordan began to be seriously scared.

So far as he knew he had no enemies, and he had no idea where they might be taking him or why. What if this was a case of mistaken identity and his kidnapping hadn't been orchestrated by Willett or his minions?

One thing he knew for sure: if he didn't present himself at the stables ready for track work the following day, he could very well lose his job. He had seen Willett sack people at a moment's notice before, caring nothing for any word-of-mouth agreements or even contracts. But did he really want to go back there and continue to work in such an environment? Race-fixing and holding a good horse back to lengthen the odds might be just the tip of the iceberg; there could be a lot

11

more to Willett's shady activities, as his brother had implied.

At last he heard the car crunch over some gravel and swing to a stop. The boot of the car was opened and the sudden blaze of sunlight effectively blinded him; it wasn't late enough for it to be dark. Rough hands pulled him out of his resting place and tore the duct tape from his lips. They also chopped off the duct tape binding his ankles and wrists. He rubbed them to bring back the circulation but his legs could scarcely hold him and he staggered when he tried to walk. The two men laughed at his efforts, not caring that they'd hurt him.

'Why are you doing this?' he yelled at them, panic making him shrill. 'It must be a mistake. I don't have any money if that's what you think.' He could see his captors now — thickset muscular lads in their early twenties, both with shaven heads and so similar that they were probably brothers.

'Oh, it's no mistake. We know who you are, Johnnie boy.' One of them tweaked his ear. 'We're here to teach you a lesson.'

Johnnie closed his eyes momentarily, almost with relief. So it was about winning that race. At least it was nothing worse.

'OK,' he said in a small voice. 'I take your point. You've scared me half to death. You can take me home now.'

The bully boys looked at each other and sniggered. They took an arm each, pulling him towards a building that looked as if it might be an old laundry block. Some fifty yards away the back of an old wooden mansion loomed but Johnnie didn't recognize it at all. He had no idea where he was.

'This is your home for now, laddie.'

'Oh, and where's here?'

'Aw no, you don't catch us like that. This used to be a wine cellar in the olden days but we've done it up all nice and snug just for you.'

Johnnie would have argued further but he knew it was no use. He could only hope this punishment wouldn't last long. With a sinking heart, he allowed himself to be led down some old stone steps to a cellar where there were empty wine racks, thick with dust and cobwebs. There was a filthy triangular sink in one corner of the room but no toilet. He supposed the tin bucket under the sink would have to serve. There was a rickety single camp bed with an old mattress and a dirty rug. And, although it was still warm outside, the cellar, having been built to keep wine cool, was unusually chilly. Wearing only a T-shirt, he folded his arms across his chest, shivering with apprehension as well as the cold.

'Welcome to the Hilton,' one of the boys joked. They gave one another a high five again before leaving Johnnie alone and in the dark.

1

On her twenty-sixth birthday, Larissa Barton was awake early. She had a premonition that this day might be a momentous one — and not in a good way.

After ten years of marriage to an unusually wealthy man, she was reviewing her place in his world which, only a short while ago, she had taken completely for granted. She had toyed with the idea of leaving before but had never taken it seriously. Now she was.

A week or so earlier, in the aftermath of a good dinner at home and concluding a successful deal with some business associates, Miles had grown expansive, deciding to share his favourite single malt rather than offer the usual blended variety he kept for visitors. She also suspected he wanted her gone for a few minutes while sensitive issues were discussed. Some of his business dealings weren't above board but she preferred not to know the details. He had tossed her the keys to his desk, asking her to bring down the good whiskey he kept in his study.

The bottle was where he said it would be in the back of the bottom drawer but, before leaving, she decided to take a peek in the top drawer, which he always kept locked. It would be her birthday soon and she was hoping to catch a glimpse of her present. As a husband, Miles was lacking in so many ways but he was never mean over birthdays or Christmas. She was to find out that just as eavesdroppers hear no good of themselves, snoopers are often granted a similar reward.

There was no birthday present or even a package that might contain one. But there were four mobile phones. Four? Larissa frowned. Miles had two personal mobiles already as well as an office of several staff to keep track of his business affairs. What could he possibly want with four more cell phones?

She knew she should get back to the dinner party quickly or Miles would come looking for her, but curiosity overcame her and she couldn't resist a quick peek. The first one she tried was locked, but Miles always used the same code — his birthday or her own. The phone responded to his birth date and she saw there was only one person listed in the directory — someone called Lynne. She pressed the key for speed dial and after a few rings was greeted with a smoky female voice, sounding amused.

'Miles,' it said. 'What a pleasant surprise. I thought you were busy. I didn't expect to hear from you tonight — '

With her heart pounding Larissa ended the call and switched off the phone. She picked up another — the code was her own birthday this time — and, as before, the only person listed was another woman — Nadine. Quickly, she switched off the phone and flung it back in the drawer before locking it securely. Shocked by this discovery, she had a lot to think about. Her husband, over thirty years her senior, was clearly cheating on her — and not with just one woman, there seemed to be at least four. But for now she must show no sign that she was aware of it. She picked up the bottle of single malt and hurried back to the dining room.

'There you are,' Miles said, clicking his fingers for her to return his keys. She did so reluctantly and saw that his good mood had evaporated while she'd been away. 'What were you doing up there? What took you so long?'

Larissa murmured an excuse and smiled at his guests, feigning weariness and saying she needed to go to bed. In fact she wasn't tired at all; she wanted some time alone to think about what she should do.

They hadn't shared the same bedroom for over a year now. At the time she had thought nothing of it but, after tonight's discovery, everything fell into place. Although Miles kept insisting that this was the way to keep the romance in their marriage, Larissa didn't believe a word of it. Not now. It just made it easier for him to see other girls.

A year ago she had tried to talk about having children, but Miles wouldn't hear of it. He told her they were a disruptive influence and that a beautiful woman was like a flower — her beauty would fade soon enough without being ruined by childbirth.

Then she thought back to the early days of their marriage. She was his third wife but that hadn't given her any cause for alarm. Not at the time, anyway. At sixteen years old, she had been confident in her burgeoning beauty, delighted with this older man who showered her with gifts, sweeping her off her feet and rescuing her from the mundane existence of school, her overbearing, ill-tempered father and the boring prospect of college.

He had established her in his three-storey mansion in Brighton, run so efficiently by his housekeeper, Joan Hudson, that Larissa soon realized she had nothing to do but keep herself beautiful — and amused.

As Miles Barton's trim and sporty-looking child bride with a naturally clear complexion and unusual dark-blue eyes, magazine editors were always pleading with her to let them photograph her for their covers. She became a minor celebrity and was no longer surprised or embarrassed when conversation halted and all heads turned towards her when she entered a crowded room. Although she remained a country girl at heart, she learned to spend a lot of time keeping herself as shiny and newly minted as any film star; her manicurist and hairstylist were the most sought after and fashionable in town. Her hair, naturally a dark chocolate brown, was a halo of subtle blonde highlights, conditioned into shining obedience. Miles never complained about the expense; in fact he revelled in her show-stopping abilities, enjoying her seemingly effortless social performance.

In the early days of her marriage and having so many other adjustments to make, Larissa did not miss either her mother or the racehorses that had once been so much a part of her life. Her husband owned thorough-breds too and this was how he had become so friendly with her father, but she was disap-pointed to find that he spent little time with them, leaving all the 'hands on' work to his trainer, William Willett, and others.

For her eighteenth birthday, Miles bought her an Audi sports car and hired a good instructor to teach her to drive it — a woman of course. He could see no point in putting temptation in some young man's way and wanted a tutor whose mind would stay on the job. The car contributed much to her sense of freedom and happiness. And, for a while, she had been happy — or so she had thought. Now she realized it had all been a sham and that Miles didn't love her at all, certainly not as a partner or his equal. She was just another of his possessions — a pampered pet.

And now that she had made this discovery of his secret phones, she couldn't help watching him covertly, waiting for him to go out alone. No longer the naïve, sixteen-year-old bride with stars in her eyes, she could now see the flaws in her marriage as well as in her ageing husband, and realized, almost with a sense of panic, that she had never been happy with Miles — not at all. Preferring to keep her at a distance, he had never been willing to share a mutual love.

Ten years earlier, flattered to come to the notice of one of her father's friends, she had been more than ready to convince herself that he was 'the one', as might any young girl in the throes of romance with a powerful man. And Miles, with his smouldering dark eyes, tanned good looks and well-kept figure had known how to charm her into marriage and into his bed. In those early days, he had seemed like a fairy godfather, granting her every wish and giving her everything she could possibly want from dance instructors to gold credit cards. He had even allowed her to join an exclusive women's tennis club to keep fit. At one time it had been suggested that she might be good enough to play professionally and she had raised the subject with Miles one night over dinner. He wouldn't hear of it.

'It's not possible, Rissa. We can't have you gallivanting all over the world on the tennis circuit,' he said, smiling indulgently and leaning across the table to pat her hand.

'But Miles, I'm the best player they have — ' she had started to argue with him.

'I don't care. It's out of the question, my darling,' he said, kissing the tips of her fingers. 'I need you here with me.' And there the subject was left, never to be raised again. At the time Larissa accepted it because she thought he loved her so much, he didn't want to let her go. Now she thought it was because he wanted to keep her under his thumb.

She was reminded of a rare lunch away from home with her glamorous cousin Morina. Her cousin lived in Brisbane but she travelled the country doing make-up demonstrations in department stores. The two girls had spent many school holidays together and remained firm friends. As a general rule,

Miles disapproved of 'girly lunches' as he called them, aware that, left to their own devices, women would compare notes and that wine would loosen their tongues. This particular day was no exception. Morina was having one of her 'all men are bastards' days.

'Oh, Rissa,' she had sighed, stirring the coffee she had ordered to sober them up. 'I'm so tired of those department store Casanovas who think that giving me a nice dinner — on their expense accounts of course — will automatically grant them a night in my bed. And if I'm lonely enough to get caught in a weak moment and let them, they're always a disappointment; creeping away in the early hours of the morning, trying not to wake me. You don't know how lucky you are to be married to Miles. An older man — all that sophistication and finesse — I'll bet he knows how to give you an orgasm every time?' And she cocked an eyebrow, waiting for her cousin to take up her cue and expand on her love life. Instead, Larissa just smiled, looking down at her coffee. How could she tell her cousin the truth? Morina was hoping to hear of romance and fantasy and all she had to offer was disillusionment.

'Now don't you dare to say you're not happy because I won't believe it.' Morina continued to probe. 'I was your bridesmaid, remember? I saw you on your wedding day. I've never seen a girl so much in love.'

In love with love, certainly, Larissa thought. *I wish someone had warned me about that.* 'Morina, we were only sixteen,' she said, once more avoiding the question. 'We still believed in Cinderella and her Prince Charming.'

'So what are you saying? Miles isn't Prince Charming, after all? Don't tell me he's turned into a frog? Or was he always a frog?'

'I didn't say that — don't put words into my mouth. And anyway, what happens behind closed doors is strictly between me and Miles.'

Morina pouted. 'Oh, don't be so prissy and uptight. You never used to be such a clam. Time was when we used to tell one another everything.'

'So we did. When there was very little to tell.' Larissa lowered her voice to a whisper, making Morina lean forward eagerly to catch what she said. 'I'll let you into a secret. I made up most of those stories to fill in the gaps.'

'Oh, you!' Morina glanced at her watch. 'Damn. I have to get back to work. I'm doing a make-over for a bridal party at two.'

Larissa stood up and gave her cousin a hug. 'It's been great to see you,' she said. 'Good to catch up.'

'I don't think we caught up on anything.' Morina studied her. 'In my line of work I know all about women and I know you, Larissa Barton — you're keeping something back. I can tell from the strain around your eyes. I just wish I had another spare hour to worm it out of you.'

'There's nothing, really,' Larissa said, trying not to think of that locked drawer and those treacherous mobile phones. 'Call me when you're next in town.' She watched her cousin leave the café, dark curls bouncing, handbag swinging and high heels clicking on the marble floor.

It would have been a relief to spill the beans and tell her cousin of her suspicions, but then Morina would have expected her to take action and she still hadn't made up her mind what she wanted to do.

★　★　★

This year her birthday had fallen on a Sunday, so Miles wouldn't go anywhere — either to his office in town or to the track. He ignored Sunday race meetings, despising them as second-rate although he was reliably present on all the major race days, when one or more of his champion thoroughbreds would be in the field.

Miles smoked only cigars and drank only rarely but he did like to gamble for high stakes, both at the casino and on the track. Like many a wealthy man who regularly made more money than he could use, for Miles there was never enough. He lusted for more. She was starting to realize that her husband might well be one of the greediest men on the planet.

Idly, as she pondered her situation, she wondered if he would remember her birthday at all. Perversely, she was half hoping he wouldn't. Then she'd have a legitimate reason to sulk and leave the house on her own. Miles often went out alone — sometimes all night — but now that she had found out his secret, she knew better than to question him about such things.

But even as she was thinking along those lines the bedroom door burst open and Miles was there, laughing and filling the room with his boisterous presence, bringing her a breakfast of croissants and coffee on a tray. The housekeeper must have prepared it, of course. Miles would never think of adding a fresh napkin and flowers but she would have to pretend it was all his own work. She tried not to see that he was naked under his open dressing gown, with an erection already in evidence.

'Happy birthday, my darling!' he carolled, making her wince, as he set the tray down on the table beside her. 'I can't believe we've been married for almost ten years.'

Larissa could. Lately, it was beginning to feel like twenty. All the same, she summoned her most engaging smile and tilted her head for him to kiss her cheek. Miles ignored the offer and pounced, straddling her and pressing her back on the pillows as he came in for a sloppy one, all saliva and teeth, his erection hard against her thigh. He tasted mostly of toothpaste but, even so, it took all of her concentration not to shudder in response.

'Mmm. You smell delicious,' her husband murmured, pushing her nightgown up and feeling between her thighs — a move she recognized as his usual prelude to sex. He wasn't one to waste time on foreplay.

'Miles, wait.' She struggled free of his grasp. 'What's the point of bringing me coffee and croissants if you're going to let them get cold?'

He sighed, rolled off her and sat up, leaning back against the embossed, velvet covered headboard. 'Come on, then. Let's eat them quickly and get down to business.'

'No, Miles, I want to savour it. After all, how often do I get to have breakfast in bed?'

She sat up and pulled the tray on to her knees to forestall any further argument, busying herself with pouring coffee for both of them.

'Trust you to ruin the moment.' He wrinkled his nose at her. 'Ah well, you might as well have this now.' Without ceremony, he tossed her a small box wrapped in gold paper — professionally wrapped by the store. Miles's clumsy fingers could never have arranged such tiny bows. It had to be perfume or jewellery. She had reached a stage where she didn't care which. Miles liked those strident, modern perfumes that lingered while she preferred something more subtle. 'Go on then.' He was starting to get impatient. 'Open it.'

'I'm sure it's lovely, whatever it is. But not until after breakfast.' She set it aside, put some jam on a piece of croissant and pushed it towards him. Scarcely bothering to chew, Miles swallowed it, chasing it with a huge gulp of coffee.

Larissa watched all this with distaste. 'Sometimes I wonder which planet you're from,' she murmured.

'What's that?' Miles snapped, making her grateful for the increasing deafness to which he didn't admit. The remark had slipped out before she could prevent it.

'Nothing, darling.' She dimpled at him.

27

'You're always so good to me.'

'My pleasure,' he said, still unsure whether he had been insulted or not.

At last, Larissa set the breakfast tray aside and opened her package. It was indeed jewellery, as she had expected. A small suede pouch containing a bracelet of half a dozen small pink crystals on a silver chain. It was beautifully crafted and sparkled as she held the jewels up to the light.

'Oh Miles, they're so pretty.' Her smile was genuine this time as she kissed the corner of his sulky mouth. 'And shine so beautifully they could almost be diamonds. Thank you.'

'They shine like diamonds because that's what they are!' he yelled, shocking her and making her blink. 'Are you such a fool that you can't see those are pink diamonds — the rarest jewels on the planet? And that chain isn't silver — it's platinum.'

'Oh, Miles. It's quite lovely, of course. But I can't possibly wear it. Not if the diamonds are real.'

'Sell the damn thing, then.' He shrugged, prickly and offended. 'Do what you like with it. I don't care.'

'Thank you, Miles,' she said, realizing she had sounded less than grateful. With the expensive bracelet lying across her hand, she felt almost guilty about the way she had been

28

thinking of her husband in recent times. Until she remembered those girls and the mobile phones. 'You're so good to me. I really don't deserve it.'

'Sure you do, Rissa. You've done a fair enough job so far. Although the façade is just starting to crumble; you're getting a bit past it now.'

'Past what?' She stared at him, shocked by his callous remark. 'I'm only just twenty-six. And you're a fine one to talk — you're well on the way to sixty.'

'But we're not talking about me, are we?' He placed a finger on the lines of stress that had appeared between her brows. 'Look at the wrinkles on that grumpy face. And here — you're just beginning to get some lines around your mouth.' He traced them with the same finger until she batted his hand away.

'I do not have wrinkles. I have beauty treatments twice a week. But OK. I'll see about getting some botox as well, if you like.'

'I don't like. There are some clever doctors around but nothing can really stop the march of time. Look at this?' He pinched the tender flesh of her upper arm, making her wince. 'Used to be firm and smooth as a peach but now you're stringy from all that tennis and working out. Sorry, darl, but there's nothing for it. I'll have to make a fresh start.'

'A fresh start?' She stared at him, suddenly apprehensive. 'In what way?'

'With another girl.' He sighed as if she were being unusually slow. 'I can see I'll have to spell it out. I'm not a complete fool, you know. I've known about your feelings — or lack of them — for some time. So we've come to the parting of the ways. I'm divorcing you, Rissa.'

'On what grounds? I haven't cheated on you or betrayed you — '

'No. But don't say you haven't considered it.'

'Considering and doing something about it are two very different things.'

'To be sure. But are you still so naïve that you believe witnesses can't be bought?'

'You wouldn't.'

'Oh yes, I would. I've done it before. Judges are ready to believe anything of lovely young wives.' He changed tactics. 'Look at what happened this morning. Do you think I can't sense it? You'll do anything rather than have sex with me.'

She dropped her gaze to her hands, knowing the accusation to be true. All the same she was upset at the thought of losing the comfortable lifestyle to which she'd become so accustomed. Her bedroom, for a start. She gazed out of her windows at the magnificent view of the bay with sailing boats and ships on the horizon and fingered the silken sheets on her king-sized bed. Opposite was her collection of high-heeled shoes that filled an entire wall of her walk-in wardrobe. The other side was packed tight with clothes she would never have time to wear. Was she really prepared to let Miles turn her out? To leave all this behind?

'We can try again, can't we, Miles?' she said in a small voice, not at all sure that this was what she wanted. If only he had given her some time to think. 'Please?'

'No, Larissa. My mind is made up. It was good between us at first when you were young and willing but things have gone sour now. I don't like to labour the point, but your freshness has gone. You're getting too cynical and too old.'

'Stop saying that.' She was close to tears. 'I'm only twenty-six.'

'Yes. But I need someone younger now. Someone who'll look up to me as you used to do.'

'Are they so much younger than I am, then? Those girls on your mobile phones?'

'Some of them,' he said without thinking. Then he frowned, staring at her. 'How d'you know about them?'

'Never mind.' She turned on him. 'You

know what you are? Nothing but a dirty old man — one step away from a paedophile.'

'Not at all. I just like young, willing flesh in my bed. Ask any honest man and he'll tell you the same. You know what they say? It's women who have to age — men only season.'

Looking at it critically, she held up the expensive bracelet on the tip of her finger. Somehow it had proved to be the catalyst for all these harsh words. 'So why give me these rare diamonds if you want rid of me?'

'Ah, well, let me explain.' Miles's smile was wolfish. 'I always offer pink diamonds to my ex wives — it's my way of saying *farewell and thanks*. It's worked very well in the past.'

'How's that?'

'The deal is this. You take the diamonds and don't contest the divorce. I like things left nice and tidy with no loose ends. But if you persist in clinging to your version of the truth — that you are the innocent party — I will produce reliable witnesses that you have cheated on me for the whole of our married life.'

'What did your first and second wives do?'

'They were sensible girls. They took the diamonds, of course.'

Suddenly, Larissa felt vulnerable, lying in bed in a flimsy nightgown. Had she allowed it, her husband would have had sex with her this very morning, knowing all the time that he meant to be rid of her. So she sprang out of bed and, turning her back on Miles, put on the underwear she had worn the previous day. She dressed quickly in jeans and a T-shirt and thrust her feet into a pair of sandals. She ran to her wardrobe and seized a suitcase from one of the top shelves. Then she proceeded to pack it with casual clothes. She took trainers, jeans, T-shirts and a few simple summer dresses, ignoring the glamorous clothes she had worn to functions with Miles. She had never allowed him to buy her furs.

'OK. I can see that you've made up your mind to leave and that's fine with me.' Miles stood watching her from the doorway, arms folded across his chest. He still hadn't bothered to fasten his dressing gown. 'So what do you think? Will you take the diamonds and let me divorce you or not?'

For a lady of leisure, Larissa was unusually fit. She worked out at least twice a week and played tennis regularly with a group of near professionals. She picked up the diamond bracelet, which was lying unheeded on the bed, and she threw it as hard as she could, aiming for Miles's patronizing, self-satisfied face.

She felt no remorse as she saw blood spurting from a cut eyebrow as her soon to be ex-husband howled in surprise rather than pain. Injured and for a moment unable to see, he managed to retrieve the diamond bracelet and thrust it into the pocket of his silk dressing-gown.

'I don't want your diamonds, Miles. I'd rather keep my good name. But as your wife for ten blameless years, I will have what's due to me. You can do whatever you like with your trumped-up witnesses. In view of your past record, I'm sure any sensible judge will see through them. And I have an excellent lawyer — he's an old family friend. See you in court.'

She fastened her suitcase and picked it up. It wasn't heavy and she knew she would have to rely on the goodwill of their housekeeper, Mrs Hudson, if she wanted to retrieve anything more. Remembering her own generosity over the years, giving the woman good clothing as well as extra free time, she could only hope Joan Hudson would be on her side.

'And you needn't think you're taking the Audi . . . ' Miles began as he saw her pick up her keys from the dressing table.

'Oh, Miles, of course I'm taking my car.' She was more than weary of this discussion now. 'It was a birthday present and it's registered in my name. And anyway, what would you want with a car that's eight years old?' She edged past him, keeping the suitcase between them. Having injured him physically, she didn't trust him not to take his revenge. She knew, from experience, that he could be brutal when his temper was roused. When they were first married, after watching her conduct a mild flirtation at a party, he had punched and kicked her when they got home. She had taken care to avoid one-on-one conversations with men ever since.

Today, he made no move to stop her but watched her go, pressing the heel of his hand to his bleeding eyebrow. It was only when he heard her slam the front door behind her that he realized how badly he had handled the situation.

'Dammit!' he swore softly under his breath. 'And damn the bitch to hell.'

2

Sally Arkwright glared at her mother, not at all pleased with this latest news.

'But why, Mom? Why does Larissa want to come back and live here? Got her own home, hasn't she? Three times the size of this one.'

'Not any more. She says Miles wants a divorce.'

'Thought it was too good to last.' Sally was heartless as only the young and uninjured can be. 'So why the divorce? Did she get bored and play up with a younger man? Serves her right for marrying an old one. Miles is almost old enough to be our grandfather.'

'Don't make assumptions, Sarah.' Stella never called her younger daughter Sarah unless she was annoyed with her. 'I don't know what happened to your sister's marriage and I haven't asked. If you want to know the truth, you must talk to Rissa yourself.'

'No point. She thinks I'm a kid — never tells me anything. Forgets she was married at my age.' In sudden apprehension, she fixed her mother with a look. 'Hey, I hope she's not expecting to have her old room back?'

'I don't know, Sally.' Stella sighed, more

than usually irritated by her younger daughter. 'She's not even here yet.'

* * *

Larissa arrived that afternoon, late and with a car full of packages. She looked exhausted, Stella thought, and quite unlike her usual well-groomed self. She went to meet her, hugging her daughter close as soon as she got out of the car.

'Been doing a little retail therapy?' she said mildly, glancing at the back seat full of parcels.

'Just a few sensible clothes before Miles cancels my credit cards.'

'Will he really do that?' Stella winced. 'I'm so sorry, Rissa.'

'Don't be nice to me, Mom,' Larissa said, her voice full of tears. 'I'll only howl.'

'Maybe you should. Better to let it all out than bottle it up.' Stella walked them slowly towards the house, a protective arm around her elder daughter. Larissa left her suitcase and packages in the car, forgetting that here there would be no eager servant to retrieve them and put everything away.

They went into the big, farmhouse kitchen that served also as a family room. Larissa sat down at the table and leaned back, pushing her hands through her lion's mane of hair.

'Oh, God.' She closed her eyes and let out a long breath. 'You've no idea what a relief it is to be home.'

'That bad, huh?' Stella wouldn't press her, but she hoped her daughter would elaborate before Sally joined them and brought their confidential chat to an end. At this moment, she was upstairs at her desk, finishing the homework she would need to give in the next day.

'Oh, Mom. These last few months — you have no idea.'

Stella pushed a strong cup of tea in front of her, adding milk and two generous spoonfuls of sugar.

'Mom, stop! I'll get fat as a pig. You know I never take sugar.'

'Today, you do. Best thing when you've had a shock.'

'It's not so much of a shock as a revelation. Because Miles is so much older than me, like a fool I assumed — ' She broke off with a small, bitter laugh, shaking her head. She didn't feel ready to mention Miles's phones connecting him to those other women.

'Rissa, you don't have to tell me anything, if you don't want to. And you're welcome to come back here for as long as you like. I can use a hand with Sally, she's impossible these days — just discovering boys.'

'I'm not sure I'm the best person to offer advice.'

'Whatever. And then Sue, my right-hand girl, has just left to get married and live up country. I can use some extra help in the stables.'

'Are you sure? You're not just saying this to make me feel better about coming back home?'

'No, we're really short-handed. I need you.'

'OK. Great. Do me good to shovel some horse shit and get some dirt on my hands.' She smiled at her mother, a woman of almost fifty, who looked very much like an older, stockier version of herself. Stella, of course, never bothered to colour her greying hair and never wore make-up or nail varnish. For all that, she was still a handsome woman with the fine bone structure inherited by both her daughters. 'I've missed the day-to-day life with horses much more than I thought I would. Miles owns more than half a dozen thoroughbreds but he doesn't have any real contact with them. He just wants them to keep winning so that he can show off.'

Stella bit her lip, recognizing the bitterness in her daughter's voice. Things had clearly gone very wrong. She sighed as Larissa went on with her tale.

'Recently we lost a lovely mare. She broke

down on the course and had to be shot. I cried my eyes out for the rest of the day but all Miles could think about was the money he'd lost. He is a selfish, cruel man and I can't think of anything cold enough to describe his heart.'

'Whew!' Stella said when she came to the end of this outburst. 'You do know I never wanted you to marry him, Rissa? I always knew it would end in tears.' She shrugged. 'But Miles had your father fooled and he seemed to be a friend, so I let them persuade me.'

'It's not your fault, Mom. I was as much to blame. I couldn't wait to get out of school and lay my hands on the glittering prizes. And Miles could turn on the charm and was handsome enough in those days. I convinced myself he looked like George Clooney.'

'Oh, Rissa.'

'At least Pop isn't alive to see what a hash I made of it. I'd never have heard the end of it. Miles wants to trade me in for a younger model. Can you believe it?'

'Who?' Stella almost choked on her own cup of tea.

'I dunno. It's just an idea he has. I don't think he's met her yet.'

'But you're only twenty-six — in the prime of life. Is he getting senile or what? He's over thirty years older than you are.'

Larissa shrugged. 'That's what I said. I even offered to go the botox route but no dice. To quote his own words — he needs younger, more willing flesh in his bed.'

'Someone like me, maybe?' Suddenly, Sally was there, posing in the doorway like a model and smirking at her elder sister. She had the same good bones and dark hair but she had missed out on her sister's startling blue eyes; hers were something between green and brown. 'Welcome home, sis. I hear the old man threw you out.'

'Sarah!' Stella was outraged. 'How long have you been eavesdropping outside that door?'

'Long enough.' Sally's smile was all mischief. 'It's the only way I can find out what's going on. Nobody tells me anything around here.'

Stella was quick to come back. 'If you behaved more like a grown-up instead of a spoilt brat maybe we'd tell you more.'

'Seriously though, Sis, if the job with Miles is going begging — '

'Don't even think about it, Sally. After what I've been through, no sister of mine is going to — '

'Only joking.' Sally's temper flared. 'And anyway, why shouldn't I find a rich husband? You did.'

41

'Oh, Sally, stop it right now.' Stella groaned. 'Aren't things difficult enough today without you making them worse?'

'You think I don't have difficulties of my own?' Sally's eyes filled with tears. 'Johnnie Riordan asked me for my mobile number and said he wanted us to go out. I felt sure he'd ring me or at least text but he never did. And I know it's because I'm so beastly ordinary. Why can't I have streaks in my hair and be glamorous like Rissa?'

'Much good all this so-called glamour has done for me,' Rissa said, not without bitterness. 'Miles is threatening to drag me through the courts on trumped-up charges of adultery and — '

'Rissa!' Stella spoke urgently. '*Pas devant . . .*'

'What children, Mom?' Larissa said softly, once more pushing her hair away from her face. 'Sally's right. She should know what's going on — she's not a child any more. We Arkwrights are a team of three now and we have to stick together.'

★　★　★

Larissa slotted back into her old life at home as if she had never been away. She didn't antagonize Sally by reclaiming her old room but took the large bed-sitting room at the

42

back of the house that had been her grandmother's refuge some years before. She was pleased to find it had been left largely as it was. Most of her grandmother's things were still there — her rather garish Staffordshire dogs on the mantelpiece, the old snowstorm ball that Larissa had been allowed to play with as a child, as well as the antique toby jug that played 'Another little drink'. She wound it up and listened, smiling at the old-fashioned tune.

She had little time to brood or dwell on her situation as her mother was right; the stables were very short-handed and there was plenty of manual work to be done, making her pleased she had kept her fitness during her years with Miles. She had been home for over two weeks now and still there was no word. She wouldn't have known what to say to him, anyway. There were already reports and pictures in the social pages showing him looking sleek and urbane as ever, squiring various young women around town but he was curiously silent about the divorce. So far as Larissa was concerned, she wasn't greedy but she would like a fair settlement to be reached as soon as possible so that she could put the last ten years behind her and get on with her life. But, knowing Miles as she did, she didn't think anything would be as simple and straightforward as that.

This particular afternoon, with Sally safely upstairs listening to CDs, her mother could speak frankly about the business, explaining that times had been hard and that the stables had taken some time to recover after her father's sudden death of a heart attack five years before. She avoided saying — although Larissa knew it to be true — that in some ways her father's passing had been a relief. He had been irascible and quick to fly off the handle in his later years, probably because he was unwell and unwilling to share his concerns.

'But Mom, why didn't you tell me you were struggling financially?' Larissa said, wishing she had been more observant and less involved in her own affairs. 'It wouldn't have hurt Miles to help you.'

'I didn't want your husband's money.' Stella was quick to come back. 'He was your father's old friend rather than mine. He would have been patting my head, calling me 'little woman' and trying to tell me what to do. No. I preferred to push on alone. And now, as you see, we're starting to do OK. Moving from the high profile stables at Caulfield and consolidating here at Warrandyte was definitely the right thing to do. It left me with money enough to renovate the old stalls and people are now coming back to me with good horses. I'm even starting to make a name for myself on my own.'

'Well done, Mom. And I'm here to help you now. I'm sure Sally will, too, when she gets through her final exams.'

'How much good she'll be, I don't know.' Stella smiled ruefully. 'She isn't a natural horsewoman like you, and she's too busy chasing after the boys.'

'She's only young. Give her a chance, Mom.'

The next day Larissa was in one of the stalls, humming softly to herself as she groomed Golden Czarina, her mother's most recent and promising acquisition. She was a magnificent filly who had been lightly raced, as Stella was hoping to train her up for the Spring Carnival; she didn't believe in pressing a young horse to its limits too soon. She had discovered the filly when she came up for sale but couldn't afford to buy her alone, so she shared ownership with the family lawyer, Roger Timpson who was also Sally's god-father — an old friend she could trust. At one time Larissa had wondered if Roger might get together with her mother one day but nothing had come of it so far. Roger was reliable enough but rather pedestrian while her father had been a steam kettle of unpredictable emotions; a hard act to follow.

Thinking of Roger, Larissa sighed. She would have to get in touch with him when she eventually heard from Miles about the divorce.

Larissa was grooming Czarina, admiring the distinctive gold mane and tail which had given the filly her name.

'You're a beauty, aren't you?' she murmured, brushing the animal's shining rump. 'A girl with good child-bearing hips.' She had always been interested in breeding although she'd had little real contact with thoroughbreds over the last ten years, apart from leading Miles's champions back to the mounting yard. It was only now she was home again that she realized how much she had missed the 'hands on' contact with horses. Idly, she wondered if she could persuade her mother to embark on a modest breeding programme here at Warrandyte. There was certainly enough room, and when she received her settlement from Miles she would offer to divide one of their larger paddocks and build a new stable block to keep the breeding mares separate from the racehorses. This was her dream of the future, anyway.

Her thoughts were interrupted by a man's voice calling from the open door at the rear of the stables.

'Hello there! Anyone about?'

Knowing that sometimes sports reporters turned up unannounced, hoping to sniff out some news, Larissa came out of Czarina's stall and closed it firmly behind her.

'Just go into the office,' she called back. 'Be with you directly.'

She washed her hands quickly and dried them on her trousers as she hurried to see what the man wanted. Dressed in jeans, cowboy boots and a striped cotton shirt, he was youngish, even-featured, tall and dark-haired, but so thin that his cheekbones and chin were unusually prominent. The pallor of his skin accentuated this impression. He smiled a greeting but his dark eyes were troubled and she could see purple shadows beneath them. He didn't look like a reporter searching for gossip.

'Hi,' he said. 'Sorry to bother you in the midst of a working day but I was hoping to see Mrs Arkwright. I did go up to the house first but there's nobody there.'

'That's right. She's gone into town. Maybe I can help you, Mr — ?'

'Oh, I'm sorry. Riordan. David Riordan.'

'And you'll be a jockey, won't you? I can see no other reason why a tall man like you should be so thin.'

'Good observation — you're right there.'

47

He grinned ruefully. 'Sometimes I wonder how I survive on just vitamins and rabbit food. And you — you must be Mrs Arkwright's forewoman?'

'No. I'm her eldest daughter, Larissa. Back home for a while, filling in.'

'Larissa — unusual name — and I thought you looked familiar. You'll be Mrs Barton, then. Miles Barton's wife.'

'Not for much longer.'

'Really?' For a moment he looked unsure what to say. 'I'm sorry.'

'Don't be. Because I'm not.' She was quick to change the subject. 'So what can we do for you, Mr Riordan? If you're looking for rides, it isn't for me to decide. You'll have to talk to my mother.'

'Call me David, please. And no, it's not that — although I'd be happy to ride for Mrs Arkwright some time.' He hesitated as if he was unsure how to proceed. 'This is probably going to sound all too silly — but I'm wondering if you've seen or heard anything of my brother?'

'Your brother?'

'Johnnie Riordan. He's a jockey as well — a few years younger than I am — a lot smaller, too. I can't ride under fifty-seven kilos. He took a ride for your mother a few weeks ago and then disappeared, leaving his motorbike behind at the course. We haven't seen him since. He's not shown up for track work and hasn't been in touch, which is quite unlike him. And I have to tell you we're worried sick.'

'Of course.' Larissa could now see the reason for his hollow-eyed look. 'But what made you think he'd be here?'

'I didn't, but I'm clutching at straws now. The last time I saw him, he said he was making a date with Stella Arkwright's daughter and . . . ' he hesitated, 'I don't think he was talking about you.'

'No.' Larissa smiled. 'That would be Sally — my little sister. She's only sixteen. And she was very put out when he didn't call.'

'So she didn't hear from him either?' David sighed. 'There's nobody here who can help me to find my brother?'

'I'm afraid not.'

David's shoulders slumped. Murmuring thanks, he turned to leave.

'Wait a minute.' Larissa placed a comforting hand on his shoulder, startled at how fragile the bones felt. 'You look all in. Come up to the house and sit down and let me make you some coffee. I could do with one myself.'

'I really ought to get back home.'

'There's no hurry is there? Not if you still

don't have any news.'

'I suppose not.' Listlessly, he followed her up the path by the paddocks which led to the back door of the house. She opened it and gestured for him to come inside.

'Nice place you have here,' he said, gazing around, admiring the big family room adjoining the kitchen as Larissa brewed coffee and invited him to take a place at the big table, obviously used for meals as well as the preparation of food. 'My mother would love it. A real country homestead with horses. She misses them so much.'

'So your mother is a horsewoman, too?'

'Used to be. Until arthritis caught up with her. She hasn't the strength in her hands now and her knees are too painful. She and Dad always worked around stables — mostly at Caulfield. Johnnie and I grew up around horses, so it was only natural for us to take up riding.'

Larissa poured the coffee, offering him milk and sugar, which he refused. 'It must be hard for you when you're not naturally small.'

He shrugged. 'I get by. I just have to watch what I eat.'

'You could still work with horses, if you took up training or breeding instead.'

'And never be more than a hired hand, working for somebody else.' David smiled.

'This way I have at least a chance at the big time. But I've always wanted to breed a good horse and train it myself. Years ago, before we came down to Melbourne, my father worked on a ranch in New South Wales. We were there for just over a year and I thought it was heaven. My mother and I could have stayed there for ever but he got restless as usual. I was only small but for me it was one of the best times in my life. I loved to see the foals stand up on their wobbly legs, so soon after they were born. Since then it's always been my dream to breed thoroughbreds, if only on a small scale.'

'You could still follow that dream.'

'Dreams remain dreams unless they're supported with money. And my mother still needs my help. I have to work around that.'

'Is she an invalid, then?'

'Not really.' He looked away, discomfited. 'It isn't exactly that.'

'Forgive me. I'm being nosy. I always ask too many questions.'

He was saved from answering as they heard a car drawing up outside and moments later Stella came into the kitchen, weighed down with grocery packages and looking surprised to see a stranger sitting at her kitchen table. Sally followed, wearing school uniform and lugging a massive bag full of books which she

51

kicked under the table. David sprang to his feet to help Stella with her packages.

'Thanks, they were starting to weigh a ton.' She smiled at him and held out her hand. 'You'll be a friend of Rissa's?'

'No, he's not.' Sally stuck out her chin belligerently and confronted him, hands on hips. 'I know who he is — Johnnie Riordan's older brother. And when you see that little rat, you can tell him from me — '

'Sally, shut up!' Larissa broke in, coming to their visitor's defence. 'David is here to tell us that Johnnie's gone missing — has been for several weeks. You, Mom, and Sally were among the last people to see him that day at the races. Nobody's heard from him since.'

'Oh!' Sally sat down heavily at the table, looking stricken. 'How awful. And here I was, thinking the worst of him.'

'Understandable, I'm sure,' David said. 'Young as he is, Johnnie fancies himself as a bit of a ladies' man.'

'So what's happened to him?' Sally's eyes filled with tears as all kinds of unpleasant possibilities sprang to mind.

'We don't know. And the longer he's gone, the more likely it seems that he must be in serious trouble.'

'And what have you been doing to find him so far?' Stella asked him, ever practical. 'Are the police involved?'

'Not yet.' David stared into his coffee, looking uncomfortable. 'Although I'm beginning to think they should be. You see, Johnnie got on the wrong side of the cops when he was scarcely a teenager. An end-of-term party turned into a bit of a riot and he was caught spraying a newly painted wall with graffiti. The magistrate wanted to make an example of him and he was sent to a juvenile detention centre for three months. That may not sound like so long but it gave him time enough to bond with some tough young criminals while he was there.'

'That's always a risk in such places,' Stella murmured. 'So you think he might have embarked on a life of crime?'

'Let's hope not. I thought when he got a job as track rider and apprentice to a high-profile trainer like William Willett, he might turn his life around. But no. Willett is a criminal of a different persuasion, if no less dangerous. Each day we've been hoping that Johnnie'd turn up before we needed to bring in the police.'

'Well, I think you should go to them now,' Stella said gently. 'How old is your brother? Seventeen? Eighteen? I wasn't sure.'

'Just eighteen.'

'Hmm. Officially a man but still very much

a boy. Or so he seemed to me, anyway. Has he taken himself off like this before?'

'No. Never.' David hesitated before going on. 'Look, I probably shouldn't be telling you this — and he shouldn't have told me — but the last time he rode for Willett, he disregarded instructions. He was supposed to keep a low profile and let someone else win the race. But he felt the colt was ready and rode him to win, expecting Willett to be pleased. Instead, he was white-faced with anger — almost scared, Johnnie said.' David thought of mentioning the money that had fallen out of Willett's pocket but decided against it for now.

'Do you remember the name of the horse?' Larissa said, hesitating to rake up old memories. 'Miles has several horses in training with Willett, although I've never liked the man — he reminds me of a weasel with those crooked pointy teeth.'

'Not sure I remember.' David screwed up his face, thinking. 'Robin Hood maybe, or something like it.'

'Roxy's Robin?'

'That's it.'

'Yes, I remember overhearing Miles talk on the phone. He said it was a good horse but he wanted to keep it under wraps until it was racing at long odds. Then he could be certain of making a killing.'

'Race fixing?' Stella said, pursing her lips.

'Miles wouldn't call it that. He'd say it was business. He wants to wring the last drop out of everything,' Larissa said. 'He's rich as Croesus already but he's like an old dragon, guarding his nest of gold. There's never enough. And your brother ruined his plans by letting that horse win too soon.'

'Johnnie seemed a bit down at the time. Said there might be consequences.'

'There must be more to it than that. Even if they wanted to punish him, surely no one would go so far as to — ' Larissa hesitated, unwilling to state her fears.

'Kill him, you mean?' Sally was the only one unafraid to say it.

'Wait. Let's back up a minute,' Stella said. 'It's easy to imagine the worst when Johnnie's been missing so long but let's think this through rationally. If he wanted to disappear until the heat died down, where would he go?'

'He wouldn't.' David insisted. 'He loves Mum and he wouldn't want to upset her. Besides, he hasn't enough money to go anywhere.'

'And your father — what does he think?'

'Nothing.' David's mouth twisted with bitterness. 'He deserted us and took off for the Northern Territory fifteen years ago. We haven't seen him since. I used to make up stories that he'd been eaten by crocodiles and that's why he didn't come back.'

'So Johnnie wouldn't have gone off to look for him?'

'No. He was only three when Dad left. He can scarcely remember him.' David took a deep breath and stood up, suddenly ill at ease with his emotions. 'But I shouldn't be worrying you with all this. You've been very kind and I've already taken up far too much of your time.'

Impulsively, Stella stood up and hugged him. 'I just hope you'll have news soon. I feel awful that Johnnie went missing shortly after taking my ride. And, in spite of his previous record, I do think it's time to call in the police.'

'That will depend on Mum. She has an aversion to authority in any form. I had enough trouble persuading her to apply for a disability pension when she couldn't work any more.'

'The police are there to help you, David.'

'Let's hope I can get her to see it that way. But thanks for your advice, Mrs Arkwright.' He turned to leave, making Stella certain he had no intention of taking it. Larissa accompanied him to the door.

'Keep in touch, David,' she said as they walked to his car. As he offered his hand, impulsively she pulled him in closer and kissed his cheek, making him open his eyes wide to stare at her. Clearly, he didn't come from a demonstrative family. 'And let us know as soon as you have any news.'

She watched him get into his stylish, metallic purple truck and waved as he drove away. How old could he be? Twenty-four? Twenty-five? His brother was just eighteen so he might even be younger than that. *You idiot!* she told herself. *You have no business to be taking a fancy to David Riordan — or anyone else for that matter. Not until you're free of your marriage to Miles.*

With this uncomfortable thought still nagging at her, she went back to her mother and sister, bracing herself to hear their opinion of David Riordan.

3

The more she thought about it, the more Larissa felt that her soon-to-be ex-husband must have some idea of what had happened to young Johnnie Riordan. All the same, ruthless as Miles was in business and no doubt angry that his plans for Roxy's Robin had been thwarted, she couldn't see him getting personally involved. Not so William Willett. She knew, as the Riordans did not, that in spite of being a licensed trainer of thoroughbreds now, Willett had once inhabited the fringes of the criminal world. And he still had plenty of contacts; people more than willing to carry out the unpleasant tasks, leaving himself and, more importantly, Miles, squeaky clean and smelling of roses. On many occasions when she had been curled up in a wing chair in his study, reading a book, Miles would forget she was there. Out of sight in the chair, she was also out of mind and although she tried not to pay attention when he was on the phone, there were times when she learned far more than he would have liked her to know about his business dealings and other nefarious plans. Although in the eyes of most people he was fabulously wealthy, there had been times when his finances were stretched and he had been forced to 'rob Peter to pay Paul'.

Of course, Miles was unlikely to answer her questions directly but she had lived with him long enough to know when he was lying. When David Riordan told her that Johnnie was still missing she decided to pay him a visit.

She went to his office in town rather than call at the mansion that until so recently had been her home. Aside from Mrs Hudson, who was a friend, the woman who came in to do the heavier cleaning work loved to gossip about her wealthy employers. To avoid giving Miles the idea that she was there to impress him, she turned up in the clothes she wore to the stables; riding boots, jeans and a simple T-shirt as the weather was going to be hot. Now that she was living away from the tensions that Miles always created around him her face was glowing with good health, free at last of the exotic face paints and glamour he loved, her hair tied back in a simple ponytail. The blonde streaks were already growing out but she didn't care. She wouldn't be going back to those fashionable beauty salons again.

On arrival at the reception desk she saw that the door to Miles's office was closed.

Sitting at the front desk was a new personal assistant whom she hadn't met before; young and pretty, like most of the girls Miles employed. She smiled at the girl and introduced herself simply as Larissa Arkwright, asking to see Miles.

Blonde and supercilious, the girl looked her up and down, dismissing her as unimportant because of her lack of style and the casual clothes. After a moment spent admiring her own newly manicured nails, she announced that Miles was already in conference with a visitor and wasn't to be disturbed. In any case, he wouldn't see anyone without an appointment.

While the receptionist was imparting this news, Larissa became aware of raised voices behind the closed door. Miles was trying to keep the noise down and sound conciliatory but she knew him well enough to sense that his temper was scarcely controlled. The younger voice was also one that she recognized: Luke Dennison, the son of a man who had been once been one of Miles's closest friends. She knew Miles never kept friends for long and certainly not Frank Dennison, who had ceased to be of any use to him. Unfortunately, she had cause to remember Luke as well. Not just because he was young and sexy but because he was the one who had flirted with her at

60

that party ten years ago when she and Miles were first married. On her part at least, the flirtation was innocent, conducted in front of everyone, but Miles had shown her a side to his character she hadn't seen before. It was the first time he had shown her he was capable of such jealousy, and his fury had shocked her. He'd said nothing at the time, but later that evening, when they got home, he had kicked and slapped her around the bedroom, leaving her with a bruised body and a black eye she'd had to conceal for almost two weeks. He didn't stop until she was weeping with pain and fear.

'Never, never make a fool of me like that again!' he had screamed before slamming out of the room and spending the night in his study.

It was a cruel lesson but one quickly learned; she was careful never to flirt in her husband's presence again. In fact, it was safer never to flirt at all; hidden cameras might be anywhere.

She wondered whether Miles remembered the incident, whether that was part of the reason he was tormenting the young man now. Most likely not. Having chastised her, he would consider the matter settled, banishing it from his mind.

'If you want to wait perhaps you should do

so outside,' the receptionist suggested, breaking into her thoughts.

'Where?' Larissa gave a mirthless laugh, nodding towards the outer door. 'You expect me to stand out there in that draughty corridor? I don't think so.'

The girl shrugged. She had done her best and was covered if Miles complained of their eavesdropping. They both returned their attention to the conversation clearly audible behind the glass door. Larissa could see Miles's face reddening behind the frosted glass. He was seated behind his desk and Luke was standing opposite, leaning aggressively towards him.

'You stole my inheritance, you bastard. My family home.' She could hear the young man's voice break with emotion, wavering out of control. 'I had scarcely the time to collect my personal things before your bully boys turned up and said I was trespassing, threatening to throw me out.'

'They shouldn't have done that,' Miles said. 'I'll speak with them.'

'Too late. I'm not going back there now. The place just isn't the same since you've stolen it.'

'I've stolen nothing from you. It was a crumbling edifice, with you and your father reduced to living in two rooms. If you must know I paid him a fair price, far more than the old ruin was worth. You don't have to believe me — just ask his solicitors. Everything was legitimate and above board.'

'Easy for you to say.' Luke stabbed a finger rudely towards him. 'My father has been less than capable since he had that stroke and you've taken advantage. You probably caused his illness in the first place. All that stress. I remember you when I was a kid. Always hounding him to invest in this or that scheme for getting rich quick.'

'Only trying to help. The business world has been turmoil for the past twenty years; if you'd paid more attention instead of driving around in those fancy American sports cars, you'd know. We've all been in damage control — trying to salvage what we could.'

'And you salvaged plenty, I'll bet.'

'Luke, I'm trying to be patient but you're really pushing your luck. I acted only out of friendship and respect for your father and with his best interests at heart. Yarraview House is nothing but a handsome shell — a Victorian dinosaur that needs a lot of money spending to make it habitable. Money that you and Frank no longer have. Your father said it was a relief to be rid of it — he was grateful to me for taking the place off his hands.'

'Oh, you're such a saint.'

'Luke, face the facts. Your father needed to move into that nursing home. He can't live without care any more and certainly not in that draughty, broken-down pile.'

'But it was my home, too. Where am I supposed to live?'

'I don't know. Where do most young people live? A nice apartment maybe? A new house on one of those modern estates? It must be easy for a young man to get a mortgage at your age. Oh, but I'm sorry, I forgot. You don't even have a job, do you?'

'I do so. I'm a journalist on a suburban paper.'

'I'm impressed. Weddings and funerals, is it?'

'I'll be looking forward to writing up *your* funeral, Miles.'

'Is that a threat, Luke?' Miles was suddenly very upright, very still.

'Take it any way you like. I'd like to ruin your life as you've ruined mine. Yarraview House has belonged to our family since the eighteen hundreds. In his right mind, my father would never have sold it — never. So what if it's falling down and in need of new wiring? It's *our* piece of history, *our* heritage — not yours. I don't even know why you want it. You already own a mansion in Brighton — you can't live in two places at once.'

'Ah, but let me explain. A new wife can be touchy. She doesn't like to move so completely into her predecessor's shoes.'

'What new wife? From what I hear, you're not quite free of the old one yet?'

Miles didn't rise to the bait, sitting back in his seat instead. 'You know what they say, Luke. If you want to capture and keep a beautiful bird, you must first get a birdcage.'

'I don't know what you're talking about. You're so full of crap, Miles.' Luke was determined to have the last word. 'I'm sorry I didn't push it harder with Larissa when I had the chance. Poor kid. Married to an old geezer like you — she must have been gagging for it.'

In the outer office the women recoiled, hearing Miles finally lose it, He pushed back his chair and stood up to confront the younger man.

'How dare you say that to my face. Get out! You filthy-minded little bugger. Get out now.'

Larissa turned aside as Luke strode out of Miles's office, watching him out of the corner of her eye. It would be embarrassing if he were to recognize her after what she had overheard. But Luke had other things on his mind. Breathing heavily with the effort of holding his emotions in check, his eyes were shining, his lips almost twitching into a smile

65

of triumph. He was satisfied to have drawn blood.

'Whew!' Larissa gave a weak smile at the PA, knowing neither of them had missed a moment of the row they had just heard, but the girl just shrugged, curiously unmoved. It occurred to Larissa that she probably witnessed such scenes on a daily basis. Miles was ruthless in business and didn't know the meaning of tact.

'I think you should leave,' she said to Larissa, sitting up at the computer, hands hovering over the keys. 'Mr Barton won't be in the mood to see anyone now.'

She was wrong. And the girl blushed with embarrassment when Miles came out of his office looking as if nothing had happened, greeting his ex-wife as if he really was pleased to see her, suppressing the fact that he had been seething with temper just moments before.

'Elaine! Why didn't you tell me Larissa was here?' he said, before turning his back on the girl. 'Always lovely to see you, darling.' He placed a possessive arm around Larissa's shoulders, drawing her into his space. She tensed, fearing he was about to kiss her but that didn't happen. He smelled as he always did, of Chanel Egoiste and expensive cigars. 'We must have a word later, Elaine,' he murmured over his shoulder. His tone was soft but the girl blushed even more deeply, biting her lip. 'You really must learn not to make assumptions based on appearance.'

Miles's attitude made Larissa all the more pleased that she had come to see him here in his office, rather than at her old home. His conversation with Luke Dennison had been very revealing. The economy in Australia wasn't as stable as before, particularly after the floods up North and the catastrophic earthquake in Japan. Now, after paying old Dennison for his house, Miles could be financially stretched.

Even so, she couldn't find it in her heart to be sorry and, instead of allowing him to steer her towards the couch and sit next to her as he had done in the past, she chose the more formal visitor's seat opposite him at his desk. Patiently she waited while he went through the ritual of lighting an enormous cigar. It was a ploy she had seen him use many times to intimidate others, but she just smiled at him, allowing it to have no effect.

'Well, then,' he said at last, leaning back to study her. 'I see you've reverted to scrubbed-up schoolgirl since I saw you last. It's not going to work, though.'

'Surely you don't think I'm here because I want you to take me back?' She stared at him in amazement. The man's ego was past belief.

'How should I know?' he said drily. 'I have long since given up trying to read the mind of any woman. I'm hoping you've come to your senses and you're here to accept my offer. I have the divorce papers all ready for signature and the pink diamond bracelet right here in the safe. We can conclude our business to the satisfaction of all parties. Now. Today.'

'Miles, I'm not here today to talk about the divorce — although I realize that may be a priority for you, particularly if you wish to marry again?' She raised an eyebrow, tucking a stray lock of hair behind her ear.

Miles ignored the question, preoccupied with gazing at her hands. 'What have you done to yourself?' He gave a slight shiver of revulsion. 'Look at the state of your nails. You look as if you've been digging a field with your bare hands.'

'It's just honest dirt from my mother's stables. In the last few weeks my life has been much more grounded, more real to me, than the whole ten years I spent with you.' The words were out before she could stop them and she took a deep breath to calm herself, not wishing to say any more. 'No. I'm sorry. I didn't come here to fight with you, Miles.'

'So why are you here, Rissa?' he said softly. 'Time is money, you know, and I don't like to waste it.'

'A young jockey has gone missing.' She came directly to the point, hoping to catch him unawares. 'Johnnie Riordan. He's apprenticed to William Willett so you must know of him.'

Miles shrugged. 'Maybe. I don't concern myself with the little people. I leave that to Willett.'

'You never change, do you? Such a snob! Johnnie rides for Willett some of the time and also for my mother.'

'So?' Miles sat back, uninterested, his expression bland. 'If the boy has fallen out with Willett and run off, why should that be any concern of mine?'

'Because he was last seen on that Saturday race day at Caulfield. He rode Roxy's Robin for you. It seems he disregarded Willett's instructions and — '

'Cost us a packet of money.' Miles's gaze narrowed. 'Yes, I remember it now. Willett was almost having a stroke. Afraid the kid would blab and there might be a stewards' enquiry. Idiot. I said he should put on a good face and act like it was meant to happen. The stewards don't often waste their time investigating a horse that can win.'

'I see.' Larissa paused, almost afraid to ask. 'So it didn't bother you, then? You didn't ask Willett to take any steps to silence the boy?'

'Silence him how?' Impatiently, Miles tapped off the burnt end off his cigar. 'I hope you're not suggesting anything crude?'

'Only that accidents are easy to arrange.'

'Oh dear, oh dear.' Miles sat back again, regarding her. 'I can see how far I have fallen in your esteem. Isn't it more likely that the lad became scared when he realized how much trouble he'd caused and has simply run off?'

'Yes. We considered that possibility but his brother said he hadn't the money to go anywhere.'

'And who is this brother? How does he come into it?'

'David Riordan — he's a jockey as well, a few years older than Johnnie. He called on us because the boy rode for my mother that same day.'

Miles sat back, smiling and clearly enjoying himself. 'Oh, well. That rather muddies the waters, doesn't it? How am I supposed to know any more than she does about this pathetic runaway.' He stood up, glancing at his watch. 'If you're still not prepared to accept my offer, we have nothing more to discuss. Not today. Think about it, Rissa. You could have taken my bracelet and lived a life of luxury until you were inclined to marry again. But no. You'd rather stink of horse shit

70

and work in a stables.'

'I assure you, Miles,' she too stood up, determined to have the last word, 'the stink of horse shit is much cleaner and purer than the stink I am breathing in here.' So saying, she turned and marched out of his office, resisting the temptation to slam the door. She felt a welling resentment towards her ex-husband who didn't seem to care about anyone but himself.

*   *   *

Instead of returning straight home she decided to drop in at the address David Riordan had given her: the unit near Caulfield racecourse that he shared with his mother and brother. With any luck Johnnie might have come home.

The Riordans lived in a small, old-fashioned block of six units, similar to many others scattered all over the eastern suburbs in a zigzag pattern so that, as far as possible, they wouldn't be overlooked. Theirs was the largest unit at the rear of the block, the only one to have a small but well-kept garden with rosemary bushes and a couple of rose trees beside the front door.

She had to wait so long for the door to be answered that she began to believe there was no one home. At last it was opened behind a security screen, revealing a small, even-featured woman with prematurely grey hair and leaning heavily on a stick. Her face fell as soon as she saw Larissa, knowing intuitively that this wasn't someone with news of her missing son.

'Look,' she said, shoulders slumping wearily. 'I don't want to fill in a survey for money, I don't want to change my electricity account and I don't want to buy anything, so — '

'Mrs Riordan, please. I'm not here about any of those things. I was wondering if David was home?'

'Oh, so you're looking for David, are you?' Her mouth almost twitched into a smile. 'You and about six other girls.'

'Really?' Larissa squinted at her. 'David didn't strike me as being a ladies' man.'

'He isn't.' Mrs Riordan smiled properly this time. 'That's what makes him so appealing.'

Larissa thought it was time to set the record straight. 'I'm not one of his girl friends — well, I'm a friend, but you know what I mean. I take it that Johnnie still hasn't come home?'

'Know about that, do you? It's over two weeks since we've seen him and I can't help

fearing the worst. The longer he's gone . . . '
She broke off and shivered, glancing at the
unit across the driveway where curtains were
twitching. 'You'd better come in,' she said.
'No point in giving that woman's nose a
treat.'

She ushered Larissa along a short corridor
lined with racing photographs and into a
small but cosy kitchen. 'Tea?' she offered.

'Yes, please — milk and no sugar.'

Mrs Riordan busied herself with the
preparation of tea and offered Larissa a plate
of mouth-watering, home-made melting moments.
Larissa took one and crunched it greedily.
With all the manual work she was doing, she
no longer had to deny herself sweet things as
in the days when she was with Miles.

'The boys love them.' Mrs Riordan smiled.
'Although poor David doesn't eat enough to
keep a sparrow alive. But you didn't come
here to talk about biscuits, Miss — ?'

'It's Mrs — for the time being, anyway. I'm
married to Miles Barton.'

Mrs Riordan's smile widened. 'Good luck
with that.'

'You know my husband?'

'Let's say our paths have crossed.' Mrs
Riordan didn't elaborate. 'I never like to see
my boys riding for him. And Willett has
always been bad news — even as a kid. He

73

had a ramshackle place in the hills in the eighties when I was just a girl. It was a rainforest jungle in those days and he grew marijuana hidden behind a hedge of brambles.' She smiled at the memory. 'But that's a long time ago now. He's progressed to something a lot more sophisticated than growing a bit of weed.'

'Such as?'

'That'd be telling, wouldn't it?' Deftly, she changed the subject. 'So, Mrs Barton, why are you here? What do you want with me?'

'My mother and I would like to help find your son. He was last seen after riding a winner at Caulfield for my mom — Stella Arkwright. She feels somewhat responsible. If he hadn't been riding for her on that day he would have come home earlier with David.'

'Don't let her think like that.' Mrs Riordan covered Larissa's hand with her own. 'Let's just hope Johnnie's gone off on some ploy without telling anyone.'

'Is he likely to do that?'

'No.' The older woman's lip trembled and she stared into her half-empty cup of tea. 'But it's the only way for me to keep thinking he's still alive.'

'Mrs Riordan,' Larissa said gently, 'don't you think it's time to go to the police?'

'No!' The woman looked up and glared at

her. 'What are they going to do? Twist everything so it looks like whatever happened to Johnnie must be his own fault.'

'Not all policemen are like that. Some genuinely want to help.'

'I know what I know.' Mrs Riordan picked up the teacups and carried them to the sink, indicating it was time for Larissa to leave. 'You keep your opinion, Mrs Barton, and I'll keep mine.'

'Tell David I called,' Larissa said as she walked to the door. 'It may be that Johnnie is being held somewhere against his will.'

'Why?' Mrs Riordan turned to face her. 'He's just a boy. Why would anyone want to do that?'

'To stop him answering any awkward questions about Roxy's Robin. Remember, the longer you leave it and do nothing, the less likely it is that he'll be found alive.'

'How dare you come here, saying such dreadful things.' The woman blushed scarlet, upset and enraged. 'Go away, girl. Get out of my house.'

Larissa went. Her tactless remark had made her an enemy but she hoped she had stirred up Mrs Riordan sufficiently to make her go to the police.

* * *

When she reached home it was after four and no one was home. Stella must have gone to fetch Sally from school. In some ways Larissa was relieved. It gave her the chance to think. She made herself a cup of tea and sipped it, mulling over the day's events. When the telephone rang she was preoccupied and answered it at once, without wondering who it might be.

'Would that be Larissa? Larissa Barton?' It was a young man and his voice sounded eager and vaguely familiar.

'Who wants her?' she said, wishing she'd let the call go through to answering mode.

'It's Luke here. Luke Dennison.' He sounded jaunty, confident. 'I'm sure you'll remember me. At least from today?'

'Oh. Yes.' She was cool, remembering the uncomplimentary things he had been saying about her. 'So you did recognize me in Miles's office?'

'Of course. But I wasn't going to say so. Not in front of the blonde watchdog.'

'What can I do for you, Luke?'

'Ooh, don't get me started. Sorry, no — please don't hang up.' He corrected himself. 'That was rude. I was wondering if you'd like to go out for a meal? Or maybe just a spin in my new Corvette?'

'I don't think so, Luke. It isn't a good idea.'

She was grateful that neither her mother nor Sally was home to hear even one side of this conversation. Awkward questions would have been asked.

'OK.' He seemed unperturbed. 'Can I give you my mobile number in case you change your mind?'

'As I've already said, this isn't a good idea.'

'OK. I get it. Be seein' ya, Rissa!'

'Not if I see you first. 'Bye, Luke.'

She stared at the land-line after he'd gone, wondering whether to take it off the hook for a while. Why was it that as soon as a woman left her marriage, most men considered her to be fair game? In the end she left it, hoping that Luke would take the hint and not call her again.

*　*　*

Luke Dennison slammed the phone down in a bad temper. Used to calling the shots, he wasn't accustomed to being turned down. What was wrong with that Rissa Barton? Most divorced women were almost pathetically thrilled to get any attention, especially from him. He must be losing his touch.

Having been thrown out of Yarraview House, he was presently lodging with Peter, the last of his friends from college, but he knew the arrangement couldn't last. In a studio apartment intended for one occupant, at present there were three. It would have been crowded enough with two people but Peter's girl friend had just come to live there as well. The bitch was doing her best to get Luke thrown out, accusing him of trying to watch her in the shower. As if he'd bother. The girl was like a praying mantis with nothing to see on a bony figure as flat as a board, making him wonder how Peter managed to get it up with her at all. Of course, it was stupid of him to have made the mistake of saying so; it had only brought everything to a head. Now he was faced with trying to find a new port in the gathering storm.

Being a creature of habit, he did what he always did when he was upset and too restless to stay indoors. He took his new sports car, bought with the last of the money his grandmother had left him, and drove slowly down Toorak Road, looking for someone to goad into giving him a chase.

He didn't have to wait long. In no time at all a driver in a black Porsche took up the challenge. As it was night and the car had darkened windows Luke couldn't see the man's face, but the signs were unmistakable as the Porsche drove past him and then moved in front of him suddenly, forcing him to brake. All they needed now was to leave the city behind and find a stretch of highway long and empty enough for the real battle to commence.

The Porsche took off towards the western suburbs, using a highway that was unfamiliar to Luke. But he trusted his yellow Corvette to be the match of any regular Porsche, although he hadn't yet had it converted from left-hand drive.

In the middle hours of the evening there wasn't much traffic about. People were home or out at some entertainment, not yet on the streets for the late run home.

The two cars began their duel as before, chasing, overtaking and cutting in on each other until Luke detected a certain change in the game. The driver of the Porsche was becoming still more aggressive, moving dangerously close and threatening to force him off the road into a steep ditch on his left hand side.

It wasn't a buzz any more and Luke was seriously frightened. He thought about trying to call a pax to show he was giving up, making a U-turn and going back home. But the driver of the Porsche wouldn't have any of it, continuing to hog the road and controlling the game, refusing to let Luke communicate with him and forcing him to drive faster and faster to keep out of his way.

In the end Luke was so busy watching the car behind him, wondering which side the next attack was coming from that his whole attention was centred on his rear-view mirror. He just didn't see where he was going and had no time to react when his powerful car drove at full speed into the only tree standing at the side of the road.

The next morning, Larissa watched the news of a grisly accident on a country highway. Television cameras hovered over what had been a handsome yellow sports car as firemen tried to wrench it from around a tree. It had struck the tree with such force that it was a total write-off; a smash that no one could possibly hope to survive. There was but one fatality — the driver, Luke Dennison, who had been alone in the vehicle at the time.

Larissa's first thought was that if she had accepted his invitation to go for a spin she might not now be alive, and that made her shiver. Her second thought was that Miles no longer had anything to fear from Luke Dennison. For some reason the second thought made her even more uneasy than the first.

4

Johnnie had no idea how long he had been kept in this freezing wine cellar. During the day there was a tiny bit of light to be seen through a thick glass window high up on the wall, enabling him to distinguish day from night. It was too small for him to climb out of, even if he could reach it and break the glass.

Food and lukewarm water arrived at any odd hour of the day or night. Usually it was cold burgers and chips from Macca's; leftovers half-eaten by somebody else. To begin with Johnnie ignored this disgusting fare, so different from the healthy, appetizing food his mother made, but in the end he was forced to eat some of it. If he were to stand any chance of escaping from here, he knew he was going to need all his strength.

One day he stood at the top of the steps with his brimming toilet bucket, hoping to throw it at his captors, taking them by surprise and making good his escape. Instead the two bully boys were quick to wake up to his ruse and punished him by squashing the half-full bucket of excrement over his head.

Then laughing derisively, they left him there shivering and ready to puke at the smell of himself. It took him a long time to rinse his hair and his clothes in cold water at the tiny sink afterwards and, without soap, it was impossible to get rid of the stink entirely. He shivered uncontrollably, hoping he wouldn't catch his death of cold. His captors ignored him for some time after that, leaving him without food for the rest of the day.

At night his dreams became vivid and terrifying. He knew he must be feverish as a worsening cough burned in his chest and kept him awake. Gradually, he started to give up hope, beginning to feel he might even die here, and eating less and less of the unappetizing food.

Rescue came at last from an unexpected quarter; a boy of sixteen or so who was sometimes sent down with his meals.

'I wouldn't eat that,' he whispered, indicating the burger that, unusually, didn't seem to be half-chewed. 'I saw one of them open it up and spit on it.'

Johnnie groaned. For once, the food was warm and looked worth eating.

'You should get out of here,' the lad said. 'While you still can.'

'How?' Johnnie whispered back. 'Those two move fast as snakes, the pair of them.'

'Not tonight they don't.' The kid grinned. 'Someone gave them a big bottle of Tullamore Dew from the airport and they're well pissed. This is the best chance you'll get.'

'What about you? Won't you get into trouble when they find out you let me go?'

'You'll have to knock me out. Make it look like you jumped me.'

'How? I don't have a weapon and I'm too weak to knock you out with my bare hands.'

'Excuses, excuses!' The lad sighed. 'They gave me this baseball bat to defend myself in case you turned ugly. Not my fault if you take it off me.' He handed it over. 'Don't kill me now, but you'd better hit me hard enough to make it look good.'

'I can't do that. I might really hurt you.' Johnnie was seized by a fit of coughing.

'And if you stay down here with a cough like that, you'll be dead in a week,' the lad urged. 'Nobody ever comes out here, you know — the power's off an' the place has been empty since the old owners left. Belongs to some rich bloke who's plannin' to get it done up.'

'Who?'

'How should I know? Look, are you goin' to stand there askin' questions all night or what?'

'But I don't understand.' Johnnie was still

reluctant to do as the boy asked. 'Why would you do this? Why should you run such a risk for me?'

'If you die I don't want to be charged as an accessory to manslaughter or murder. Those idiots up there are my sister's husband and his brother. They don't have half a brain between them, but if they go down they'll make sure I do, too.'

Johnnie picked up the baseball bat and found that he couldn't bring himself to swing it. 'I can't do it,' he said. 'Not in cold blood.'

'Don't, then.' The kid snarled at him. 'Be a coward! Just stay here an' rot.'

Johnnie swung the bat then, striking the boy a blow on the back of the head. He was terrified that he might have hit him too hard but, although the lad was unconscious, he was breathing evenly and his pulse was steady. His story would be believed.

Cautiously, Johnnie crept up the stone steps, realizing how weak he had become in the weeks that he had been held prisoner here. He was breathless by the time he reached the top and was trying to stifle his cough. Limbs trembling and shaking with fear, he crept out of the building, grateful that it wasn't part of the main house. The old mansion itself looked deserted, standing in darkness except for the flickering light from some candles in what was most likely the kitchen downstairs. He imagined the bully boys sprawled across the kitchen table in a drunken stupor. Although there was no sound of human activity, not even snoring, he thought it best not to investigate further. He winced as his boots crunched on the gravel outside — there was nothing he could do to deaden the sound — and his heart thumped in his chest as he expected any moment to hear the hue and cry of pursuit. But not even a dog barked; there remained only silence and the darkness of a moonless night.

Once he was well clear of the main house he hopped and hobbled along the driveway, making his way to the road, not knowing which direction to take. He had no idea where he was and hoped it wasn't too far away from the suburbs. It would be so much easier for them to recapture him in an isolated country area.

He would have to flag down a lift although he was all too aware of his daunting appearance. After the incident with the bucket and living in the same clothes for more than two weeks, he must look and smell like a vagrant. He found himself on a minor road that was busy enough although most vehicles passed him by with a derisive hoot of the horn. At last, a small and dusty truck with an empty tray pulled up at the side of the road under a street lamp, waiting for him to catch up. The driver leaned across to open the door on the passenger's side.

'Good God, what happened to you, lad?' The driver peered at him. He was a man in his late sixties, with a gingery-grey beard and wearing a battered felt hat. But underneath it his eyes were youthful, blue and twinkling with good humour.

'It's a long story,' Johnnie sighed. 'And you might prefer that I ride in the tray. I'm afraid I stink.'

'No. Hold on an' I'll put some old newspapers over the seat.' The old man scrabbled behind him to pick up a handful. 'Never travel without a pile of old papers — soak up anything from oil to blood.'

'Blood?' Johnnie hesitated as he was about to climb in. After his recent experiences, he wasn't prepared to trust anyone.

'Sometimes I go shooting hares. The missus goes spare if I leave the car stinking of blood. Get in, then. Are you comin' with me or not?'

'Yes, please.' Johnnie climbed in and sank down gratefully on the pile of newspapers.'

'Phew! Not kidding, are you. What have you been doin,' son? Crawlin' about in a sewer?'

Johnnie ignored the question to ask one of his own. 'This might sound stupid, but where are we? I have no idea where I am.'

'This road leads to Ringwood, sonny. Where do you want to go?'

'Not sure. But I don't think I can go home.' He could well imagine those bully boys catching up with him on his mother's doorstep.

'Well, I think you should.' The old man peered at him as they drove along. 'No matter what you've done, the folks'll forgive you and want you back safe with them.'

'It's nothing that I've done. It's what people have done to me.' Without really meaning to, Johnnie poured out his tale to the old man, who thought it strange enough to believe.

'It's disgraceful. You should go straight to the police and lodge a complaint. Do you know who's behind this plan to abduct you?'

'Not for certain. But I have a good idea.' Johnnie tried to suppress a cough and didn't succeed. 'And I can't go to the police — I have a juvenile record, you see.'

'All right,' the old man said, thinking. 'But you need to see a doctor about that cough before it gets any worse. I'd take you home with me but the missus will go spare. Says I'm always bringing lame ducks home, expecting her to take care of them.'

'No. Look, you've done more than enough. You've been very kind. If you let me off here, I'll — '

'You'll do what? You look ready to drop. You must have a friend, surely? Some place where you can lie low for a bit?'

'Not really . . . ' Johnnie hung his head despondently. 'Except . . . '

'Yes? Except what? You've thought of somebody?'

'There's a lady I ride for sometimes. She's real nice an' she has a stables at Warrandyte. If we're on the way to Ringwood, we can't be too far from there.'

'Warrandyte it is, then.' The old man looked relieved. 'D'you know the address?'

'I'm not quite sure — but the name's Arkwright.'

'Unusual name. Wouldn't be Stella Arkwright, would it?'

'Yes!' For the first time in ages, Johnnie felt as if his luck was turning around. 'You know her?'

'I've known Stella and her family ever since she married Bob Arkwright, grumpy old wretch that he was in his latter years. Whenever she needs a farrier, she always calls on me first. Cobbler's the name — Tom Cobbler — although I fix shoes for horses, not people.' He held out his hand and didn't flinch at the smell as Johnnie shook it. 'I'll have you over to Stella's place in two shakes, no sweat.'

'Wait a minute.' Johnnie looked at the clock in the car. It was registering ten past eleven. 'It's a bit late to drop in on racing people — they have to be up at the crack of — '

'This is an emergency.' Tom grinned. 'And I'm sure Stella won't mind.'

★ ★ ★

Stella didn't. The three Arkwright women greeted their visitors in their dressing-gowns, relieved to see the young jockey and eager to hear of his adventures. Unwisely, Sally hurled herself into his arms until the smell hit her and she recoiled, gagging.

'Oh wow! Where have you been?' She covered her mouth with both hands. 'Did you fall down a drain or what?'

'I'm sorry,' Stella said, also covering her nose. 'But would you take a shower first? Explanations can come later. And I'd better burn those clothes in the boiler downstairs. You'll never be able to wear them again.'

'But they're all I — ' Johnnie started to protest.

'No argument.' Stella said as if she were

speaking to Sally. 'Into the shower with you.' She gave him a new bottle of shower gel and a towel, ushering him towards an old downstairs bathroom off the kitchen. 'And take it as hot as you can stand.'

Before he came out, she had found him an old dressing gown that had belonged to her husband. The lad emerged from the shower room, smelling much sweeter but still shivering and sweating.

'You're not well, John.' Stella looked at him, realizing how much weight he had lost in the past two weeks. He had been thin before but now he was gaunt. 'You need to go to the hospital.'

'No, please!' he said, giving way to another coughing fit. 'I'll be OK after a good night's sleep an' something to eat.'

'All right,' Stella said. 'But if you're no better in the morning, I'm taking you to the doctor.' She turned to the farrier who was now gratefully nursing a small glass of whisky. 'What about you, Tom? Can we offer you some supper before you go home?'

'No, I'd better be off.' The old man glanced at his watch. 'I'll be in trouble enough with the missus already.'

'Thanks, Mr Cobbler,' Johnnie said, trying not to cough. 'You saved my life.'

'Well, I dunno about that,' the old man

replied, picking up his battered hat and preparing to leave. 'I'm jus' happy everything turned out the way it did. See yez all later an' thanks for the Scotch.'

'Irish, actually.' Stella grinned.

'Whatever. It sure hit the spot.' Tom said.

Nothing more was said until Johnnie had devoured two bowls of Stella's nourishing home-made vegetable soup with chunks of fresh bread and butter.

'Thanks,' he said as his spoon hit the plate. 'Best food I've had in weeks.' He sat back, smiling rather shyly at Sally, who was devouring him with an intense and adoring gaze. 'I really should let my mum know I'm OK. And David. They'll have been worried sick.'

'Tomorrow.' Stella said firmly. 'It's after midnight and a few more hours won't make any difference now.' She knew John had no idea how he looked after spending a fortnight in a cellar. On top of that he was almost asleep on his feet. 'I'll take you down to the doctor first thing and then drive you home.'

★　★　★

Fortunately, Johnnie's cough turned out to be nothing more sinister than a touch of bronchitis. Stella's doctor prescribed a course of antibiotics and said there was nothing wrong with him that good food and a few nights' decent sleep wouldn't cure. Larissa, hoping to make peace with Mrs Riordan, offered to drive him home. Stella had dressed him in some of her husband's old clothes but they were much too large for him and made him look smaller and more wasted than ever.

Patsy Riordan, delighted to have her youngest back where he belonged, insisted on making tea and cutting a cake that was being kept for somebody's birthday.

'I'm sorry for what I said to you before,' she murmured softly to Larissa so that Johnnie shouldn't hear. 'I'm afraid I was very rude.'

'It's forgotten already,' Larissa said. 'But I still feel you should report this to the police.'

'Why?' Mrs Riordan looked troubled. 'He's home safe now. He can stay here with me as long as he likes.'

'That's just it, Mum, I can't.' Johnnie had picked up on the end of their conversation. 'I've got a living to earn and if I don't front up at Willett's stables as soon as I can, he'll fire me — apprentice or no. He might even have done so already. And he's mean enough to tell everyone I'm unreliable so I won't get another job. I've seen him do it before.'

'But you're sick. You shouldn't go anywhere until you get better.'

'I know you don't like me working for him, Mum. But whatever you say, it's a good job with a high-profile stables — I don't want to lose it.'

'There are plenty of other trainers you might have gone to.' The woman's lips set in a stubborn line. 'Nice lads who play the game honestly. I wish you'd never gone anywhere near that man. He's a known villain and I'm sure he's at the root of most of your troubles.'

'We don't know that, Mum.'

'I do. I've known that weasel since I was a girl. And who else had reason to lock you up so as to keep you quiet?'

'I don't know.' Johnnie looked pained, tired of the argument that seemed to be going round in circles. 'Maybe it's something else and they think I know a lot more than I do. Maybe it was just a case of mistaken identity. I didn't recognize those men — I never saw them before.'

Soon afterwards Larissa made her excuses and left. While she was happy to have delivered John Riordan home to his mother, secretly she had hoped to see David again. She did her best to hide her disappointment and seem uninterested when Mrs Riordan said he was riding for one of his regulars at a race meeting up country. She had to make do with a brief call to his mobile, telling him his brother was home safe and sound. He did sound pleased to hear from her and promised to catch up soon, but she wasn't entirely sure she believed him.

The next day happened to be a Monday so, resisting his mother's urging to take just one more day off, Johnnie rose at dawn, showered, dressed and got ready to present himself at work; thoughtfully David had fetched his motor bike from the racecourse. That, too, was a bone of contention with his mother, who would have preferred to see him driving a car.

His cough was clearing up rapidly, thanks to the antibiotics, but he was tired after sitting up late talking to his brother. Contrary to their mother's wishes yet again, David agreed that he should return to Willett's stables and look out for anyone who seemed surprised to see him. It might be the best way to find out whether Willett or anyone there was responsible for kidnapping him.

Johnnie parked his motorbike under the trees alongside the vehicles belonging to other hands. Only the foreman, together with his wife and sons, lived in a comfortable cottage close to the stables — all other hands lived out. Willett's black Mercedes was already parked in the spot reserved for it alongside the main door. Johnnie felt a sinking of his stomach as he looked at it, more than ever certain he had been riding in the boot of that car.

But he thrust his hands in his pockets and, whistling softly, tried to look nonchalant as he entered the stables.

'Well, well. Look what the cat's brought in. His lordship's finally seen fit to grace us with his presence.' Rick Murphy, Willett's foreman, greeted him hands on hips. He was a stocky, grim-featured man; a hard taskmaster who liked to work his lads till they dropped. Nevertheless, the stables reflected his almost military discipline, the stalls kept clean and smelling of hay and straw. 'Think you can shove off on holiday for more than two weeks without so much as a 'by your leave' and just turn up again when it suits you, eh?'

'I've been sick.' Johnnie resurrected his cough to prove it. 'On antibiotics.' He took the packet out of his trousers. 'Look.'

'You might have called in and said. We're short-handed here.'

'I know. But I'm here now, aren't I? Bright-eyed, bushy-tailed and ready for work. Who d'you want me to take out for track work today?'

Murphy's mobile phone rang before he could answer this question. 'Yes, sir, he's here. Right away, sir.' He grinned maliciously at Johnnie, jerking his head towards the office. 'The old man will answer that question for you. He's heard you're back and wants to see you, pronto. Hope you've got a doctor's certificate handy.'

Johnnie said nothing. Murphy was a miserable sod, liking nothing better than to see other people in trouble, chiefly because it kept the boss's attention away from himself. He smiled at Murphy as if he hadn't a care in the world but he wasn't looking forward to this encounter.

He knocked and went into the office to find Willett barking orders to someone over the phone. The old man gestured for him to close the door and abruptly ended his conversation. He sat back in his chair, glowering at Johnnie.

'All right,' he said at last. 'Nobody goes absent from my employ without giving me a good explanation. You're supposed to be an apprentice here as well as our regular track rider. Who are you to go swanning off without a word to anyone for more than two weeks?'

'I — '

Willett stabbed an accusatory finger at him. 'Then you turn up out of the blue, expecting life to go on as if nothing happened?'

'Everyone seems to think I was enjoying myself.' Johnnie felt his temper rising and didn't care. 'I was doped and snatched from the jockeys' room. I spent two miserable weeks bailed up in somebody's wine cellar. I almost caught pneumonia and died in there.' At this stage he didn't care whether he sounded disrespectful or not. 'And what's more, I think you know a lot more about it than I do — sir.'

'Now, now John, calm down. This is no time for ridiculous accusations.'

Johnnie smiled. The fact that Willett was trying to placate him made him even more certain he was on the right track.

'And don't you go smirking at me, you cheeky beggar.' Willett glared at him. 'This time I'll give you the benefit of the doubt but don't let it happen again. Go on — get back to work and make up for lost time. Tell Murphy I want to see you out there on Maximo's Curse.'

Inwardly, Johnnie winced but he wouldn't give Willett the satisfaction of seeing it. Maximo's Curse was a new acquisition from Ireland; a talented brute with an unpredictable temper. On a good day Johnnie could work him well, but if the colt was feeling out of sorts and bad-tempered he would try to bite other horses and run into fences, doing his best to dislodge his rider. Once free, he was hard to catch, so Johnnie and the other hands spent a lot of time chasing him round the paddocks until Max got tired of the game and gave himself up.

Today, fortunately, 'that Irish bastard' as the boys called him, was in a relatively good mood, allowing Johnnie to walk him before giving him a swift gallop around Willett's training track. He was to race at a city meeting at Caulfield the following Saturday.

The rest of Johnnie's working week progressed without incident and he was booked to ride Maximo's Curse as well as another of Willett's best horses on that day. At this time of year there were no major races and the prize money was small but, on account of his skill as much as the light weight, he managed to grab first place with both of them. Willett, still holding a grudge, was too mean to offer congratulations. Only David, who brought in a winner himself that day, had any praise for his younger brother.

'Ungrateful old devil,' he said of Willett. 'I saw him out there in the winners' circle, ignoring you and lapping up all the owners' plaudits for himself.'

Johnnie shrugged. He and Willett had little respect for each other these days and he had made up his mind to leave the moment his apprenticeship was over and he was free to find a better job. He might even take his chances interstate.

His mobile rang and he fished in his bag for it, groaning when he saw who the caller was. 'I'd better take it, Bro. She'll give me no peace till I do.' He put the phone to his ear. 'Hi there, Sally.' He tried to suppress a sigh as he listened to the girl's excited voice. 'Yes, I've been busy. A party tonight? No, sorry. Had a big day at the races and I'm bushed. But thanks for askin' — I'll be seein' — ' He tried to cut off the conversation but Sally interrupted, talking quickly, unwilling to let him go. 'Sorry,' he said again at last. 'Can't make it tomorrow, either. Say thanks to your mum for the offer of supper but I've arranged to do something with David. See ya.' This time he succeeded in cutting her off, blowing out a long breath of relief.

'What's that all about?' David said. 'I thought you liked Sally?'

'I do. But she goes on as if we're almost engaged. She's only sixteen for heaven's sake.'

'Try to let her down lightly. A girl's feelings at that age can be pretty intense.'

'She's intense all right. Calls me at least ten times a day as if we're going steady. I'm starting to dread the phone ringing. And Michelle's coming down from Sydney for the races next week. I'll want to spend time with her.'

'Ah, Michelle.' David smiled, thinking of the little blonde Sydney jockey who had taken a shine to Johnnie on her last visit.

'I know.' Johnnie brightened with a sudden idea. 'Maybe you could speak to Sally's sister for me.'

David's eyebrows shot up. 'Mrs Barton? Larissa? What d'you want me to say to her?'

'I dunno. But you seem to get on OK. Could you ask her to get Sal to chill out a bit?'

'Hmm,' David said. 'I'll try. But don't blame me if it puts us on the outer with both of them.' Having said this, he smiled to himself. He had been looking for an excuse to contact Larissa and his brother had just handed him one on a plate.

5

'But why?' David said on the phone to Larissa the following morning. 'Why won't you let me offer you Sunday lunch?'

'Because it's no fun for me to eat a square meal while you sit opposite me with a plain piece of fish on a salad.'

'OK. I see what you mean. Let's go to a movie instead then. D'you fancy one of those new films in 3D?'

'No. Because I'd rather sit somewhere quietly and talk.'

'I know. That's why I suggested lunch.'

'Back to square one, then,' she said, biting her lip until she had a sudden inspiration. 'Have you been to the Dandenongs lately? There are lots of cool, shady places to sit, and with autumn coming the gardens are lovely at this time of year.'

'The hills? No. I haven't been up there for years, not since I was a kid.'

'Then pick me up on Sunday at noon. I'll bring a picnic and you can eat as little or as much as you like.'

'Hold on. I was the one who asked you out to lunch.'

'All right, then. You can bring something to drink. Tell me now, is there anything you don't like to eat?'

'I do like chicken or fish but I don't eat red meat or ham. I hope you don't mind.'

'Not at all. Your diet sounds pretty similar to mine. I can't face steak at all, not after seeing . . . ' She broke off in confusion, realizing she had been about to criticize Miles, who liked to consume his steak rare with the blood running out on the plate.

'After seeing what?'

'Never mind. I'll see you on Sunday then.'

When Larissa came off the phone she danced around the stables with a millet broom, feeling like a teenager again, about to go on a first date.

'What's got into you?' Her mother arrived just in time to see her. 'Won the lottery or something?'

'No.' Larissa grinned. 'David Riordan asked me out.'

Her mother's expression clouded. 'Oh, darling, is that wise? Until you are properly divorced from Miles it might not be sensible to go on a date. He could have someone watching you.'

'I can't be that paranoid, Mom. And anyway, it's not really a date. I'm just meeting a friend for lunch.'

'Oh?' Stella cocked her head on one side. 'So why so excited that you're dancing around with a broom?'

On Sunday the weather turned on one of those mild, sunny mornings that only March in Melbourne can provide. The wind, which had battered the trees the day before, had dropped to a gentle breeze. David appeared on time, wearing jeans and one of his signature cowboy shirts, and she saw that his purple truck had been given a thorough wash and brush up before he arrived. Although Larissa herself wore jeans, comfortable sandals and a floral silk top, she had taken greater care with her appearance than she had since leaving Miles. Her hair, tucked behind her ears and worn a little shorter now that the blonde streaks had almost grown out, was brushed into shining, natural curls. Her make-up was subtle, looking as if she owed more to nature than artifice, her eyes were fringed with darkened lashes, making them look huge. Only Stella pulled a little moue of disapproval, knowing how much trouble her daughter had taken to go on a simple picnic.

Larissa had packed the picnic hamper with several salads, bringing prawns and oysters with slices of lemon, as well as several portions of cold chicken without any fat. She included a flask of coffee but no cheeses or dessert, thinking David wouldn't eat them.

They chatted easily on the journey to the hills, David remarking on how much development had taken place since he'd last come this way. Most of the roads from the suburbs had been widened to accommodate the new housing estates branching out on either side. Huge supermarkets had arrived to service these new residents, as well as furniture stores, office equipment supplies and car yards, not forgetting the usual fast-food outlets.

Soon they were taking the steep, winding road up to Belgrave and beyond. They passed the most popular picnic ground with the tour buses parked outside the coffee and gift shops and travelled on, taking the road to Olinda. There was a smaller picnic ground on that road that not everybody had found. Sometimes it was almost deserted. Larissa hoped that that would be the case today.

There was just one family seated at one of the tables near the barbecue when they arrived, but another car followed them in and a couple climbed out, taking a table not far from their own. They must have been tourists because they brought out a camera to photograph a pair of kookaburras who were watching the picnic ground keenly from a nearby gum tree, waiting for scraps of food that people might leave behind. Then the tourists started taking pictures of each other. David offered to photograph the two of them together and they agreed, looking slightly embarrassed.

'Nice camera,' he mentioned to Larissa after returning it to the owner. 'Those things cost a bomb.'

He reached into the cool bag and brought out a bottle of local Chandon, warning Larissa that she would have to drink most of it as he was driving today.

'Well, you could drink it and I'll drive us home.' She smiled at him, amused to see him searching for a response that wouldn't offend her. 'Only teasing,' she said. 'You should see your face. I know men don't like other people driving their cars.' She was thinking of Miles, who would have a fit if she asked to borrow one of his sports models.

'I suppose it's difficult for you.' David must have been reading her mind. 'After having all that — the best seats at the theatre, holidays at exclusive resorts and designer clothes. It must be hard to adjust to an ordinary, everyday life.'

'Not really,' Larissa said, considering this. 'More like a relief after all that stress. I like being home with Mom and Sally. With Miles, I felt I had to live up to his expectations, as if

I was always on show. As if everything I did somehow reflected on him.'

'So you're not thinking of going back?'

'Good heavens, no. What gave you that idea?'

As they ate and drank the delicious, dry champagne — their good resolutions forgotten — Larissa told him everything about Miles, including his offer of the pink diamond bracelet in return for a trouble-free divorce. 'Wouldn't it have been easier to take the bracelet and accept the divorce?' He said at last.

'Easier, yes. His first two wives caved in, but I won't.'

'But why not? If you're not going back to him, Rissa, why don't you want the divorce?'

'I do. But why should I be portrayed as the guilty party when I haven't done anything wrong?'

'Does anyone care any more? Divorce is so common now that nobody remembers who was at fault.'

'OK. I know I must sound like a dog in the manger but I was loyal to Miles for the whole ten years we were married. I don't see why I should make it easy for him to divorce me now.'

'Even if that means making it hard for yourself?'

Larissa shrugged, wishing she hadn't let the wine loosen her tongue, allowing the conversation to drift on to the subject of Miles and the divorce. She repacked the picnic basket except for the flask of coffee. 'We should drink this now and sober up a bit. Neither of us will be legal to drive.'

'It's all right,' David glanced at his watch as he rose to put the picnic basket back in the car. 'It's only half past two and we've got a few hours before the mosquitoes arrive. We can go for a walk along the bush track over there — we might see some rosellas.'

'Do you like birds, David?'

'I always have.' He smiled. 'Even white cockatoos. But not in cages. To me there's no lovelier sight than a large bird swooping under the trees, flying free.'

Since the track had become overgrown David had to hold several branches aside for Larissa to pass. They saw several pairs of crimson rosellas and did hear the cry of a lyre bird, although it was too well hidden for them to see.

Halfway along the track a comfortable bench had been provided by some local worthy, and they sat down to drink their coffee, looking up into the trees in the hope of seeing more birds.

'Larissa,' David said at last, 'there's

something I need to mention. It's important.'

'That sounds rather ominous.' She pulled a face, hoping to lighten the mood. 'What have I done?'

'Not a thing.' Half-embarrassed to say it, he threw away the line. 'To me you are almost perfect.'

'Only almost?' she teased, pouting.

'No, please be serious for a moment. I promised my brother I'd speak to you about your sister.'

'Sally? Yes. The kids have been dating, haven't they?'

'In a manner of speaking. But it's gone further than that. Sally's almost stalking him, Rissa. She's spoiling what should be a care-free friendship between two young people. She calls and texts him a dozen times a day and gives him no peace.'

Suddenly Larissa sat up very straight. 'And what do you expect me to do about this?'

David hesitated, seeing this wasn't going well. 'We were hoping you might have a word with her. Get her to chill out a bit.'

'I see,' Larissa said, dangerously quiet.

'Well, that's good — because — '

'So that's why you asked me to come out today. You want me to call off my pest of a little sister because your brother is too cowardly to dump her himself.'

'It's not like that — not at all.'

'No? Well, that's what it sounds like to me.'

'This has come out all wrong. Let me start over — please listen to me.'

'Why should I? When you want to ruin a perfect day. I've heard all I need from you, David, and now I'd like to go home.' So saying, she stood up and began to march purposefully back the way they had come.

'Larissa, wait!' David had to run to catch up with her but he couldn't halt her stride. Impulsively, he caught her arm and pulled her towards him, kissing her angry mouth before she could say anything more. He put all the feeling he could muster into that kiss, hoping to show with his actions what he found so difficult to express in words. She responded instantly with a stinging slap to his face, making him release her at once.

'All right,' he said, raising his hands shoulder high in surrender. 'Maybe I deserved that. But we need to back up for a moment here and calm down.'

Larissa stared at him. Her reaction had been way beyond what was necessary and she was shamed to see the red imprint of her fingers on David's face.

'I'm so sorry,' he said. 'I'm no diplomat. I didn't handle the subject as tactfully as I might.'

'I'm sorry, too,' she replied. 'I shouldn't have hit you so hard.' The truth was that she had been startled and disturbed by the passion in David's kiss and her own instinctive response to it. It seemed right and almost familiar, although she scarcely knew him at all. The memory lingered with her still and was far from unpleasant. 'And I didn't want to admit it but you're right about my little sis. She's grown into a spoilt only child since I've been gone. Because Mom's so busy, she takes the line of least resistance and rarely says 'no' to her. Sal's used to getting whatever she wants the moment she wants it and right now she wants your brother. She expects him to follow her around like a tame puppy and the fact that he doesn't only makes her keener still.'

'So what are you saying? I should tell John to go to the other extreme and smother her with attention to put her off?'

'I'm ninety-five per cent sure it'll work. Sal's nothing if not contrary. If she thinks Johnnie's really in love with her, she'll quickly transfer her affections to somebody else.'

★   ★   ★

It took the best part of a week but the strategy worked. Sal came home from school

110

the following Monday, full of complaints about Johnnie. For several days now he had been bombarding her with texts and phone calls since the early hours of the morning, even when he knew she would be in school. And, although she had turned the phone off to avoid her form teacher's displeasure, she found it filled with missed calls and messages from him when she switched it back on. As if to confirm it, the jaunty ring tone started up yet again.

'I've had to recharge it three times this week already,' she muttered, glaring at the little screen. 'He leaves me no time to talk to anyone else and, if I ignore him, he'll only start ringing again.' She put the phone to her ear. 'What is it now, John? Look, you have to stop. I can't live my life like this. I'm sorry if you think you're in love with me but it's no good. I can't take any more. You have to back off and give me some space. Just leave me alone!' So saying, she snapped the phone shut and flung it down on the table. 'Hateful boy!'

Hearing this, Larissa concealed a smile. Later she telephoned David to give him a progress report and they congratulated each other on a job well done without too much hurt to anyone.

'I'm going to be riding at Werribee on Saturday,' he said. 'But only in the first three races. I can take you to tea at Werribee Mansion afterwards.'

'What a good idea,' she said. 'I haven't seen the mansion for years, not since it was done up.'

'Then you're in for a nice surprise.'

'Who was that?' her mother asked when she came off the phone. 'Not David Riordan again? Oh, Rissa.'

'Don't *'Oh, Rissa'* me. It's no bad thing for me to take a look at a country course — we might like to send one of our own horses one day.'

'All the way over there? On the other side of the city? If I want to compete in the country, I'll go to Cranbourne or Pakenham, thanks. And, as I've already said — and Roger Timpson agrees with me — you should curb your social life until the divorce from Miles can be properly finalized.'

'I didn't know you'd discussed me with Roger.'

'Well, it's time you engaged him officially. It's no good letting things slide until it's too late.'

'Too late for what? Miles doesn't seem to care. I don't think he spares me a moment's thought from one week's end to the next. He's far too busy keeping up with his latest squeeze.'

'It may be more comfortable for you to think so but you shouldn't underestimate his power and influence — for David's sake as much as your own.'

'What?' Larissa stared at her mother, shocked by this last remark. 'You can't be suggesting that Miles would hurt David?'

'I'm just saying you should be careful. You don't need me to tell you how mean he can be when he's crossed.'

Just how mean was made clear to her only a few days later.

Rissa went with David to Werribee and he brought in two winners out of his three rides. Mindful of her mother's warning, she dressed simply in jeans and a T-shirt, hiding her face under a wide-brimmed straw hat and dark shades.

'Ooh!' David teased when he saw her. 'Mata Hari today?'

Larissa smiled but she didn't share with him her mother's anxiety, not wishing to spoil their day. At Werribee he introduced her to his racing connections as Rissa Arkwright but several people squinted at her as if trying to place her.

'Is your girlfriend a model, David?' one of the older women asked. 'She looks rather familiar to me.'

'No,' Larissa said, trying to pass attention

away from herself. 'I just have one of those common faces. This happens all the time. People are always mistaking me for somebody else.'

'You don't seem that common to me.' The woman refused to let it go. 'I'm certain we've met before.'

'Sorry to leave you up to your eyes in it, Riss, but I have to go,' David leaned in to whisper. 'Don't worry. We'll get away as soon as I've weighed in after this race.'

'That's it. I've got you now!' the woman crowed, delighted to have placed her. 'You're Larissa Barton — Miles Barton's wife. Oh, you must remember. We met at that awful reception in a tent at Flemington. Dreadful do. Lot of old bores and nowhere near enough food.'

'I think,' Larissa whispered, 'you're confusing me with someone else.'

'Oh no, dear. I never forget a face.'

Larissa smiled weakly and excused herself to go to the rest rooms. She didn't return to the party she'd left behind but went to stand by the winning post to watch David come in.

The course was small with everything in close proximity and Larissa enjoyed being near enough to see the leaders pounding towards her, fighting it out at the finish to reach the winning post. This time David's mount was unplaced. He didn't leave her waiting long while he weighed in and went to change before gaining permission to leave as he had no more rides that day.

'Sorry about that old woman bothering you,' he said when he rejoined her. 'Don't let her spoil our afternoon.'

'I won't.' Larissa smiled, happy to have him to herself again. 'It's my mother who's paranoid about Miles — always expecting him to exact some frightful revenge.'

'And is that likely?' he said softly as he opened the passenger's door to his truck and handed her in. He had showered, changed into his jeans and a shirt and now smelled of fresh citrus soap and cologne.

'I don't know. And today I refuse to let myself care.' She took off her sunhat and glasses. 'I'm starved. Let's go for the tea and buns.'

It wasn't tea and buns. It was a Devonshire tea with freshly baked scones, thick cream and strawberry jam, accompanied by a pot of strong English breakfast tea.

'This is awful. I can't resist a Devonshire tea,' David groaned as he embarked on his third scone. 'I'll have to survive on lettuce for a week after this.'

'No,' Larissa said. 'We'll do the tour of the house and then you can do a quick jog around the gardens.'

The mansion had been restored to its full late-nineteenth-century glory, together with shining brass beds, Persian rugs and antiques. Larissa stalked down the main staircase, lightly touching the well-polished banister as she went.

'Imagine how it would have been to live in that time,' she said. 'Nothing but hunting parties, banquets and balls.'

'You could still have all that — or something similar — if you stayed with Miles.'

'That isn't an option,' she answered lightly. She had told him about Miles's offer of the pink diamonds but not about her discovery of his collection of pre-paid phones. It still made her feel queasy to think about them.

'All I know is I like being with you, Rissa. Let's just take it a day at a time.'

'A day at a time,' she echoed, letting him take her hand and thinking how right it felt — a horseman and woman together with their slightly calloused hands.

They strolled around the gardens afterwards, hands clasped as if they had been friends for years instead of just a few weeks. For Larissa, it was a rare treat to spend time with a man close to her own age and with similar tastes; someone who laughed at the same things and wasn't always waiting to catch her out or take her down a peg.

He showed her the folly in the garden, composed of dozens of seashells and the nearby rose garden, although most of the flowers were spent and past their best at this time of year. At no time did he attempt to kiss her and, although she knew that was only sensible in such a public place, she couldn't help feeling a bit disappointed.

He brought her home shortly before 7 p.m. and refused her invitation to supper, or even to come in, somehow intuiting that Stella might not be pleased to see him. While he allowed her to give him a sisterly hug before leaving, he made no attempt to repeat that extraordinarily unsettling kiss. Having been married to Miles for ten years and with little experience before that, Larissa felt she might be unusually lacking in the ways of modern courtship. She found David charismatic and loved being in his company, but having reacted so violently when he kissed her before she didn't know how to move past it and encourage him now. So she smiled and waved him off as he drove away, feeling rather unsettled that he hadn't asked to see her again.

Inside the house, it was obvious that her mother and younger sister had had a row. In the kitchen, Stella scarcely bothered to greet

117

her and two spots of angry colour burned in her cheeks. Upstairs, Lady Gaga could be heard, belting out a song at full volume.

'OK, what's happened?' Larissa put her arm round her mother's shoulders. 'She's just at that awful in-between age, Mom. You shouldn't let her get to you like this.'

'Oh, I know, but she's impossible sometimes. Last week was all about Johnnie Riordan — who did at least seem to like her. This week it's a new boy at school, a migrant from somewhere in India. I can understand Sally's interest; he's a lovely-looking boy. His name is Sanjay, but it seems his mother doesn't want him to have anything to do with Australian girls.'

'Why have they come to live here, then?' Larissa smiled.

'That's what I said. And it would have been OK if I'd left it there. But I went on to tell her she should forget about boys for a bit and concentrate on her school work.' Stella winced. 'She lost her temper completely and said I wanted to turn her into a crabby old swot who never had any fun. Then she flounced off to her room saying she didn't want any supper.'

'I'll go up and talk to her, Mom.'

'Well, I hope you have better success than I've had.'

Outside Sally's door Larissa hesitated, making up her mind what to say.

'Sally!' she called, knocking gently. 'Can you turn the music down a bit and let me come in? I'd like to talk.'

She heard Sally turn off the music and come to lean on the other side of the door. 'What for? To tell me off for being rude to Mom?'

'We can't have a proper discussion when I can't see your face. Please let me in.'

Sally unlocked the door quickly and ran back to sit cross-legged on her bed. Her eyes were red and it was obvious that she had been crying.

'Oh, Sally.' Larissa went to sit beside her sister, trying to hug the stiff little body. 'Don't think I don't understand. I used to fight with Mom all the time when I was your age.'

'No, you didn't.' Sally glanced at her with resentful eyes. 'You were married at my age.'

'True. But it's hardly turned out to be the fairytale everyone hoped.'

'I know and I'm sorry.' Sally bent her head as fresh tears welled. 'I shouldn't be mean to you or to Mom but I don't know what gets into me sometimes.'

'We should both try to be kinder to her. She has a lot on her plate these days and you know she wants only the best for us.'

'Yes, I do know, Sis. But sometimes she gets so bossy and all she can think about is school and stuff. She told me once that you married Miles to get out of going to college. She doesn't want me to make the same mistake.'

'Won't you come downstairs with me and have supper now?'

'I'm not hungry,' Sally said, her growling stomach giving the lie to it. 'I can't apologize just now, Rissa. I'd feel a hypocrite.'

'Don't say anything then. But do come and have some supper.'

Over a simple supper of baked cauliflower cheese, the three women were at last able to relax. Larissa opened a bottle of wine and, in spite of Stella's pointed look of disapproval, gave some to Sally. After that, they watched an old DVD of something so silly it made them all laugh and, although no official peace had been made, they all felt a lot better when it was time for bed. After all the drama at home, nobody thought to mention Larissa's day out with David.

★ ★ ★

Since Stella had employed a new girl to feed and take care of the horses at weekends, they had the unaccustomed luxury of sleeping late on Sunday morning. Nobody arrived in the kitchen until nearly midday. While Stella and Rissa prepared a brunch of mushrooms, tomatoes, scrambled eggs and toast, Sally went down to the gate to pick up the Sunday papers, rolled up in plastic to keep them from getting damp. They were all starving, so nobody looked at them until the food was all gone. Sally unwrapped them while Rissa made more toast and opened a new pot of raspberry jam.

Both Stella and Rissa turned towards her as they heard her clap both hands to her mouth to stifle a shriek.

'What's wrong?' Larissa teased. 'Is Johnny Depp coming to Melbourne or has a UFO landed in the middle of the MCG?'

Sally at last found her voice. 'You won't think it's so funny when you've seen this,' she said, spreading the paper out across the table for dramatic effect.

'Oh, my good Lord,' Stella murmured, looking over her younger daughter's shoulder.

On the front page of the most widely read tabloid in Melbourne was a clear photograph of Larissa and David, taken in the Dandenongs and showing her slapping him shortly after he had kissed her. The headline screamed: LOVERS' TIFF?

There weren't many words because no

interview had been given but inside the paper were a lot more pictures of both of them enjoying their picnic and watching birds. Enlarged and in the centre of all of them was a photograph of that torrid kiss.

'Those bastards who sat at the table next to us,' Rissa murmured. 'Reporters. And all the time we thought they were tourists. No wonder they looked so embarrassed when David offered to take a photograph of them together.'

'Oh, Rissa.' Stella sank into a chair, her head in her hands. 'What's going to happen now?'

'I don't know.' Larissa scrabbled in her handbag, looking for her mobile. 'But first I have to warn David. He might not have seen this yet.'

'Oh, you wish.' Sally shook her head. 'If he hasn't, his friends are nothing like mine.'

Larissa called David's number and went outside on the back veranda to talk to him. Much as she loved her mother and sister, she wanted this call to be private.

As soon as he answered the phone, she knew that he'd seen it.

'Larissa, please,' he said. 'Don't you go off the planet as well. My mother won't let up — she's been prophesying doom since the early hours of the morning.'

'I'm so sorry, David. I suggested that picnic. I had no idea we'd be followed and watched.'

'Try not to worry. You know the old saying — yesterday's news is wrapped around tomorrow's fish and chips. Some people don't even buy newspapers at the weekend.'

'And some people read them from cover to cover — like Miles.'

'Your husband needs to get over himself. After all, he's the one who wanted to end the marriage.'

'Oh, I know. It's just . . . ' Larissa paused, biting her lip, wondering how to explain her husband's dog in the manger attitude. Miles might no longer want her to be a part of his life but his pride would be damaged if she were seen to find happiness in the company of a younger man. Although it was the first time she had gone out with David, the fact that she had slapped him suggested a more intimate, much longer association.

'I'll come over and see you,' David said. 'Convince your mother nothing's going on.'

'It's a little late for that.' Larissa pulled a wry face. 'She's looking at me as if I'm Jezebel reincarnate. David, it might be better if I don't see you for a while — at least until all the fuss dies down.'

'OK, then. But do try not to worry. I'm

sure it'll blow over in a day or so.'

Larissa didn't answer this but she couldn't help feeling he was wrong.

It was just bad luck that there had been no more gripping news item to claim the front page of the newspaper that day. Miles had many powerful friends in the media and they'd be only too delighted to show her up in the worst possible light.

When she came back inside, it was to hear that Stella had already fielded two calls on the land-line from the editors of women's magazines, offering to pay for her daughter's side of the story.

'I hope you weren't rude to them, Mom.' Larissa said, having had more experience of dealing with editors and reporters than Stella. 'Give them nothing and they'll only make up something worse.'

'Well, what do you expect me to say?' Stella's nerves were on edge. 'I'm not going to say *I told you so* but — '

'No. Please don't do that.'

'But you seem to be rushing headlong into danger without any thought for the future. I can't help feeling that Miles will turn this situation to his advantage.'

'There *isn't* a situation, Mom. David and I are — '

'Just good friends?' Sally finished the

sentence for her. 'After seeing that picture in the paper who the hell is going to believe that?'

'Sally!' Stella began.

'Yeah, yeah! I'll go to my room,' Sally snapped. 'I know you both think I'm too young and stupid to have anything to offer in this.'

★ ★ ★

Seeing those same pictures in the tabloids, Miles's first impulse was to screw the offending newspaper into a ball and hurl it into the waste basket, but he quickly suppressed it. If he did so, Mrs Hudson would know just how angry those pictures had made him feel and he didn't like to think of anyone, least of all his own housekeeper, sniggering behind his back. Instead, he folded the paper neatly and left it beside his breakfast plate as he always did. Mrs Hudson could draw her own conclusions.

Then he made a few phone calls and booked himself on a flight to Hong Kong as soon as it could be arranged. Fortunately, he was able to pick up a cancellation for the very next day. He had several business interests there and he hadn't been around to check up on them for some time. He smiled to himself, thinking what consternation an unexpected visit might cause. He liked to keep his staff on their toes and didn't believe that any employee, however well-paid and loyal, should be left without supervision for too long. Also he had been meaning to pay a visit to China to firm up some new contacts he had made at a recent trade fair. He could arrange the next leg of his journey from the office in Hong Kong. He asked Mrs Hudson to pack him a bag to take with him in the morning and told her that, if she liked, she could take few days off.

The following morning he called in to his office to inform his staff that he was leaving that day and would be out of town for at least three weeks. Everyone was careful to say nothing about those newspaper articles when he came in but he saw his new PA hiding a smile as she secreted a newspaper under a pile of documents. Word was well and truly out concerning his errant wife and he'd like to strangle Rissa for making him look such a fool. At the same time, he had no intention of remaining in Melbourne to become the laughing stock of his enemies or so-called friends.

His PA allowed him time to settle and check his messages before she brought in a pile of documents for him to look over, as well as letters to sign.

'Not now, Elaine.' Impatiently, he waved them away before she could place them in front of him. 'Something's come up. I'm on my way to the airport — flying to Hong Kong. Then, if my plans work out as expected, I'll be travelling on to Beijing.'

'But Mr Barton, you can't go now, you're too busy — you have people coming from Sydney to see you and business meetings set up all week — '

'Cancel them. This is far more important.'

'But when will you be back?'

'Not sure. I'll be in touch.'

'But what shall I — ?'

'Don't argue with me, Elaine. Just do it.'

'And then there's Mr Willett.' Elaine didn't want to think about that rude man who had been ready to swear at her, accusing her of blocking his calls. 'He's been on the line every ten minutes since I arrived. He says he must speak to you immediately and it's urgent.'

Miles sighed. He knew exactly what was so urgent. Willett wanted more money. William Willett had yet to find out that so far as Miles was concerned, their partnership had run its course; he couldn't wait to be free of it. After so many years of living in hope and being disappointed more often than not, Miles now believed that owning a racehorse was rather like throwing money into a bottomless pit. The 'inside information' he'd hoped to glean as an owner had proved to be a total myth and the sooner he could distance himself from Willett and his money-pit of a stables, the happier he'd be. These days he had bigger fish to fry. Casinos and poker machines didn't break down and cost a fortune in veterinary fees and, like most rich men, Miles was always open to change. He was bored with the old and familiar and could easily be distracted by the prospect of something new.

Anxious to avoid speaking to Willett, he decided to leave his office and go to the airport early to wait for his flight. On the way he remembered to call Lynne and tell her where he was going.

'But why do you have to go away now, Miles?' She sounded unusually petulant. 'I wanted us to have a big engagement party so I can show you off to my friends.'

Miles winced. Lynne was adorable and he had every intention of marrying her at some time in the future but he didn't care for the prospect of being shown off as a prize catch to her friends.

'Bit premature, darling.' He lowered his voice to the 'big cat' purr that she loved. 'I'm not quite divorced yet, remember?'

'But you will be, Tiger. You promised.'

'Don't worry. I'll bring you a really nice present from Hong Kong.'

'What sort of present? A big diamond ring?'

'Maybe.' Miles closed his eyes again. He had thought that divorcing Rissa would be no more complicated than it had been with his first two wives. Why couldn't she just accept the pink diamonds and leave? Instead, she had taken up with this journeyman jockey who wasn't even a champion yet. How everyone must be laughing behind his back.

Before reaching the airport he used his mobile again. The calls he made this time were brief and to the point. He repeated his instructions twice to make quite sure they were understood. After that, he sat back and enjoyed the rest of the ride to the airport, thinking it was amazing what a few well-placed words could do.

6

It took David almost two weeks to realize that something was wrong. It seemed at first to be a series of coincidences. He had two rides cancelled in a mid-week city meeting, the trainer calling to say both horses had been scratched. Then he was due to travel up country to a meeting at Echuca the following weekend. The trainer called the day before, sounding embarrassed and telling him not to bother as he had changed his mind, engaging a local jockey to ride for him instead.

Over the next few days, one by one, his opportunities disappeared. Even those trainers who had thought well of him previously were now passing him over in favour of someone else.

'I can't understand it,' he said after nearly a week of being home with no rides and nothing to do. He was beginning to dread the sound of his mobile in case it was yet another trainer dispensing with his services. 'Maybe it's because I don't work through an agent. I've never thought I needed one.'

'I don't think it's that.' His mother looked sad and defeated. 'It's because of that woman, isn't it? After seeing all that in the papers, her husband is using his influence against you. I told you he wouldn't be pleased to find out she was seeing you.'

'We don't know that. Not for sure. Rissa says he doesn't care what she does.'

'She'd have to say that, wouldn't she? That woman is using you, David. You're just a convenient prop to help her get through her divorce.'

'Now you know that's not true, Mum.' He stared at Patsy, shaking his head. 'I don't know why you're so set against her. She's always been civil enough to you.'

Patsy ignored him, sniffing and pursing her lips while David continued voicing his thoughts. 'Maybe I should go and see some of these trainers face to face. Find out what's really going on.'

Impatiently, Patsy ran hot water into the kitchen sink to do the washing up. She added too much detergent so that it foamed up, fizzing and making her cough.

'I know what's behind all this, even if you don't,' she said. 'I tried to warn you but no, you had to go your own way. When I think of all the single girls you could have chosen — nice girls with no strings attached — and you have to take up with a married woman — an *older* married woman at that.'

'Oh, stop it, Mum. You make it sound awful and it's not. Larissa's only a few years older than I am.'

'She's still married, though, isn't she? And this is her husband's way of punishing you and taking revenge.'

'Don't be so melodramatic — even Miles Barton doesn't have that much power and influence. And anyway, Larissa and I are just friends — we're not sleeping together.'

'I should hope not.' Patsy glared him.

'We're getting paranoid. It might be no more than coincidence that I'm losing these rides. Let's wait and see.'

But another week passed and still no one engaged David's services.

For the want of anything better to do, he went to Flemington to support Johnnie who was riding for Willett that day. He also hoped that if some other jockey failed to take a ride, the trainer might overcome his scruples sufficiently to hire him rather than scratch the horse. Although it was a mid-week meeting, there was a large crowd because it was Anzac Day and the gates were open for all the old 'diggers' who were allowed to go on course for free. As well as the usual race card, there would be various entertainments and spectacles including the traditional, old-fashioned game of 'two up', to be played after the last race.

132

Apart from the first race on the card, which he won, Johnnie had only one other ride for the day, on Maximo's Curse. He wasn't looking forward to it — the big horse wasn't in the best of moods. Mares were competing alongside the colts and that always unsettled him. Max's nostrils flared at the scent of them and he played up, whinnying and pawing the ground to get their attention. He tried to follow one into her starting gate and threw a vicious kick towards the barrier attendant who stopped him. Johnnie had to dismount and let the attendants wrestle and push the unwilling beast into his own stall. With his eyes rolling, Max was already sweating up and when Johnnie climbed back in the saddle, he knew he would be in for a difficult ride. He was thankful that it was only a quick dash down the straight. With Max stirred up like this he knew he had no hope of winning; he would be lucky to finish the race in one piece.

There was no time for further thought because they were off. Pursuing his own wishes, rather than those of his jockey, Max forced his way through the field to take up the lead, racing erratically and exhausting himself with this early push to the front. Johnnie couldn't have stopped him, anyway, but instead of capitalizing on his four-length advantage and heading for the winning post, Max changed direction unexpectedly and ran into the inside fence. Crashing through it, he dislodged his rider before coming to a standstill on the other side, dazed and scarcely aware of what he had done. Johnnie felt himself hurled through the air at speed, knowing he must land on the course in front of the other runners. In spite of his helmet and the protective jacket beneath the silks, his whole body was shaken as he crashed to the ground. Mercifully, he knew no more.

It all happened so quickly that David, who had witnessed it all, was momentarily stunned and unable to move. Although most of the runners managed to swerve and avoid him, his brother was kicked and trampled by at least one other horse.

Ignoring various commands to stay out of the way, David jumped over the fence and charged on to the course to join the paramedics at the scene. Allowing them to do their work without hindrance, he saved his questions until they were all in the ambulance, siren screaming as the vehicle tore through the streets of the city at speed.

'He's going to be all right, isn't he?' David asked, scarcely able to speak through dry lips. His brother looked half dead already, unconscious and white-faced under the oxygen mask.

'We think it's his spine — and there may be some internal bleeding from injuries we can't see,' the younger of the two paramedics started to explain until he was silenced by a meaningful look from his older colleague. 'They'll know more at the hospital when they've taken some X-rays.'

'Don't you worry, son.' The older man spoke with false heartiness. 'I've seen all this before. These lads are young and tough — it's amazing what they can withstand.'

David wasn't so sure. In his opinion, Johnnie was small, fragile and not completely recovered from the chest infection he'd picked up some weeks ago when he'd been held prisoner in that wine cellar. And how was he going to tell his mother that Johnnie had been taken to hospital, critically injured?

That was one thing he didn't have to do. As it was one of the feature races on an important day, television cameras had recorded it all and replayed the disaster at least half a dozen times. Patsy was already at the hospital in East Melbourne, waiting for them when they arrived.

As the still form of her younger son was whisked away into an examination room, she pounced on David, demanding answers.

'Is he conscious yet? Can he speak? Just tell me he's going to be all right?'

'I can't tell you anything, Mum.' David felt as exhausted as if he, as well as his brother, had suffered an injury. 'There will have to be X-rays and tests. One of the paramedics said it might be his spine — '

'His spine? Oh, dear God. He'll spend the rest of his life in a wheelchair.'

'If he lives.' David had lost the ability to be gentle with his mother; he was too tired.

'Ah, Jesus, Mary and Joseph!' Patsy reverted to the speech of her homeland. 'Don't be tellin' me that.'

'I'm sorry, Mum. I don't know anything, really.'

'I never wanted him to work for that man. And talking of Mr Willett, where is he? Where's his concern? He should be here at the hospital, asking after my son. Oh dear Lord,' Patsy murmured a prayer almost under her breath. 'Just let him live an' I promise I'll come to mass every Sunday again an' spend the rest of the day on my knees.' David looked at her, shaking his head. Patsy was a lapsed Catholic who hadn't been near a church in years.

Although the Riordans stayed at the hospital long into the night, William Willett never appeared. Late in the evening, David went outside to switch on his mobile and see if there'd been any calls but, apart from various messages from the media, trying to get a story out of it, there were only two calls. One from Murphy, trying to ascertain how seriously Johnnie had been hurt, and a message from Rissa, offering her support.

Patsy wasn't pleased to hear it. 'That woman can nick off and stay out of our lives!' she snapped. 'Larissa Barton is at the root of all our troubles.'

David disagreed but, realizing that his mother was already at the end of her tether, he didn't argue further.

In spite of various nurses telling them to go home, get some sleep and come back in the morning, the Riordans stayed in the almost deserted waiting room while Johnnie remained in surgery long into the night. Minutes stretched into hours without any news. Then, at about 3 a.m. an exhausted young surgeon came to tell them that they had done all they could and it remained to be seen if Johnnie could rally and make a reasonable if not a complete recovery.

'What do you mean — not complete?' Patsy was quick to pounce on this distinction. 'Are you saying my son will not ride again?'

The young surgeon sighed. He was tired and all he wanted was to get out of his scrubs and into a shower. He would have preferred the consultant or the registrar to have this conversation with them in the morning.

'We can't really say what will happen — it's too soon,' he said. 'We've done our part, putting him back together as best we can. I don't want to give you false hopes but nor do I want to tell you he'll spend the rest of his life in a wheelchair. It can go either way.'

'But Johnnie is scarcely eighteen,' Patsy wailed. 'An' you're telling me he'll spend the rest of his life in a wheelchair.'

'That's not what I said.' The surgeon closed his eyes momentarily. Tired as he was, he was trying to be patient with the boy's mother. 'It's too soon to know. I suggest you both go home and get some rest, if you can.'

'I'd like to see him before we do.' Patsy said.

The surgeon looked at the woman's distraught face and decided against it. Early impressions after such an accident could be vital to John's recovery. The last thing he needed was to see his mother sobbing over him and talking of life in a wheelchair.

'Best if you don't. It was a long operation and John is still in post-operative care. He'll sleep for some hours now, and when he wakes up he'll need to see both of you smiling and saying encouraging things about his future in the morning.'

'But . . . ' Patsy would have protested

further but David had taken her firmly by the arm and was now leading her towards the door.

* * *

They returned to the hospital in the morning to find that John had been transferred to a ward. He was lying flat on his back and wearing a neck brace.

'They're feeding me through a straw,' he croaked. 'I can't even get a decent meal.'

'At least you want one.' His mother took his hand. It felt frail and cool in her own. 'Get well and I'll soon have you home, eating three meals a day.'

'Have you heard from Murphy or Willett?' he asked, attempting to move. He frowned, finding he couldn't. 'And how's Max? Did he survive?'

'I believe so.' Patsy sniffed. 'I'm surprised you care after what he did to you.'

'Not his fault. They shouldn't have raced him with mares. At least one of them was on heat and that's what upset him. Will you speak to Willett for me. Say I'll be back as soon as I can.'

Patsy exchanged a meaningful glance with David. He hadn't spoken as yet.

'How's the drought going, David?' Johnnie

looked up into his brother's worried brown eyes. 'Maybe you can take some of my rides? Not permanently, though. Just till I'm better.'

Taking his hand, David smiled at him. 'You just concentrate on getting well, Bro. I spoke to Michelle and she wants to come and see you before she goes back to Sydney . . . '

'No. Say I'm not up for it. I don't want her to see me like this.'

'Don't be silly. Michelle won't care. She's your friend.'

'Just do as I say — please.' Johnnie glanced at his mother. 'Could you go to the café and get me a decent cup of coffee, Mum? The stuff they give us here tastes like cat's — '

'And that's enough of that sort of talk, young man.' His mother once more pursed her lips. 'At least if you're making jokes, you have to be feeling better.'

'OK.' David said as soon as his mother was out of earshot. 'What did you want to say that you didn't want Mum to hear?'

'I need you to go and see Willett. There must be some workers' compo or insurance I'm due for and Mum's going to need it when they send me home. I want the wheels set in motion soon as poss.'

'I'll do it, of course. If that's what you want.' David tried not to show how little he relished the task. 'But isn't there a social worker or someone from here who can handle all that?'

'I suppose so — but I'll be at the bottom of some list and they'll take for ever. I'll need to know quickly if there's nothing to get.'

'What do you mean, nothing to get? You're his apprentice, aren't you? Of course there's insurance — there are laws and systems in place to cover accidents on the course like this.'

'I don't trust Willett or Murphy to pay for anything they don't have to unless someone's breathing down their necks. Please, Bro. Just drop around there and see what you can find out.'

They had to terminate the conversation as Patsy returned with the cup of coffee, complaining about the length of the queue at the café.

While Patsy fidgeted, putting John's night-clothes and a dressing gown in the wardrobe, David saluted John and said he'd be off.

'Today!' Johnnie mouthed behind his mother's back.

David nodded but he didn't feel happy about taking himself uninvited to Willett's stables. Not at all.

★ ★ ★

Although this was normally a quiet time in the working day of a racing stables, David

141

arrived around 3 p.m. to see Willett's big black Mercedes parked outside the front door. With a sinking heart he parked his truck alongside it and went inside to the foreman's office. He tapped gently on the door and opened it before waiting to be invited to go inside.

Willett and Murphy were seated together at the desk, peering at a computer and some printed lists of figures, which Murphy quickly threw into a drawer.

'Well, if it isn't David Riordan,' the foreman said, not looking pleased to see him. 'What brings you here today? I suppose you've come to tell us about that careless brother of yours.'

'Careless? In what way?' David felt his temper rising and his fists clenched automatically but he knew it was no use getting riled. Offering violence was not the way to get the information he wanted, so he took a deep breath to control himself instead. 'If you put an apprentice of frail build on a colt bent on chasing mares, I'd say you were the careless one, rather than John.'

'Come on, Riordan.' It was Willett who spoke this time. 'We know this isn't a social visit. What do you want?'

'My brother is flat on his back in the hospital. Don't you even care how he is?'

'He's young and resilient, isn't he?' Willett shrugged, his smile cool. 'Broken bones mend.'

'Not broken spines,' David snapped back. 'I want you to put me in touch with your insurance people. John may be invalided out for some time and, even if his medical expenses are covered, he'll need money to survive.'

'Oh, dear.' Willett didn't miss a beat. 'Didn't you advise him, Rick, on taking out some insurance of his own?'

Clearly surprised by the question, Rick Murphy stared at his boss for a moment with raised eyebrows, but David broke in before he could answer.

'Johnnie is apprenticed to you, William Willett. Work cover insurance must have been provided for him. As I understand it, that is the law. Until his apprenticeship is completed and he is freelance, like me, he shouldn't be expected to pay for his own.'

'Now look here.' Willett leaned forward, confronting David and narrowing his eyes. 'It's all very well for you to throw accusations around when things have gone wrong. When your brother was absent from work for more than two weeks without any word, I stopped the payments. How was I to know he would ever return? Why should I throw good money after bad? I was already thinking of taking on someone else to replace him. We let him come back out of the kindness of our hearts, didn't we, Rick?' He glanced at Murphy who nodded vigorously. 'So I don't see that we should be blamed for forgetting to reinstate his insurance.'

'If it was ever there in the first place. John was afraid of something like this. That's why he asked me to chase it up.' David moved towards the door. 'Don't imagine, for one moment, that you've heard the last of it.'

'Are you thinking of suing me?' Willett smiled.

'If we have to. I'm hoping it won't come that.'

'Oh? And what will you use for money?' Willett's words were soft but menacing as if he had shouted them, making David turn sharply to meet his gaze. 'We hear you're at a bit of a loose end lately, Riordan. Not getting too many rides yourself.' Willett tutted with false sympathy. 'And you such a talented horseman, too. What a shame.'

'You'd know all about that, wouldn't you?' It took every ounce of David's self control not to punch Willett's nose and wipe that mocking smile off his face.

'I didn't start it but it doesn't take much,' Willett said. 'A whisper here and a rumour there, especially from a reliable source.'

'What sort of rumours?' David's heart beat faster and he could feel his temper rising.

'You should know.' Willett shrugged. 'Nobody wants to employ a jockey who takes recreational drugs.'

'That's a filthy lie and you know it.' David felt his heart step up its beat. This wasn't going at all the way he'd intended. 'I think twice before I take pain killers and I never drink within twenty-four hours of racing.'

Willett continued to smile. 'You don't have to justify yourself to me, Riordan. I think you'll find the damage is already done.'

After all that had happened, including a sleepless night, David's temper finally snapped. Taking hold of the desk he pushed it towards them, trapping Willett and Murphy in their chairs against the wall behind them. While Murphy looked shocked that David's attack should turn so physical, Willett cried out in fright as the sharp edge of the desk bit into his paunch.

'Now you listen to me,' David said. 'You might think you've ruined me but I still have friends in this business and I'm sure they'll be interested to know what you've done.'

'It wasn't me,' Willett bleated, struggling against the hard edge of the desk.

'I don't care if it was or not. I can take

certain tests to prove that I don't do drugs and I'll get my reputation back. But I won't let you sideline my brother and make him a victim in this. You'll reinstate his insurance and make sure it's valid and paid up to date. Now. Today. I'll be calling you later to make sure it's done. If not, I might not be quite so gentle the next time you see me.' He glared from one to the other, satisfied to see both men blanch. They had badly underestimated him and they knew it. Willett, for all his swagger, was just an old man and, like all bullies, Murphy went to jelly when he himself was threatened with violence.

Almost astonished at his own bravado in there, David marched off, slamming the door as he left. He managed to hold himself together, not starting to shake until he was back in his truck. As a rule, he wasn't a violent man, and it was only their smug overconfidence that had tipped him over the edge.

Back in the office, Murphy shoved the desk back into place, releasing them both.

Rubbing his injured belly, Willett could scarcely draw breath to ask for whisky, indicating the bottom drawer of his desk.

Murphy reached in to pull out a bottle of Slate — the American bourbon they kept for guests, and two glasses. Without asking permission he poured a glass for Willett and also a generous measure for himself, taking a quick gulp of the fiery liquid.

'Are you letting him get away with it?' He nodded towards the yard where David could be heard driving away. 'Or shall I call the lads? Get them to teach him a lesson he won't forget?'

'After the cock-up they made of looking after his brother?' Willett muttered, nursing his own glass to his chest. 'It'll be a cold day in hell before I call on those two again.' He shivered, suddenly chilled. 'Nah! Leave him be.'

'But we have to do something — '

'Leave it, I said.' The old man could still scarcely speak above a croak. 'And see the insurance people are paid up to date — make sure young Riordan's covered.'

'If you say so, boss. But it could be seen as a sign of weakness. I don't mind telling you.'

'Just do it!' Willett snarled.

'All right. Keep your hair on.' Murphy turned away, hiding a smirk. This was something new; the first time he'd seen the boss seriously rattled.

★   ★   ★

David didn't contact Larissa until much later that night, when his mother was sleeping with

147

the help of pills. He wasn't in the mood for another of her tirades, citing Larissa as the cause of all their woes.

'David, at last.' Rissa sounded relieved to hear from him. 'I've been waiting for you to call — I've been so worried but I didn't want to disturb your mother at home. How's Johnnie?'

'It's too soon to tell. His body's a mess but his mind is active enough. He's smart enough to be concerned about his insurance.'

'Don't tell me Willett hasn't paid it? He's always had a lazy attitude toward 'the intangibles' as he calls them. It used to drive Miles crazy. Whatever else you say about Miles, he always covered his legal obligations.'

'I went to see Willett today at his stables. He and Murphy tried to bluff their way out of it all and threaten me but I turned the tables on them — quite literally, I'm afraid. I imagine the last thing they want is a full investigation of their shoddy practices by the racing authorities. I tried to put the fear of God into them and I think they believed me.'

She laughed — it was the first happy sound he had heard that day. 'Ooh. That doesn't sound like mild-mannered David Riordan.'

'If it was only me, I wouldn't care — I can look after myself. But they'd better not do any more harm to Johnnie. After seeing

Willett today, I'm all the more certain that he was involved in Johnnie's kidnapping. No proof, of course.'

'And without a solid motive, that might be hard. Unless John can pinpoint the property where he was held. There can't be that many old-fashioned mansions near where he was picked up. It can't be so hard to find.'

'He thinks it was at the top of quite a steep hill but he was in such a hurry to escape that he didn't take too much notice of his surroundings. We've driven all over the north-eastern suburbs but nothing seemed familiar. Of course he was kept in a cellar and half starved — he can't even remember how long he was walking before the farrier picked him up.'

'But?'

'How do you know there's a 'but'?'

'It's obvious, isn't it?' Larissa said. 'Johnnie wanted it all forgotten and his life to go on as before. He wanted to go back to work for Willett and forget that it ever happened.'

'You could be right. But the accident changes everything. Even if Johnnie recovers, he may never ride professionally again.'

7

Over the next few weeks, David's gloomy prophecy was proved correct. Although his brother had recovered the use of his arms and the top half of his body, he still had no feeling from the waist down and was unable to move his legs. Although the surgeons weren't prepared to say he would never walk again, he faced a long journey of rehabilitation and would be confined to a wheelchair for some time. Everything possible would be done to get him mobile again but they weren't making any promises. His mother was with him when the surgeons eventually broke this news and John didn't take it well.

'Why?' Chest heaving with emotion, he raged at them, tears of frustration and anger pouring down his face. 'Why did you save me, if it was only for this? If I can't ride any more, I have nothing. I'd be better off dead.'

'Now then, John.' Equally distressed, his mother tried to reason with him, swallowing her tears and taking his hand. 'That's a wicked thing to say when everyone has worked so hard to do their best for you. Saving your life.'

'What have they saved it for?' The boy snatched his hand away. 'What sort of life can I have, trapped in a useless body like this?' He slapped his unfeeling legs.

'You may improve.' The surgeon was anxious to find a positive. 'There's hydrotherapy — many chronic sufferers enjoy the warm water pool. And with physiotherapy some people even manage to walk again after a while.'

'Yes! Lurching along like a cripple.' Johnnie glared at them. 'Oh, go to hell,' he muttered, sounding defeated. 'Please, everyone — just go away and leave me alone.'

As his depression deepened, he let Michelle go back to Sydney without seeing her; she was still involved in the career he loved and he couldn't bear to hear her talking about it.

★ ★ ★

Despite Larissa's protests that, after the unfortunate incident with the reporters, they should put their friendship on hold until she was properly divorced, David insisted on taking her out to dinner.

'We have to get on with our lives,' he said. 'There's no point in letting them win by making us miserable. Anyway, I might as well eat. What's the point of starving when I still

151

haven't got any rides?'

'All the more reason not to spend the last of your money on me.'

'I'm not destitute yet, Rissa. I was doing quite well until this happened.' He laughed ruefully. 'And what about you? Any news from Miles's lawyers about the divorce?'

'No and I can't understand it. After those reporters supplied him with all the evidence he needs.'

'Then maybe we should provoke him by providing a little more.'

'Oh, David, this is no time to be flippant. You don't know Miles as I do. He can be very vindictive. Much as I'd like to see you, I think we should be discreet about this.'

'And so we will. I have a friend who has a nice little restaurant tucked away up in the hills — it's a new place and kind of a well-kept secret. Not many people know of it yet. I've known Conor for years and his middle name is discretion. And I won't take no for an answer — I've already made the booking.'

He didn't mention that this same friend had a series of private cabins set among the trees where guests who didn't want to drive home might spend the rest of the night. Not that he had any thoughts of spending such a night with Larissa. To give her dinner and see her relaxed and happy would be more than enough.

So far as David was concerned, these feelings were new. He was by no means an innocent; young men who worked around stables were seldom allowed to be innocent for long and jockeys were always a target for girls who believed their lifestyle to be a lot more glamorous than it was. But he had never been promiscuous and had slept with no more than a couple of the girls who had thrown themselves at his head. He was one of those men who preferred to have feelings for someone rather than indulge in meaningless, casual sex. He had known Larissa was special the first time they met. He'd never asked but he wouldn't have cared if she'd had a dozen lovers in addition to her husband, Miles. He was beginning to believe in love at first sight.

And Larissa, succumbing to David's wry humour and charm, agreed to fall in with his plans. All the same, when she came off the phone she sighed, knowing she would have to answer some hard questions from her mother. This was the one disadvantage of moving back home; Stella had fallen into the old habit of treating her as if she were the same age as Sally, behaving like a mother hen guarding her chicks. Larissa wasn't wrong. As soon as Stella returned from the races and saw her daughter preparing to go out, the inquisition commenced.

'You have a busy social life all of a sudden. Off out again?'

'Umhmn.' Larissa peered into a mirror applying lipstick so that she'd be unable to answer. But her mother wasn't to be put off; she seemed to have a sixth sense about David.

'It's that boy again, David Riordan, isn't it? Oh, Rissa.'

Unwilling to get into the same old argument, Larissa said nothing, concentrating on her reflection in the make-up mirror.

'Don't you think you should stay clear of him after what's happened?' Stella persisted. 'At least for the time being?'

Larissa put the lipstick away in her handbag and turned to her mother. 'I don't know why you object to David. He's been a good friend to all of us and I won't turn my back on him. Not when he's having such a hard time.'

'Yes. Largely because of you.'

'All the more reason I shouldn't desert him now.'

'Larissa, all I want is your happiness — you must know that. But this relationship is already affecting David's life and not in a good way. That isn't going to stop so long as you're married to Miles.'

'Mom, just remember one thing — it was Miles who threw me out. Not the other way around.'

'Technically, he could argue that you left him. Who's to say otherwise?'

'Well, there's Mrs Hudson for one.'

'Really? Joan Hudson knows only that you left home in such a hurry that she had to bring you the rest of your clothes. She's still Miles's housekeeper, don't forget. Ultimately, her interest lies in keeping her job.'

'So what do you want me to do? Stay at home and live like a nun until Miles decides to divorce me?'

'You should have sense enough to be discreet.'

'Why?' She twitched one shoulder. 'Miles isn't discreet. Far from it.' She was thinking of those four secret mobile phones he kept locked in his desk and the women to whom they were linked.

'And what does that mean? If there's something you know that has a bearing on the case, Roger Timpson should be told.'

Momentarily, Larissa closed her eyes. 'Please don't hassle me, Mom. Can't I have one night without thinking of Miles and what he might do?' She kissed Stella, leaving a smudge of lipstick on her cheek before rubbing it off.

'Stop worrying about me and don't wait up. I have no idea when I'll be home.'

'Oh now, you're not thinking of staying out all night?' Stella murmured, glancing towards the door, wondering if Sally might be listening outside. It had happened before.

'Mom, I'm not a teenager any more, I'm all grown up. Time you stopped worrying so much and let me look out for myself.'

'I just wish you were better at it, that's all,' her mother retorted, determined to have the last word.

'G'night, Mom,' Rissa said, picking her soft blue cashmere wrap and throwing it around her shoulders. It was one of her favourite things, which Joan Hudson had managed to bring from her old home. It didn't really go with her casual outfit of jeans and a plain blue shirt but she needed that extra little bit of luxury and warmth. The leaves had fallen and winter was on the way, with the weather much cooler at night.

Miles's housekeeper — a plump and motherly woman — had proved to be both a friend and an ally, firmly on young Mrs Barton's side. At a time when she knew Miles would be absent from home, she had raided the walk-in wardrobe and filled her car with half a dozen bags and cases containing most of Larissa's everyday clothes. At Warrandyte the Arkwrights had greeted her like a heroine and, in return for her kindness, Rissa had given permission — in writing in case of any objections from Miles — to put all her unwanted cocktail and evening gowns on eBay, agreeing to split the proceeds when they were sold. Such luxury items were snapped up quickly, most of them were already gone with Miles none the wiser. Like many men of his type, he didn't see his housekeeper as a person but as part of the furniture in his home. He wouldn't doubt her loyalty or expect her to have any wishes or feelings of her own. It certainly wouldn't occur to him to wonder about his wife's empty wardrobes and shelves.

Hearing the sound of David's powerful truck pulling up outside, Larissa skipped out of the house before he could be waylaid by Stella. She was determined to enjoy every moment of this evening without allowing her mother's concerns to dampen her spirits.

'OK, what's wrong?' David said as soon as he saw her. 'Your shoulders are hunched and you're almost vibrating with tension. What's happened?'

'Oh, nothing,' she answered, smiling and forcing herself to relax and lower her shoulders. 'Just the usual cautionary tales from my mom.'

'Why? Is she saying that I'm an unsuitable swain?'

'No, it's not that. She thinks I'm ruining your life for you, that's all.'

'So does mine.' He laughed. 'But isn't that something for me to decide?'

'You don't really know my mom. She's the original control freak. She rules my little sis with a rod of iron.'

'Then I'm glad I'm not your little sis.' He settled her into his car and gave her a lingering kiss on the cheek, making her shiver with pleasure. 'You look gorgeous tonight.' He studied her, tucking a stray wisp of hair behind her ear. 'And what is that heavenly smell?'

'I dunno. Something in a black bottle by Tom Ford.'

'Who?'

'Never mind.' Larissa smiled, changing the subject. 'How's your mum bearing up? And how's Johnnie?'

'Not much change there, unfortunately. Sometimes I think Mum enjoys fussing over him. It'll drive him crazy when he gets home.'

'Is that likely to be soon?'

'Not really. They're sending him off to a rehab hospital where they've got an army of physiotherapists to try and get him moving and all sorts of ologists to check on his mental state. He's not prepared to make any adjustments — he wants his old life back. Short of a miracle, that seems highly unlikely.'

'Poor kid. But miracles do happen sometimes, you know, especially for the young.'

'Let's hope so.' He turned up his headlights as they headed for a narrow, almost deserted road in the hills.

'I love the trees at night,' Larissa said, looking up at the huge mountain ash they were passing. It had years of moss growing up its trunk and massive branches reaching up into the night sky. 'They're so incredibly spooky and old. Like something from *The Lord of the Rings*.'

David smiled but he didn't answer as he was concentrating on negotiating the narrow, winding road as it climbed. At last they turned into a gravel driveway and pulled up in a small car park outside a well-lit ranch-style restaurant half-hidden among the trees. Visitors would have to be 'in the know' as it couldn't be seen from the road. Although it was newly built, the style was reminiscent of an old-fashioned log cabin, with the entrance concealed by a large pergola which had an ancient, knotty wisteria climbing all over it. It might look odd now but in summer it would be covered in bright green leaves and drifts of spectacular lilac-coloured flowers. While a large sign proclaimed that the restaurant was open for lunch only at weekends and dinner at night, there was a smaller sign underneath advertising *Fernleigh Cottages — Overnight Accommodation Available — Ask at the Front Desk.*

Inside, the tables were set in individual private alcoves and were decorated with posies and little red-shaded lamps in the centre of each one. Surprisingly, in view of the long climb and the remote location, the restaurant was almost filled to capacity, with not many vacant tables. The dining room was heated by a huge and welcoming log fire crackling in a huge central fireplace in order to warm both sides of the room. The fireplace was the only concession to modern decor. The rest was reminiscent of a mid-twentieth-century English pub; all dark wood, old gilt-framed mirrors to make the room look larger, stags' heads and wooden-framed pictures of Scottish lakes and highland cattle. As they stood in the doorway, David's friend, Conor, came over to greet him with a hug, releasing him only to stand back and admire Larissa as he waited to be introduced.

'And this must be the new girl friend?' he said in a stage whisper. 'You've done well for yourself this time, David. She's gorgeous.' He took Larissa's hand and bowed over it. 'Conor Parker Barrington — at your service, ma'am.'

Slightly embarrassed, Larissa retrieved her hand.

'This is Rissa,' David said, clearing his throat. 'Rissa Arkwright.'

Larissa smiled at Conor, relieved that he seemed to have no idea who she was. So many people recognized her as Miles Barton's wife.

Conor showed them to an alcove not far from the open fire and brought them complimentary glasses of pink champagne. Then he left them to study the menu and the 'specials' for the night. Conor's list wasn't extensive but sounded delicious, catering for all tastes.

'You can have steak if you want,' she said bravely. 'I don't eat it myself but if that's what you'd like, I won't mind.'

David, who suspected Miles would have eaten rare beef and veal just to torment her, declined. 'Conor doesn't rely on a conventional menu here. He has a Vietnamese chef who specializes in seafood,' he said. 'He cooks Western fare to perfection, if that's what you want, but his chilli mud crab is to die for. It's on the 'specials' board tonight as a banquet for two. But I should warn you although the flavour's fantastic, it can be messy.'

'Bring it on.' Larissa smiled. 'I love spicy food and I haven't had crab for ages.' It had been out of bounds during her marriage to Miles who was allergic to any kind of shellfish — or so he claimed.

To begin with, they had simple, natural oysters with a spicy, lemony dressing. This was followed by a large oval plate of the crab, set in front of them piping hot in more ways than one and smelling delicious. Larissa spread the generous white napkin across her knees and dug in. Apart from various murmurs of enjoyment, conversation stopped while they gave their attention to the meal.

When there was nothing left but a ruin of crab shells and a few grains of rice, Larissa made use of her finger bowl, dried her hands on the no-longer pristine napkin and sat back with a contented sigh.

'David, thank you so much for bringing me here. It has been a wonderful evening.' She hesitated a moment, unsure whether to say what was on her mind. 'It does seem a pity it has to end.' Surprised by her own forwardness, she stared down at her hands, suddenly unable to face him and half hoping he had missed what she said. With a jolt she realized that she was still wearing Miles's wedding ring; the wide, gold band seemed to wink at her in reproach. Quickly, she put that hand in her lap.

'But it doesn't have to, Rissa. Not yet.' David spoke equally softly, reaching across the table to take her other hand. Although slightly rough, his hand felt warm and capable and she wanted to grasp it, holding on for dear life. 'By now you must know how I feel about you. I'm not very good at hiding it.'

Larissa took a shuddering breath. Now that the moment had come she didn't know how to handle it or what to say. Although she had been married to Miles for ten years, her life had been sheltered and the confidence she had displayed in public was largely a sham. Apart from showing her off when it suited him and allowing her to pursue her sporting activities, Miles had kept her in his own private purdah. She had been watched all the time, never allowed to conduct the mildest flirtation or even to keep in touch with her old friends. Recently, she had come to suspect that her younger sister might have a far greater experience of boys than she had ever had.

'Coffee?' The waitress came up to the table, ready to take their order and intruding on this moment of intimacy.

'Dessert? There's mango ice cream tonight

or a raspberry sorbet with — '

'Just coffee, thanks,' Rissa murmured, looking up at David and trying to read his expression.

'Will that be espresso, latte or — ?'

'Plain black, thank you, for two. Just bring it,' David said, not taking his gaze off Rissa. He knew he was being abrupt but inwardly he was cursing the girl for intruding on such a pivotal moment.

'Oh, David,' Larissa said, letting go of his hand. 'I don't know why I said that — I don't know what came over me . . . '

'No, it's me.' He shook his head and sat back, leaning against the back of the bench as he stared at the ceiling. 'You must think I'm crazy, declaring my feelings when I have no work any more and we've only just met. Of course it's too soon. Forget I said anything. We'll have coffee and I'll take you home.'

She realized he meant it and would do just that if she didn't speak up at once before it was too late. 'Yes, but what if I told you that I don't want to go home? That I've already told my mother not to wait up for me.'

'Larissa.' He captured both her hands and held on to them. 'Will you please say that again. It's much too important — I don't want to misunderstand you or get it wrong.'

'All I'm saying,' she leaned forward to

smile into his eyes and feeling much better as she concluded that he was just as shy and diffident as she was, 'is that I saw the notice when we came in. If there is overnight accommodation, I think we should take advantage of it.'

There! It was out in the open and up to him now.

'Wait here,' he murmured, leaving her at the table while he went to pay the bill for their dinner and speak to Conor.

Conor lived up to his reputation of being discreet and said nothing as he led them up a winding path through the trees to one of his cabins, lighting their way with a flashlight.

Inside, the room was larger than Larissa had expected; half of it was set up as a sitting room with a coffee table and easy chairs, the other half was taken up by a luxurious king sized bed. She was thankful that Conor played it straight and didn't make any smart remarks. The air-conditioning in the room was surprisingly warm and he showed them how to adjust it. Then he pointed out the small bar fridge where they would find drinks or some milk to make coffee or tea.

'In the morning we do a simple French breakfast of coffee and croissants and you don't have to leave in a hurry,' he said at the door. 'I wish you a pleasant night.'

They both murmured their thanks and neither spoke until they were quite sure he was gone when Larissa had a moment of misgiving.

'Tell me, David,' she said. 'This is the first time, isn't it? You haven't come up here and done this before?'

'No, never!' He looked quite shocked. 'How could you think that of me?'

'I'm sorry — so sorry.' Suddenly, she felt close to tears. 'I'm just not used to this sort of thing.'

'And you think I am? What do you take me for?' He knew he was ruining the moment but he couldn't seem to help it. 'Larissa, if you've changed your mind, it's all right. We don't have to stay. I'll take you home.'

She could see there was only one way to mend the situation. She moved in close, taking his face in her hands, subjecting him to a deep and lingering kiss.

8

The following morning Larissa had been sleeping so soundly that when she first awoke, she didn't remember where she was. As this bed was huge and comfortable, quite unlike the hard mattress on the single at her mother's home, for a moment she imagined herself to be lying in the luxurious bed she had occupied in the house at Brighton Beach. It was only when she looked across at the window and saw the peaceful woodland scene outside and bright, early-morning sunshine dispersing the mist through the trees, that she fully remembered where she was.

She had behaved like a wanton last night but she didn't care. She stretched and sighed, falling back on the pillows with a sigh of relief, almost purring like a contented cat. David was lying half out of bed on the other side, still deeply asleep.

When Conor had departed last night, leaving them for the first time truly alone, they had been unsure how to make the first move. Having taken the first step towards this advancement of their relationship, she was suddenly shy. They seemed to have such high expectations of this night but what if it was all a mistake? What if she disappointed him?

But David had been wonderful. Seeing her shyness and hesitation, he had taken control of the situation right from the outset. Unlike Miles, who was greedy and could sometimes be rough, attacking her as if she were a three-course meal, David was all she could ever have hoped for in a lover, passionate yet always considerate of her changing moods. After spending half an hour kissing her and fondling her until her lips were swollen and she was half-drugged with desire, he left her to go and fill the enormous, old-fashioned bath with warm water, planning for them to get in it together.

'But I had a shower just before we came out,' Larissa protested, anxious to get back to the kissing, so exciting and different from Miles's clumsy and selfish advances.

'That isn't the kind of bathing I have in mind,' he said. 'You're still tense and this has a lot more to do with soap and seduction than scrubbing each other clean.'

Then, as she sank into the warm water, fragrant with extravagant bath salts, he had taken a sponge, washing her body so slowly and sensually, she thought she would die from wanting him. But still he kept his distance, scarcely allowing her to touch him in return. And when the water began to cool, he lifted her out and dried her with the softest of white towels before setting her down at last between the crisp, linen sheets of the bed.

'That's better,' he said. 'Delicious it may be but I'd rather not be reminded of a scent given to you by your husband.'

Larissa smiled, not wanting to ruin the moment by saying that Miles's taste in fragrance was so overpowering and unsubtle that the only perfumes she wore she chose for herself.

'You'd prefer me to smell of old-fashioned lavender?' she teased. 'Nanna bath salts?'

For an answer, he tickled her, making her squeal until she pulled him in close again for a deeply satisfying kiss which made them serious again.

'I do love you, Rissa,' he said at last. 'I hope you know that. For me this is a serious matter — much more than a casual affair.'

She wanted to say that she loved him in return, but something still held her back. It was early days and these feelings were all so new. Also, she realized that although she had been married to Miles for ten years, her experience was sadly lacking. Miles had been interested only in pleasing himself. This was the first time she had made love with someone who wanted to please her as well.

David was patient, understanding that she would need a lot of reassurance before she was ready to release all her inhibitions. In her previous existence with Miles, Larissa had been tense and afraid he would hurt her every time they had come together; something to be endured rather than to enjoy. But in David's arms, with his slender, muscular body moulded against her own, and an erection she didn't have to tease and coax into life, she discovered a different experience. He kissed her stomach and breasts, making her squirm with pleasure but made no move to go any further until she was almost weeping with desire for him. And after he'd entered her and the moment finally came, he was able to wait until his pleasure coincided with her own, allowing Larissa to experience a full orgasm for the very first time.

'Oh, David, what happened to us?' she whispered, staring at him wide-eyed as, breathless and with hearts still thundering together, they came down to earth and began to relax in each other's arms. 'For a moment there, it felt as if I were flying or having an out-of-body experience.'

'Oh, Larissa . . . ' He rested up on one elbow and teased her gently, running a finger down her nose. 'We had an orgasm together, that's all. You're a beautiful, sensual woman.

Don't tell me you've never had that experience before?'

'All right then, I won't.' She turned her back on him, biting her lips and fighting back sudden tears, her emotions suddenly very close to the surface. Although she was the one who had been married for ten years, she also felt naive, lacking in technique and worldly experience. The irritation she felt wasn't directed against David but towards Miles. For the whole of their married life he had used her for his own pleasure, leaving her in ignorance of what lovemaking really could be. He had been almost Victorian in attitude, believing that sexual gratification was a male prerogative. It wasn't his business to care whether or not she enjoyed it.

David put a tentative hand on her shoulder. 'Don't be sore with me, Rissa. I'm a clumsy oaf and I should have realized that was a sensitive issue.'

Immediately, she turned towards him. 'Oh, David, it isn't your fault, it's me. I was thinking of Miles.' There. The name was out in the open between them. 'How could he leave me unaware of something so special. So wonderful.'

'I wouldn't know,' he said softly. 'To be honest, I'm not that experienced myself, but I've always believed the girl should enjoy it as much as I do.'

'And have there been many girls, David?' she asked in a small voice, hoping the answer would be 'no'.

'Mostly just friends. Jockeys receive a lot of interesting offers from girls. Especially around Carnival time. I had no reason to ignore them before.'

'But you do have a reason now?' She wound her arms around his neck, looking deeply into his eyes.

They had made love again until they fell into an exhausted, dreamless sleep. In the morning, when David awoke, they lay in each other's arms without speaking until they were brought down to reality by a soft tapping on the cabin door. David put on his trousers and went to answer it while Larissa pulled the bed-covers over her head, feigning sleep. After their previous experience with reporters, she didn't want to run the same risks again.

But it was just a diminutive maid bringing their Continental breakfast. She seemed shy and anxious to leave, handing the tray to David before making her escape.

It was only when they smelled the fresh croissants and the pot of strong coffee that they realized how ravenous they both were. The arrival of breakfast meant that the night really had come to an end and soon it would be time to go home and take up the daily thread of their lives.

They took a leisurely shower together, almost tempted to go back to bed again until a glance at the clock told them it was almost midday.

'Where has the time gone?' Larissa said. 'I never meant to stay away from home so long. Our new girl who helps Mom at the weekend called in sick and I should have been back in time to give her a hand. She'll be furious now — after clearing up the stables all on her own.'

'What about Sally? Won't she help?'

'Sally!' Larissa smiled, shaking her head. 'She'll be sleeping off the latest teen party at the house of one of her friends.'

'Then we'd better get you home pronto. And I'll lend a hand. I've nothing better to do, after all.' He grinned. 'Might help me get back into your mother's good books.'

Larissa grunted, having serious doubts that such a ploy would work. There were times when Stella could be more than pig-headed. But when David pulled up outside the stables, her mother came out and greeted him civilly enough, accepting his offer of help. When they were done, she invited him to stay to have a late lunch.

'It's not much — only canned soup, I'm afraid,' Stella said. 'I don't have time to make a roast dinner with all the trimmings, not these days.'

Silently and with writhing eyebrows, Larissa tried to warn him not to accept. This was an old routine of her mother's when she had some point she wanted to make; she would lull her victims into a false sense of security, feeding them before she pounced. But David missed all her signals, agreeing to stay. Stella warmed some bread rolls in the oven and put the soup in a saucepan to heat while Larissa set the kitchen table for three.

As they sat eating, Larissa realized that David had another reason for wanting to stay.

'I was wondering,' he said as they reached the close of the meal and Larissa put the kettle on to make tea. 'Who's going to ride Golden Czarina for you now?'

'I don't know.' Stella looked pensive. 'Like all fillies, she can be temperamental but she got on so well with Johnnie, I've shied away from engaging somebody else.' She sighed. 'Now it seems that I'll have to. Especially with the Spring Carnival coming up in just a few months. I expect John will be out of commission for quite some time.'

'Not just some time.' David's smile faded. 'He may not get back to riding professionally at all.'

'Really?' Stella looked shocked and turned

to her daughter. 'You never told me it was serious as that?'

'Because we kept hoping it wasn't.' David came to Larissa's defence. 'I can ride track work for you to keep the job open for him, if you like? At the moment, I've nothing else to do. Although I should warn you that hiring me might not do your reputation much good; I seem to be out of favour with most trainers, these days.'

'Well.' Stella cocked her head to one side, considering him. 'I suppose the least I can do is employ you, after my daughter single-handedly put paid to your career.'

'Mom! What a horrible thing to say.'

'Well, you know me,' Stella shrugged. 'Never one to shy away from the truth.'

'I'll do it,' David said quickly. 'I like this environment and the way you keep your stables. I'd be more than happy to work around here. Of course, I'm not as light as my brother and I no longer have an apprentice's claim.'

'That doesn't matter so much now. Czarina's won every time I've taken her out these days so she isn't as lightly weighted as she was. I'm planning on entering her in a mares' race at Flemington soon to see how she goes.' Stella thought for a moment. 'All right, David, you're on. You can ride track work for me. As for race day, I'm making no promises — it's no good if you have to starve and make yourself weak. If you can't make the weight easily, I'll have to bring in someone else.'

'Fair enough, Stella. It's a deal.' David clasped the woman's outstretched hand to seal the bargain. 'Thank you so much. You can't know what this means to me.'

'And to save travelling time, you can take over the foreman's cottage, if you like.' Stella said, surprising both of them with the offer. 'It's been vacant since Sue left to get married last summer and if it continues to be unoccupied it's going to get damp. You can take your meals with us or go out. Whatever you'd like.'

'That's a very thoughtful of you, Stella. Thank you.' David smiled.

Larissa also smiled, understanding the strategy behind her mother's apparently generous offer. If David were living here on her mother's property, it would be a lot more difficult for them to spend time alone. But at least he would be here and she would be able to see him every day.

The only person not entirely pleased with this new arrangement was David's mother. Patsy frowned when she heard he was going to work for Stella Arkwright and once more move away from home.

'Don't know what John's going to say about this,' she said. 'He's depressed enough already without you taking over his rides.'

'Somebody has to. This way, I can hold the job open for him if he ever gets well enough to come back — '

'Of course he'll get well,' his mother snapped. 'A lad of eighteen with the whole of his life before him.'

'Well, that's what we all hope, of course,' David said. 'But if I don't put my hand up for it, Mrs Arkwright will employ someone else.'

'You'd better tell him yourself then, because I shan't.' Patsy sniffed.

He needn't have worried. Johnnie was lying in his hospital bed looking listless. He was no more interested in David's news than in anything else going on around him.

'Good luck to you, Bro,' he said without enthusiasm. 'It all seems so far away from me now, I really don't care any more.'

'You'll be out of here soon.' David gazed around his brother's sparsely furnished single quarters in the rehab hospital. 'Then we can put some time into getting you well.'

'It's no good. I wanted to be up there with the real Group One jockeys of the Spring Carnival. That's never going to happen now.'

'Don't say that. Most jockeys have accidents sooner or later, some worse than

177

yours, and still get back on top of their game.'

'Not with a case as hopeless as mine,' Johnnie said, turning his face to the wall.

Before leaving, David spoke to a senior nurse about Johnnie's depression. She seemed to treat it as a criticism, insisting that everything possible was already being done.

★　★　★

Nobody knew what was in Monday's newspaper until Sally brought one home from school. Having no time to read it, no one had bothered to pick up the Arkwrights' copy left at the gate. After a strenuous but satisfying day with the horses, Stella, Larissa and David were seated around the kitchen table, relaxing and enjoying a well-deserved glass of wine before dinner when Sally burst into the room, red-faced and almost in tears.

'I just hate it.' Sally glared at her sister as she flung the newspaper down on the table in front of them. 'It was bad enough when you were with Miles and my friends sneered at you for being married to a rich old man but this is so much worse.' She spread the paper dramatically, displaying the photo shoot in the middle pages. 'Don't you ever think of anyone but yourself? How could you do this to me?'

Romantic Tryst in the Hills! the headline screamed and the paper went on to describe the details of the evening that had been spent at Conor's restaurant. There was more than one picture, too. At dinner — the two of them holding hands and smiling into each other's eyes — and then one of Conor leading them to the cottage where they would spend the night. And the last picture — most damning of all — their departure in daylight the following morning where there could be no mistaking their identity. The report was thorough and no detail had been left out.

The four of them gazed at the newspaper in horror, unsure what to say.

'I'll kill him,' David muttered at last. 'This has to be Conor. And I thought he was a friend. I didn't think he recognized Larissa but obviously he did. He sold us out.'

'Well, whoever it was, the damage is done, isn't it?' Stella shrugged, shaking her head. 'One newspaper article might be passed off as idle gossip — but two? I hate to say it again but I warned you to be discreet.'

'Mom, that isn't helpful,' Larissa said, staring at David who was busy punching in a number on his mobile. He sounded tense and angry, standing up to move away from the table and pace the room when he spoke to the person who answered.

'I trusted you, man,' he said without preamble. 'What's going on?'

He listened for a while to the clearly agitated recipient of his call. 'OK — I get it now — I understand. I'll pass on your apologies to Rissa. Sorry I doubted you. And, yes, we're still mates. 'Bye,' he said before closing the phone.

'It wasn't Conor,' he said, rejoining the conversation. 'He has a written agreement with all his staff that nobody is to talk to the press or gossip about any well-known guests. How long d'you think his business would last if they did?'

'What happened, then?' Rissa looked up from the damning pictures in the newspaper, biting her lip. 'Obviously his system broke down.'

'He says the waitress who should have been on duty that night phoned in sick. She sent a friend in to cover for her. Conor employs the girl sometimes but she isn't a regular. Recognizing Larissa as Miles Barton's wife, she seized the chance to make a quick buck. End of story.' He shrugged.

'But I didn't see a camera all night,' Rissa protested. 'I would have mentioned it.'

'These pictures are fuzzy. Probably just blow-ups from a cell phone.' David sighed. 'It doesn't help us now but Conor fired both those girls. The one who should have been there wasn't really sick.'

Larissa surprised everyone by bursting out laughing. It was several minutes before she could control herself sufficiently to speak.

'This is no laughing matter, my girl.' Her mother was stern. 'What sort of divorce settlement can you expect from Miles now?'

'That's it exactly.' Larissa subsided into helpless giggles yet again. 'If only I'd taken Miles's pink diamonds when he offered them, this wouldn't have mattered at all.'

Sally looked at her sister as if she thought she had suddenly lost her mind. 'What pink diamonds?' she asked. 'This is the first I've heard of them.'

When she eventually stopped laughing, Rissa explained the system Miles had employed for obtaining trouble-free divorces from his first two wives.

'Oh Rissa, you're such an idiot! Why didn't you take them?' Sally said.

'I don't know. I didn't like the calculating way he sprang it on me. And on my birthday, too — as if he was getting rid of some useless old retainer. I wanted to take him to court and show him up for the selfish old villain he is, trading in wives like old cars and taking advantage of young girls.'

'Well, so far there's no sign of any new

bride,' Stella remarked. 'If Miles had someone waiting in the wings, he'd be taking full advantage of your mistakes by now and rushing through the divorce.'

'I know,' Larissa said, thinking of those mobile phones locked in his desk. His means of contact with all those other women. Her mother knew nothing of this and she wondered if she ought to mention it now, but decided against it. Miles's secret life was sordid enough without dragging it out in front of the people she loved.

David, who had remained silent for some time, spoke up at last.

'Perhaps I should leave,' he said. 'It just adds more fuel to the flames if I'm living here.'

'You stay where you are, David.' Stella rose to take the chicken casserole out of the oven. 'Whatever you do, it's not going to help — the damage is already done. Let's eat.' But, tired and hungry as they were, and appetizing as the casserole smelled when she removed the lid on the pot, no one had any enthusiasm for food.

*　*　*

William Willett didn't let much get him down but he was nervous today. Tapping his foot impatiently as he waited at the airport for Miles Barton's flight to come in from China, he reflected on how much time and money he had invested, catering to the whims of the tycoon who still treated him more like a servant than a friend. He had taken so many risks for him, including certain illegal activities that could cost him his licence if they came to the notice of the racing clubs and the stewards. He had stuck his neck out for Miles and if the man didn't fulfil his promise and come to the party now, it was more than likely that he himself would face ruin, even to the point of losing his stables.

His mind returned to a recent scene when he had gone to negotiate an extension of his credit at the bank. He had a good relationship with the manager and didn't anticipate any problems, Bainbridge had always been willing to accommodate him before.

His first setback was to find out that Bainbridge was gone without warning, replaced by a girl Willett hadn't met before and who had to check the name on his file before she ushered him into her office.

'Mr Willett, isn't it?' Slim and efficient, she greeted him with a mere twitch of the lips and a firm handshake before indicating that he should take a seat. 'Susan Collier. I'm the new manager here.'

'But what happened to Mr Bainbridge? He always had a good understanding of my business and my needs.'

'He was unwell. Took early retirement.' The girl seemed reluctant to waste time with small talk and certainly not concerning her predecessor. She put on her spectacles and opened Willett's file, letting him squirm in his seat and examining it for several minutes before sitting back with a sigh.

'I do hope you're here to tell me you have the means to reduce this rather substantial loan? Originally, it was supposed to be temporary, but it seems to have been on our books for rather a long time?'

Willett cleared his throat. He wasn't used to being taken to task by what he saw as a slip of a girl. 'Matter of fact I was hoping the bank would give me a further extension.'

'Not in the present economic climate, Mr Willett. I have been given the task of running a tight ship here and ordered to call in a large number of these temporary loans.'

'Ms Collier, I do see where you're coming from. But with respect you don't understand my business as Mr Bainbridge did. In horse racing, large sums of money flow in and out on a regular basis . . . '

Two spots of colour appeared on her cheekbones and he realized it had been a mistake to mention Bainbridge again.

'And for the last six months, it seems to have been flowing out.' Susan Collier snapped the file shut and stood up, indicating the interview was at an end. 'I will give you until the end of next month to make a substantial reduction on your present loan. It goes without saying that no further credit can be offered to you.'

Willett had resisted the temptation to say something rude. But Susan Collier had the whip hand and anything else he said could only make things worse. His only hope lay in getting his hands on the money that Miles Barton owed him for Maximo's Curse. This was why he was waiting here at the airport like a flunkey to meet the tycoon.

Miles's flight from China via Hong Kong landed at Tullamarine on time. It wasn't long before he came trudging from Customs, pushing his trolley ahead of him.

With his new plans already seething in his mind, the horse trainer was the last person Miles wanted to see. All the same, he forced himself to smile, greeting Willett breezily as if he hadn't a care in the world.

'This is a nice surprise, Will? Amazed you could spare the time. To what do I owe the pleasure? Nothing wrong I hope?'

Willett also managed to smile, although the

interview with that harpy at the bank had set alarm bells ringing in his head, making it hard for him to be pleasant.

'Not really, Miles. Nothing a bit of straight talk over a whisky won't fix.' He took hold of the trolley and steered it purposefully towards the car park. There he loaded Barton's luggage into the boot of his car.

'Ah no, Will. I can't talk business today — I'm bushed.' The tycoon yawned as he settled into the passenger seat of Willett's Volvo. 'There's a lot to talk about but I'm too tired to concentrate now. Take me home and I'll see you tomorrow for lunch. We can go over everything then.'

'That won't be possible Miles,' Willett said as he left the airport and speeded up to join the stream of traffic on the motorway. 'You've put me off long enough. I need to know where I stand — to have everything settled today.'

For the rest of the journey Miles sulked, sitting hunched in his seat in a moody silence, pretending to snooze.

In accordance with the boss's instructions, Murphy had dismissed all hands at the stables. With the day's work done and no horses racing that day, they had been told they could take the afternoon off and need not return until early tomorrow morning.

Barton sighed but didn't seem all that surprised when they pulled up outside Willett's stables. He would have preferred to talk to the trainer in the comfort of his own home, without the foreman hanging his nose over everything that had to be said. Clearly, this wasn't to be.

The stables were unusually quiet. No radios blaring or lads whistling and chatting as they went about their daily tasks. One or two horses looked out from their stalls but there were no other vehicles parked outside and no hands in sight.

'What's all this then?' He tried making a joke of it. 'Where is everyone? Got some secret project you've been keeping as a surprise? A new horse you can't wait to show me?'

'No.' Willett spoke through clenched teeth, only just holding his temper in check. 'Just an old horse you forgot to pay for when you went dancing off on your travels. And don't tell me you haven't got a fistful of traveller's cheques in your briefcase right now — I know you always take out more than you need.'

Miles felt the first tremor of misgiving, nervous to be ushered into such a large stable block with only the three of them present, but he hid it behind a bland smile. He could face anyone down if need be and didn't think he was in any physical danger. If Willett hoped to come out of this with an ongoing relationship, surely he wouldn't want to antagonize him completely? Taking command of the situation, he led the way into the foreman's office and occupied the most comfortable chair without being asked.

'Now then,' he said, 'where's that whisky you promised me.'

Willett nodded to Murphy who opened a cupboard to produce a bottle of Tullamore Dew and three glasses.

'Bottoms up!' Miles said, tossing back the first shot and extending the glass for a refill. 'What's all this about, Will? I can see you're upset.'

'As I have every right to be,' Willett began. 'About Maximo's Curse. You sent me to Ireland to get him . . . '

'I did, indeed. And I paid for your flight as well as expenses.' Miles waved an admonishing finger. 'I asked you to find me a champion — a certainty to train up for the Spring Carnival. And what do you do? You let them fob you off with a skittish nag that no one can ride. I could've gone to Ireland and done better myself, if I'd been able to spare the time.'

'There's nothing wrong with Max. He's spirited, that's all, but he's still a good horse

— a champion in the making. And you said you'd pay for his training.'

'I know what I *said*, Will, but I won't let you make me responsible. Not this time. You made a mistake in buying that horse and you'll have to wear it. Find some other patsy to buy into the deal because it's not going to be me.'

Willett glared at him. 'But there's a lot more than that, isn't there? You still owe me, Miles. For taking care of the Dennison boy and his dangerous car.'

Barton's eyes narrowed. He didn't care to be reminded of matters he thought were settled and long forgotten. 'Owe you for what? You were paid more than enough at the time — as was your associate.'

'So it seemed. But it's not easy to find an ex racing driver hungry enough to cause a fatal accident and willing to keep quiet about it afterwards.'

'The man went too far. I meant only for him to frighten the lad. Teach him a lesson.'

'Not the impression you gave at the time.'

'Oh come on, Will.' Barton's tone was still bantering. 'What are we quibbling about? It's water under the bridge. It's not like you to be so small-minded.' He smiled. 'Not trying to threaten me, are you?'

'I'm desperate, Miles. The bitch at the bank

189

is squeezing me — calling in my loan.'

'So? Threaten to take your business away. That'll bring her into line.' Miles laughed softly. 'Owe them enough and they won't let you go under.'

'That policy might have worked twenty years ago. It doesn't work now. I need the rest of the money you owe me, Miles, and I need it now.'

Miles glanced at his watch and stood up. 'I'm disappointed in you, Will, because we've always been good friends before. But in view of what's happened between us, you might as well know. I'm thinking of getting out of the racing game altogether.'

'No! There's too much at stake for you to quit now. We've been partners for years, and made good money, too.'

'Yes but we're not doing so well as we did. Horse racing's getting too hard — too many rules and regulations. Too many officials closing the loopholes and watching our every move. I'm excited by what I've seen in China, so I'm taking a different path. Casinos and poker machines are the way forward now.'

Willett frowned. 'Horse racing is a tradition here. Always has been.'

'So? Maybe it's time for change.'

'But Melbourne already has a casino.'

'With an expanding population, it can

accommodate more than one. Competition is healthy.' Miles yawned hugely without covering his mouth. 'But I can't go into all that now. I'm tired and I want to go home. Perhaps you'd be good enough to call me a cab.'

9

Another week passed and, although Larissa checked the post anxiously every day, there was still no word from Miles or his lawyers about the divorce. She couldn't help feeling this was odd. After completing the early-morning work in the stables she was enjoying a hearty breakfast of mushrooms and eggs when the telephone rang. She answered it, pleased to hear Joan Hudson's voice.

'Hi Joan, how's it going? You haven't found another stash of bling I'd forgotten, have you?'

'I wish.' Joan laughed briefly before becoming serious again. 'And I want you to know that I don't believe a word of it — that smear campaign in the papers.'

'Thank you, Joan — although . . . ' Larissa cleared her throat, touched by the housekeeper's unswerving loyalty.

'But that's not why I called. Mrs Barton, I hate to bother you . . . '

'It's Larissa now, remember? My days as Mrs Barton are long gone.'

'Er — Larissa then. I'm sorry, it's still a bit strange to use your first name after years of being so formal.'

'You'll get used to it. How can I help you?'

'It's Mr Barton. He went overseas. To China, I think. As you know, he travels all over the place so I didn't take much notice of it at the time. He said he'd be back in three weeks or so but he's been gone for over a month now and I haven't heard from him. Not a word. Um, — I don't suppose you . . . ?'

'Me?' Larissa smiled, thinking of the latest spread in the papers. 'I'm the last person he'd call. Don't worry, Joan. He's probably taken an impromptu holiday without telling anyone, combining business with pleasure.'

'Well, that's what I thought at first.'

'Have you talked to his office? They'll know more than I do?'

'Only that silly creature he keeps at the front desk. No loyalty there. She says she'll leave at the end of the month if she doesn't see her back wages.'

'Miles hasn't been paying her wages?' Larissa frowned. Whatever his faults, her husband was always meticulous about paying his staff.

'And oddly enough, *I* haven't been paid, either.' Joan seemed embarrassed to say so. 'I tried to call the accountant in charge at his office but she seems to have left as well and with no one to replace her. Nor did Mr Barton leave me any money to pay the regular household bills — he likes them to be paid on time. The cleaning lady's gone because she can't afford to work without wages.'

'Nobody can, Joan. Look, this is awful. D'you want me to send you some money to tide you over until Miles gets back?'

'No, no. I'm all right.' Joan laughed. 'I've still got quite a lot of that money we made from selling your fancy clothes. But I can't afford to keep up with the bills for the house. If Mr Barton doesn't turn up soon, I'll have to go and stay with my sister for a while.'

'Go now, Joan. Don't wait for the power and the phone to be cut off.'

'Thank you, Larissa. I thought you'd agree to let me do that.'

'Don't thank me. And you don't have to ask my permission for anything. Just give me your sister's phone number and address. I'll try and find out what's going on with Miles and I'll let you know.'

'Thank you,' Joan sounded relieved to have shifted responsibility on to somebody else.

After that conversation with her husband's housekeeper, Larissa was thoughtful. So that was why she'd heard nothing about the divorce. Miles wasn't even in Melbourne; he was overseas. Running true to type, no doubt he would be enjoying some exotic location in the company of his latest 'playmate'. Even so, it was out of character for him to leave his staff without wages and, as a rule, he left petty cash for the household bills.

She had an unhelpful conversation with Miles's PA who said she had not heard from him since he left Hong Kong for China and didn't know when he'd be back. She also threatened to leave if her wages weren't paid by the end of the month and, really, she didn't know why she had taken this shitty job in the first place. Larissa hung up soon after the girl started swearing.

All Miles's cars were accounted for with none in the long-term car park at Tullamarine. He must have taken a taxi to the airport or been driven there by somebody else.

After giving the matter a fair bit of thought, she decided to contact his lawyer, Peter Mayhall. A slender, well-preserved man in his fifties, Peter was a long-term personal friend of Miles whom she had met several times over dinner. She had always liked the man.

'Larissa.' He seemed pleased to hear from her but at the same time cautious. 'I'm not sure I should be talking to you at all. I shall be handling Miles's side of the divorce.'

'Peter, wait. I don't want to cause you any embarrassment or talk about the divorce. It's just that Miles has gone missing.'

'Ah well — you know Miles.' Peter was

trying to be tactful. 'He's probably — '

'Off with some bimbo — I know. You don't have to tiptoe around it with me. That's what I thought at first. But he was supposed to be away for three weeks and now it's more like six. On top of that, neither his office nor his household staff have been paid.'

'Oh? But doesn't his office accountant take care of all that?'

'Gone missing too, according to his 'soon to be absent' PA.'

'Really?' Peter thought for a moment 'You don't think . . . ?'

'Not for a moment.' Larissa giggled. 'She has no sense of humour at all and a face like a frog.' Once more she thought of those four mobile phones locked in Miles's desk and wondered if now was the time to mention them. They might provide some clue as to her husband's whereabouts. But yet again she decided against it. It would only confirm that she had been snooping. And really, now that she was working with horses again and Miles no longer controlled her every move, she was beginning to enjoy her new life.

'I have to go,' Peter said, making it clear that he wanted to bring this conversation to a close. 'Bit chaotic around here at present. Leave this with me, Rissa. I'll look into it from my end and let you know what I find out.'

With that small reassurance she had to be content.

★ ★ ★

It was one of those lovely crisp mornings when early fog evaporates to make way for a bright winter's day. Golden Czarina stood in her horsebox calm as a veteran and, on arrival at the course, she walked out into the sunshine, raising her head to look around, interested in all the new sights and smells that surrounded her, ears pricked. Racing against other fillies and mares, she was to carry fifty-seven kilos, meaning that David was able to make the weight to ride her. Czarina had taken to Johnnie's brother and they had bonded immediately, so that Stella was happy to leave her most promising horse in his care.

There was only one cloud on the horizon, one sour moment preventing David's enjoyment of the day. Larissa had paraded Golden Czarina in the mounting yard and when she led the filly on to the lawn for David to mount, he'd shivered, feeling someone's hostile gaze on his back. He turned, half-expecting it to be Miles Barton but it was William Willett, watching him through narrowed eyes. As soon as he saw he had David's attention, he nodded slowly and smiled. There was no friendliness in it. David looked away immediately, not wanting to communicate his jolt of anxiety to the filly; he needed to keep her calm and focused on the race. But Larissa was watching him, quick to sense his change of mood.

'What's wrong?' she said. 'Something's upset you, hasn't it? You've gone very pale.'

'It's nothing. I'm always pale,' he reassured her with a smile as he tucked his feet into the stirrups, preparing to ride away. 'We'll be all right when we get out there away from the crowd.' Out of the corner of his eye, he could see Willett bellowing instructions to his newest apprentice and poking him in the chest to emphasize his words. David felt sorry for the lad who was already nervous and red in the face as he mounted, trying to control a skittish horse.

At the start there were only ten runners so there was plenty of room for everyone to spread out and avoid getting in each other's way. Willett's filly, Pirate's Daughter, shot out of the gates and bolted to the front to take up a ten-length lead on the fence. Since the race was only 1200 metres, it wouldn't do to let her get too far ahead so the rest of field changed pace to catch up, closing the gap. At the home turn, Pirate's Daughter was still several lengths ahead and showing no sign of tiring. But, without resorting to the whip, David urged Czarina to lengthen her stride and pull level with her. Leaving the rest of the field well behind, the two fillies continued to battle it out to a photo finish. He could only hope he had done enough.

There was a groan of disappointment from the crowd, telling him that he had. Victory belonged to Golden Czarina, who had beaten the favoured Pirate's Daughter by a short head, in spite of carrying Willett's new apprentice with a big claim.

'You have a good girl, there,' David told Stella Arkwright as he dismounted, patting Czarina on the neck. 'She's a fighter all right. Doesn't want to give up.'

'Thank you, David.' Stella hugged him. Seeing it, Larissa smiled. Her mother was warming to David and seemed to have forgotten all her issues with him; she had never seen her so pleased with a jockey before.

As they had no further racing that day and Stella wanted to get back to Warrandyte before the Saturday football crowds took to the road, David sought permission to leave early and they set off for home, Golden Czarina smugly comfortable in her box as if she knew she had done well.

Sally greeted them with a tidy kitchen and a sweet temper for once, so nobody complained when she didn't volunteer to cook dinner as well. Larissa ordered several pizzas to be delivered and the four of them sat down to drink a bottle of vintage red wine and celebrate the Czarina's victory. They switched on the TV and watched the ABC news bulletin while they waited for the food to arrive. They chatted over the events of the day, having no premonition of disaster and giving the news only half their attention until a familiar name came up, halting all conversation. The anchorman lowered his voice, looking sombre as he changed the subject from the latest discussions in parliament to deliver a different item of news.

There are concerns for the safety of playboy tycoon, Miles Barton, who has been out of touch with both his office and home for some weeks now. One of his closest friends, William Willett, who also trains Mr Barton's champion thoroughbreds, spoke to us at length. Mr Willett informed us that Barton was mortified when Larissa, his wife of ten years, deserted him to take up with a younger man — a situation already widely documented in the press.

Recently, Mr Barton travelled to China on business and, although he was thought to have come back to Melbourne, no one has seen him since. The mystery deepens as no one can be contacted at either his city office or his home in Brighton, which appears to be closed and unoccupied; not even his housekeeper was available to talk to us. Also, Mr Barton has missed several key meetings with his solicitor, Peter Mayhall, prompting Mr Mayhall to bring the matter to the attention of the police. Anyone with information as to Mr Barton's present whereabouts is advised to contact either Crime Stoppers or . . .

And the news bulletin concluded as various telephone numbers appeared on the screen.

In Stella's kitchen, there was shocked silence for several moments as they absorbed this latest news.

'I knew Willett would portray us in the worst possible light,' Larissa said at last. 'He wants the police to believe we have something to do with Miles's disappearance.'

'Why?' Stella said. 'What's it to him? And what would you possibly have to gain?'

'All Miles's money, of course.' Sally said, never one to flinch in the face of an unpleasant truth. In fact she looked almost excited. 'Think about it. If Miles were to die without changing his will, Larissa stands to inherit everything, doesn't she?'

'Oh God, I hope not.' Larissa cringed, resting her head in her hands. 'That just makes it so much worse. The press will have a field day, won't they?'

'Look, I hate to leave when you're in trouble like this,' David said with a sigh. He stood up. 'But I can't help you by staying and my mother will need me. I knew Willett was up to something when I saw him today at the track. He'll do whatever he can to point the police in my direction and make things uncomfortable. Mum will be in a state of high panic by now and I should be there to support her.'

'Of course.' Larissa spoke softly, catching his hand as he reached for his car keys on the table. 'I'm so sorry, David, for dragging you into all this. You've tried to be my friend and I've brought you nothing but trouble.'

'You can say that again,' said Stella, folding her arms.

'Come on, Stella, not now,' David said mildly as he leaned down to kiss Larissa with tenderness rather than passion. She put her arms around his neck and returned it with interest, past caring what her mother or sister would think.

'We'll get through this,' he assured her. 'We know we have nothing to do with what's happened to Miles. Whatever anyone says, we've done nothing wrong.' He glanced at Stella, daring her to say otherwise. 'I won't let you down. When I've sorted things out at home I'll be back to work with the horses.'

Stella nodded stiffly, acknowledging his promise.

Once again, Larissa thought of those four mobile phones lying in Miles's desk. What might they reveal when they were recharged? She couldn't help feeling that at least one of them contained the answer to his disappearance.

* * *

Coincidentally, David arrived at his mother's home at the same time as his brother was delivered there in an ambulance car. Able to get about with the use of crutches and a wheelchair, he seemed happier than he had been for some time and pleased to be home. At last he had regained some feeling in his legs and his doctors were cautiously optimistic that if he worked hard at his exercises and did everything he was told, soon he would be able to walk with the aid of sticks. Encouraged by this news, Johnnie had vowed not only to walk but to ride again in due course. He had been following the newspaper articles and had seen the TV news bulletin concerning the missing tycoon. Now he was agog to hear his brother's side of the story.

'Don't do anything by halves, do you, Bro?' he said, waving his fists triumphantly. 'How about you? Dating the glamorous Mrs Barton. Woo-hoo!'

'Stop it, John,' his mother scolded. 'It's no matter for levity and Larissa is still a married woman. Your brother hasn't done anything to be proud of.'

John gave a thumbs up to David and pulled a face behind his mother's back.

'I saw that,' she said although she couldn't possibly have done so without eyes in the back of her head.

Inevitably, after Willett's heavy-handed innuendos, the police came around wanting to know if David could shed any light on Miles Barton's disappearance. Although they seemed happy enough with his explanations and alibis, prepared to give him the benefit of the doubt, Patsy Riordan's agitation aroused their suspicions. David told them she always behaved like this around anyone in authority, but he could see that they weren't convinced. They left him with a warning that it would be in his best interests not to leave town. For once he was less than patient with his mother after they left.

'Did you *have* to look so guilty, Mum? The

way you were acting, you'll have them tearing up the floorboards in the kitchen, looking for Barton's decomposing body.'

'I'm sorry but I hate dealing with people in authority — you know I do.'

David sighed, realizing that his mother's obvious anxiety would mean that they hadn't been struck off the list. Those detectives would be back.

★　★　★

The Arkwrights had a visit from the same officers investigating Miles's continued disappearance. They were DI Wintergreen, a dark-haired, sad-eyed man who looked too young to be a detective inspector and his even younger, fresh-faced sergeant, Andy Jensen, who stared at Larissa as if she were some kind of scarlet woman, already notorious.

'Turn the place upside down if you like but you'll find nothing here,' Larissa told them. 'Miles doesn't spend any time with anyone unless they can advance him in business, and even when we were together he never bothered to visit my mother's home. But I'd be happy to meet you at the house in Brighton and show you his desk.' She smiled encouragingly, thinking it was high time someone other than herself should discover those mobile phones.

'Mrs Barton,' the detective inspector cleared his throat, unhappy with what he needed to say, 'your — um — friendship with David Riordan has been well documented in the press. I have to ask you if you think this has any bearing on your husband's disappearance?'

For some reason, this question struck a nerve and she snapped back at him. 'If you think David has anything to do with this, you're way out of line. His brother was apprenticed to my husband's horse trainer but David is a freelance rider. They're scarcely acquainted.' Then she paused, taking a deep breath to calm herself, determined not to rouse their suspicions further by letting them see she was upset. 'Just come to my husband's home and see for yourselves. I'm quite sure you'll find all you need there.'

★ ★ ★

She drove ahead, arriving at the mansion just before them. This was the first time she had driven down those familiar streets since leaving some months ago. Fortunately, Miles had never demanded her keys to the house and she had the means to unlock the automatic gates that Joan Hudson had closed when she left. The young policemen drove in behind her, trying to look nonchalant and unimpressed by these obvious trappings of wealth.

Inside, the house smelled stuffy and uninhabited, although it was only a week since Joan had gone, leaving everything clean and tidy behind her. Wandering through the deserted rooms, it felt strange to Larissa to return to this handsome house that had so recently been her home. So much had happened since she had last been here. Only a year ago she had purchased new carpets, new curtains throughout and chosen fresh paint for the walls. It seemed so much longer now. That version of herself as Miles's biddable wife no longer existed.

Finding little to interest them in the reception and dining rooms downstairs, the two police officers concentrated their investigation on the study upstairs, a handsome room with windows giving a panoramic view of the bay. Significantly, Miles's laptop was missing; obviously he had taken it with him on his travels. Since Larissa had no keys to his desk, the police lost no time in breaking into it. They confiscated various items of interest, including the four mobile phones, all in need of charging. Larissa suppressed the urge to give a cheer when they found them. The answer to everything must lie with one of those girls.

After a thorough search of the rooms upstairs they left, asking her not to leave town in case they needed her to give further help with their enquiries.

Further help with their enquiries. Larissa almost smiled, hearing those familiar words so overused in television crime series. She had never expected to hear them applied to herself. Really, she couldn't begin to guess what had happened to Miles. But if he was out there, cavorting on some island in the Pacific, she wished he would come home to Melbourne sooner rather than later and set everyone's mind at rest.

The following day, when she was asked to make an appeal on national television, her first impulse was to refuse. Everyone knew they were separated and she would feel like a hypocrite, going on air to make a plea for Miles to return. It was Stella who persuaded her otherwise.

'If you don't go people will assume you have something to hide,' her mother advised. 'Just play it straight and be yourself. Don't ham it up or pretend to feel more than you do. Just do as they ask and make a straightforward plea for him to come home.'

Larissa was to find that this was easier said than done. In the television studio there were more people present than she had expected, including DI Wintergreen and his sergeant, obviously hoping she would scare up some new information. They greeted her with serious faces, telling her nothing and making her think they had drawn a blank with those mobile phones. She longed to ask them what progress they had made.

The appeal was due to go out live before the end of the 6 p.m. news bulletin and she was suffering from a serious attack of nerves. She tried straightening her knees to stop them from shaking but that didn't work. She didn't know how she was going to speak because her stomach felt as if it were filled with butterflies and if she opened her mouth they would all fly out.

While she was wondering if there was any way to get out of it even at this late hour, the floor manager made a final adjustment to her microphone and counted the seconds away with his fingers, telling her she was on air. Too late, she realized how badly prepared she was; she had made no notes and had no idea what to say. But she had been introduced and now everyone was watching her expectantly, waiting for her to speak.

'Miles,' she began and then paused, giving herself a few moments to collect her thoughts, glancing down at the floor and telling herself to breathe as she looked into the eye of the camera. 'I know we've had our differences and we aren't together right now but that doesn't mean I don't care. We're all worried because no one has heard from you for some time and that's scary. It's not like you to neglect your business or your staff — so please, please just let us know you are safe, even if you don't want to come home.' She took another deep, shuddering breath, realizing that, in spite of the way Miles had treated her, on some level she was still emotionally involved. 'I know you won't hear this message if you are overseas but Miles, if you are anywhere close at hand, please, please don't ignore it.' She shrugged, suddenly close to tears. 'And that's all I can say. Just be in touch or come home.'

* ★ *

Even after Larissa's emotionally charged appeal Miles remained silent. Unlike everyone else, who posted all kinds of messages on various internet sites, calling David a home-wrecker and portraying Larissa as a cheating wife whose actions had driven her rich and benevolent husband away. Even Stella received criticism for allowing David to ride for her and people snubbed them at the races. This became all too obvious when

David won for her again on Golden Czarina at Flemington. As one, the people lining the fence turned their backs on him when he returned to scale and there were random jeers from the crowd.

David was more worried about Larissa than himself. A week ago, after their visit to Miles's home, she had been so sure the police would have everything they needed to track down the missing tycoon but, as the days passed without any further developments, she was no longer so sure.

As a rule, after the races, David would ride back to Warrandyte with Larissa, but this particular afternoon she had taken off early in the Audi, saying she had a headache and needed to get home. So, after the last race, he helped Stella get the filly into her horsebox, hoping to have a serious talk with her as they drove home. Like a black cloud hanging over them, the mystery of Miles's disappearance remained unsolved, allowing no one to take any pleasure in Czarina's latest victory.

'The prize money will pay a few bills and that'll be nice,' Stella said with a wan smile. Usually she was jubilant and willing to buy champagne when she had a city winner.

It was left to David to open the conversation as they drove through the city slowly, caught up in the early evening traffic.

'She hasn't been herself at all this last week and I'm worried about her,' he blurted at last.

'Czarina? Why? We haven't been over-racing her and she's fine. We'll give her a bit of rest before the Spring Carnival,' Stella said, deliberately misunderstanding him.

'Stella, don't play games with me. I'm talking about your daughter.' David wasn't to be put off. 'Larissa's making herself ill over this. She was so sure the police would find all they needed at Barton's house. But still there's no news. And then there was that speech they got her to make on National TV. I didn't realize until then that she was still so emotionally involved.' He stared at Stella's profile as she drove. It seemed to give nothing away.

'Well, yes. She was married to the man for a good ten years.'

'Not all of it good — or so I surmised.'

'You surmised.' Stella raised quizzical eyebrows. 'So what *has* she been telling you, David? About her marriage to Miles?'

'Well, now I think about it,' he said softly, 'not a great deal.'

'Maybe that's the way she wants it.' Stella twitched her shoulder dismissively.

'That's not good enough, Stella. Just talk to me.'

She glanced at him briefly before returning

her gaze to the road. 'I'm not even sure it's your business.'

David sighed. She seemed determined to keep him at arm's length. 'I hope you're not hinting she still has some feelings for Miles?'

'I don't know. Relationships don't stay the same — they have to grow and change. And Miles was my husband's friend rather than mine. I didn't know him that well.'

'All the same, you let your daughter marry him when she was scarcely old enough to know her own mind.'

'Oh, did I?' That struck a nerve, making Stella angry enough to speak the truth. 'Don't lay the blame at my door. Larissa has always been her own person. I'd have preferred her to wait and finish her education, but no! That wasn't half as exciting as dropping out to have a big wedding. Being the centre of attention — the envy of all her friends.'

'I suppose not,' David said slowly, looking thoughtful.

'And Miles was older than all of us. To me it seemed rather medieval — a young girl marrying her father's friend.'

'So why didn't you stop it? You could have withheld your consent.'

Stella laughed shortly. 'Could I? You didn't know my husband. Everyone will tell you how charming he was, but he could be difficult and morose at home. He'd slap down anyone who defied him — sometimes literally. Besides, he wanted this connection with Miles and already had the wedding juggernaut rolling. Nobody listened to me.'

Again David thought for a moment. 'So what are you saying? This was like an old-fashioned Greek wedding — an arranged marriage?'

'Not quite. She convinced herself that she loved him, at least at first, and then she fell in love with the lifestyle he gave her.'

'I see.'

'Do you? Money can be very seductive, you know.'

'Can it?' David glanced at her. 'I wouldn't know.'

'Although things had been tense for some time, I think she was shocked when Miles wanted to end the marriage. She had no choice but to leave and come home to me. But, instead of setting the wheels in motion for the divorce as we expected, Miles let things slide and took off on this trip overseas.'

'So what does that mean? That he's changed his mind? He's hoping to get her back?'

'David, I really don't know. I've given up second-guessing either of them.'

Digesting this information, David remained

silent for the rest of the trip back to Warrandyte. Stella had told him little more than he already knew and he still wasn't sure whose side she was on. He needed to have a serious talk with Larissa.

The opportunity came sooner than he expected. Seeing that Stella was tired after driving through the Saturday afternoon crowds, he offered to settle Czarina back in her stall and make sure she had something to eat. She was a gentle creature with none of the stroppy tendencies often shown by females with the will to win. He spoke to her softly as he brushed her and she nibbled the hair on the back of his neck, making him laugh. He heard someone else laughing as well and looked up to see Larissa, standing watching him from the doorway.

'Feeling better?' he asked.

'It was just a headache,' she replied. 'And I needed some time to think.'

'What about?' He finished dealing with the horse who was now giving full attention to her haybag. He came straight to the point, deciding there was no point in skirting the issue. 'I had quite a chat with your mother on the way home. She made me think you still have an emotional attachment to Miles.'

'What?' She stared at him, genuinely surprised, before shaking her head. 'No. She's just messing with your head because she wants me to keep myself nice until the divorce is through. I was like a caged bird, living with Miles. I only stayed because I didn't know any better. I didn't know what love was.' She came in close to look up at him, speaking softly. 'But now I do.'

'That's what I thought. I'm sorry I had to ask.' He pulled her into his embrace and they kissed, tenderly rather than with passion.

Knowing the time had come to tell the truth about her husband, Larissa took a deep breath. 'I started doubting Miles when he insisted on separate rooms. But I didn't realize how empty our marriage was until I found he had at least four private mobile phones linking him to four different girls. And that's just the ones I know about — there could be more. Miles is a walking cliché — a man of power who wants also to be desirable, receiving constant proof of his sexual allure.'

'Tell me,' he said softly, holding her close, encouraging her to speak.

Quickly and concisely, she told him how she had allowed the police to discover those phones and her certainty that one of them must hold the key to Miles's disappearance.

'I'm sure that one of those girls has to know where he is,' she said at last. 'Miles treats the whole world as his playground. For him, the usual restrictions and rules don't apply. In gambling terminology, he's what you'd call a 'high roller'; a third world country could live for a year on what he can lose in one night. With the aid of Willett and his crooked foreman, he has dabbled in race fixing, bribery and anything else he thinks he can get away with because he just *has* to win. He enjoys the buzz of making illicit money.'

'So when you found out about his activities, why did you stay? Ten years, Rissa?'

'Because I *didn't* know, David. He kept me totally in the dark. It's only lately that I've begun to look behind the mask. I didn't like what I found.'

He drew her closer, letting her rest against him, silently letting her know that he understood.

She gave a shuddering sigh. 'Miles is probably somewhere laughing at us and at all the trouble he's caused right now. I just wish he'd stop playing games and come home.'

10

Later that evening, annoyed with Stella for trying to stir up trouble between David and herself, Larissa went to the foreman's cottage to visit him. Although her mother and sister were safely in bed, this time she didn't care if they guessed where she'd gone, so she didn't trouble to leave the house quietly.

'What's up?' David said as he opened the door, blinking and rubbing his eyes. With his hair on end, bare-chested and wearing only a pair of boxer shorts, it was obvious that he had been woken from sleep. Larissa slumped in the doorway, feeling guilty for disturbing him.

'Oh, David, I'm sorry. I forgot how late it is and how tired you'd be after the races. I should go and let you get back to bed.'

'Don't you dare leave,' he said, closing the door quickly behind her and gathering her into a warm embrace. 'Shall I make tea?'

'I didn't come here for tea,' she murmured, holding him close and breathing in the musky scent of his body as she looked up at him from under her eyelashes.

'I didn't think you did,' he said, kissing her

soundly as he lifted her into his arms, allowing her to lock her legs around his waist as he carried her back to his bed, which was still warm.

This wasn't the first time they had made use of the bed in the cottage but, as a rule, their encounters had been rushed and not altogether satisfying; they had yet to experience once more the lazy luxury of that night in the hills. Larissa fully intended to make up for it tonight.

As lovers, they were now comfortable with each other, aware of what was a turn-on and what was not. When David was tired, yet they wanted to make love again, he liked her to rouse him with her hand and this night they exhausted each other, making love three times before they both fell into a deep and satisfying sleep.

They were woken in the early hours of the morning by someone tapping quietly at the front door. Larissa went to answer it, expecting a confrontation and another lecture from her mother. But, of course, if it had been Stella she wouldn't have been tapping quietly, she would have hammered at the door. Larissa was taken aback to find her sister standing there.

'What is it, Sal? Bit early for you, isn't it?' She tried to focus on Sally who was wearing her red, fluffy dressing-gown and was standing hunched against the cold. 'How did you know I'd be over here?'

'Don't have to be Einstein, do I? Not after the way you slammed out of the house at midnight and not taking your car.' Sally giggled. 'Look at you? Anyone could tell at a glance what you've been up to. Ooh!' She leaned forward to peer at her sister's neck. 'And that massive bite is a dead giveaway. If Mom sees them she goes ballistic, so I make sure boys never do that to me.' She grinned cheekily at the man who had joined Larissa at the door. 'Hello, David, you look shattered. Is my sister wearing you out?'

'All right, Sally, that's enough.' Larissa felt the need to regain control of the situation. 'Thanks for coming to warn me. Is Mom hopping?'

'Not yet. I don't think she heard you leave. But it's not Mom you have to worry about. It's Sunday and Hazel will be round to see to the horses. And you know she has the biggest mouth in the business. If she sees you coming out of David's looking all sleepy and satisfied . . . ' Sally rolled her eyes significantly.

'I forgot about Hazel.' Larissa groaned and leaned forward to give her sister a hasty peck on the cheek. 'Thanks, Sal.'

'Right.' Sally was quick to take advantage. 'Just remember, you owe me. I'll expect you to return the favour when I need it.'

'I don't like sneaking around like this,' David said with a sigh, shaking his head as he watched Sally leave. 'I'll be a lot happier when we don't need to.'

'For that to happen, Miles has to come back from wherever he is and set the wheels in motion for our divorce. We're in limbo until he does,' Larissa said. 'I just wish he'd turn up.'

★ ★ ★

Miles did turn up but not in the way that everyone hoped.

Since there had been nothing to add to that first news bulletin and Larissa's appeal for his return, the media temporarily lost interest in the story of the missing tycoon. Oil spills, earthquakes and skyrocketing interest rates dominated the news as she waited with nail-biting impatience for the police to unlock the secrets of those four mobile phones.

Yet another week was to pass before there was any more news and, in accordance with usual practice, the police remained silent, giving no clue as to their progress. The strain was telling on Larissa, who was becoming pinched and hollow-eyed. She and her mother had just sat down to a late lunch of sandwiches when the doorbell rang. Having finished his morning work-out with the horses, David had gone to visit his family over at Caulfield and Sally was at school in the middle of crucial exams. The doorbell rang again, more insistently this time.

'Ignore it, Mom,' Rissa said. 'If it's important, they'll come back. Teach them to ring up and make a proper appointment next time.'

'You know I can't do that.' Leaving her half-eaten toasted sandwich, Stella had already risen from her seat at the kitchen table. 'I'll only spend the rest of the day wondering who it was.'

Moments later, she ushered DI Wintergreen and his sergeant into the kitchen.

'Oh, dear,' he said, seeing the half-eaten food at the table. 'We're interrupting your lunch.'

'Well, you're here now,' Larissa said, glaring at them and pushing her plate aside. 'And about time, too. I hope you're here to say you've found Miles safe and well and we're no longer under suspicion of doing away with him?'

'Well, yes and no.' DI Wintergreen was looking unhappy and not at all his usual confident self. 'Mrs Barton, there's no easy way to say this. A body has been found and we believe it to be that of your husband.'

Larissa gasped, no longer inclined to be flippant. 'Miles is dead? But how? Did he have an accident? A heart attack?' Over the last few years Miles had suffered from high blood pressure, which he dismissed as 'doctor's nonsense' and largely ignored. She had often worried that he might have a heart attack or a seizure.

Wintergreen cleared his throat. 'Unfortunately, no. Nothing as simple and straightforward as that.'

'So, tell me? We've been living apart for some time, pending divorce, but I wouldn't like to think anything bad happened, that he suffered at all.'

'I wish I could reassure you of that but I can't. We wanted to make sure you knew before the story breaks on the evening news. All the channels will carry the story tonight and the circumstances are suspicious. Mr Barton's remains were found in the backyard of that run-down mansion he owns.'

'That's all right, then. It can't be Miles.' Larissa let go a long breath of relief. 'He doesn't own any mansions, run down or otherwise. Apart from some commercial investments in town and an apartment on the

Gold Coast, the house in Brighton is the only property that he owns.'

'Then our information is more up to date than yours. We checked with his solicitor just to make sure. It's an old-fashioned Victorian, badly in need of renovation. We found him buried at the rear of the property, in a shallow grave.'

'No. That can't be Miles. He's probably still overseas.'

'We were following up some people connected with those mobile phones and that led us to . . . ' Wintergreen hesitated, realizing he'd said too much. 'Look, you have enough to worry about. You don't need to know all the details just yet.'

'Inspector, those details will be all over the popular press tomorrow. You might as well tell me everything now.' Larissa squared her shoulders, bracing herself for the worst. 'Aside from myself, my husband has no living relatives — not in Australia, anyway. He has a sister who went to America — I'm not even sure where. There was a rift and they haven't spoken for years. So, as his closest relative, I suppose it'll be up to me to identify the body?'

The inspector nodded. 'I'm sorry. That is one of the reasons we're here. But it doesn't have to be — '

'Let's go then.' Larissa stood up. 'Might as well get it over with.'

'Just a moment.' Stella felt bound to interrupt. 'Who is responsible? For killing Miles and burying him in this way? Do you know?'

'There's no need to go into that now,' Wintergreen said firmly. 'We should see to the formal identification first. Would you like to get a coat, Mrs Barton?' he said, nodding to his sergeant and edging towards the door. Uncomfortable under Stella's scrutiny, they were anxious to be on their way.

'Oh no,' Stella said, blocking the doorway. 'You can't leave, telling us only half the tale. Who did this? Do you have Miles's assailant in custody?'

'I'm sorry, but we're not at liberty to say.'

'That means 'no' then,' Stella said, folding her arms.

Larissa had sat down at the table again, still coming to terms with this terrible news. Her eyes were closed and her hands covered her mouth.

'Mrs Arkwright, your daughter is clearly upset.' The inspector decided he had said more than enough. 'We don't have to do this today. Maybe tomorrow when she's had time to take it in and get over the shock?'

'No.' Larissa stood up again, leaning on the table for support. She didn't want them to

225

see she was feeling giddy. 'I don't want this hanging over my head. I'd rather get it over with now.'

'You're in no fit state — you sit down,' Stella ordered. 'You too, Inspector and you, Sergeant. I think we're all beyond lunch now but I'll make some tea and you can fill us in on the details and tell us what to expect from now on. At least tell us how Miles came to be found?'

With strong tea set in front of everyone, the inspector embarked on his tale.

'Our first lead came from one of those mobile phones. An excitable young lady who was very upset when she found she was talking to the police and not Mr Barton himself. She had been seeing your husband regularly for some months and told us he'd promised to marry her when his divorce came through. Then she showed us photographs of a rambling old house in North Ringwood, saying this was to be their home when they married. It needed a full renovation and he told her she would be free to decorate as she wished. In the meantime, he said, he had business to take care of overseas and would see her on his return.

'But that was the last she heard of him. She left a dozen messages on his mobile but he never replied.'

'The run-down mansion,' Larissa whispered to Stella. 'I'll bet that's the same place Johnnie was held.'

'What did you say?' asked the inspector. 'If there's anything jogging your memory — anything at all — we'd like to hear it now.'

'It's nothing really.' Larissa smiled briefly. 'Please, go on.'

'We lost no time in finding the old house and checking it out. Most of the rooms were empty and had been for some time, but there were signs that someone had been camping out in the kitchen a few months ago. Old pizza boxes and plastic coffee cups littered the floor. Mice had been feasting on the leftovers.' He glanced from Stella to Larissa and back again. 'Are you certain you want all the details?'

'Don't stop now,' Stella said. 'Tell us as much as you can.'

'I'm not sure I should be telling you anything since the case is unsolved.' The inspector glanced at his sergeant, who shrugged. 'As I said, the kitchen was the only room showing signs of occupation and most of the gardens were overgrown and badly maintained. But, at the rear of the property, there was a vegetable patch, freshly turned over and ready for planting. Closer inspection revealed that it wasn't a vegetable patch at all but a shallow grave, containing Mr Barton's remains. A small dog, belonging to one of the neighbours, had been trying to dig him up.'

'Oh dear God.' Once more Larissa clapped her hands to her mouth, suppressing a heave.

Having a stronger stomach, Stella was determined to have all the details. 'Yes, and I suppose that girl of his will turn out to be the murderer's accomplice?'

'Not at all. What would she have to gain? She's just as shocked and upset as you are.' The inspector placed a hand on Larissa's shoulder. 'As yet we know Mr Barton died from a heavy blow to the back of the head but he didn't die where he was found. There were some tyre marks no one had taken the trouble to conceal, so we assume his body must have been brought there in the trunk of a car, most likely at night. He was a large man and one person wouldn't have handled the body alone. Two people would have been needed to carry his dead weight between them.'

'So where did he die?' Stella's voice was hoarse. 'In a hotel room somewhere?'

'We don't know. That is what we still have to find out.'

At that moment Sally burst into the room, calling out to her mother and throwing her school bag under the table before she realized there were other people in the room.

'Two fantastic exams today! Everyone else said they hated them but I'm sure I passed!'

'That's lovely, dear,' Stella murmured, distracted.

'Hey, what's up?' Sally glanced at the solemn faces seated around the table. 'What's happened?'

'Miles has been found,' Stella said. 'And he's dead. These policemen are here to give us the news. They also need us to identify the body.'

'Mom, you stay here with Sally and let me go.' Larissa stood up to grab an old coat from the back of the kitchen door; she didn't care how she looked. Not today. 'It's probably better if I do this alone.'

'Hey, can I come?' Sally's face was eager. 'I've never seen a dead body before.'

'Sarah!' Stella glared at her younger daughter. 'That's quite enough. Miles was your sister's husband. Have some respect.'

'Why? Rissa doesn't love him any more — she has David now. And Miles was ever so old — he'd have died soon, anyway.'

'Give it a rest, Sal.' Larissa sighed, too weary to be upset by her sister's tactless remarks. 'Shall we go?' she turned to the policemen who were studying her with renewed interest after hearing the new slant Sally had given them, although this wasn't the first they'd heard of a new man in Mrs Barton's life.

'I'll have words with you later, young lady,' Stella muttered, pulling Sally aside and surreptitiously pinching the tender flesh of her upper arm.

'Ow! What's that for, Mom?' Sally looked aggrieved, rubbing the place that was quickly starting to bruise. 'I come home with good news about my exams and what do I get? Nothing but abuse.'

Larissa could still hear them arguing as she opened the door for the policemen and followed them out, closing it firmly behind her.

* * *

The visit to the morgue was mercifully brief; she didn't really have time to absorb the atmosphere or the pervasive chemical smells masking something worse. Although her husband had been divested of both his watch and his jewellery, his corpse seemed somehow shrunken, diminished from the hearty figure he had represented in life. But his face was undamaged and his hair was the same. She thought he looked more at peace than she had ever seen him before. All the same, she felt oddly detached from the whole experience, as if it were happening to somebody else.

Sergeant Jensen drove her home, leaving

her to her thoughts and having little to say. She felt on the verge of tears. Although she had assured David she no longer had feelings for Miles, she felt saddened that he should have met such a sudden and brutal end.

At Stella's home the telephone kept ringing endlessly until they took it off the hook, and they turned off their mobiles. Sally, having finished with all her exams, was ordered by her mother to stay home from school.

'But why can't I go, Mom?' she asked. 'I didn't know Miles all that well and it's not as if I'm in grief or anything. Why must I stay home?'

'You know why,' Larissa snapped. She had slept only fitfully and was on a short fuse. 'We don't want you making a celebrity of yourself, filling everyone in on the gory details.'

'I don't know any gory details,' Sally grumbled. 'No one tells me anything.'

★ ★ ★

David had tried several times to reach Larissa by phone but he couldn't get through. He was worried about the three women left to run the gauntlet of all those reporters. He would have liked to be there for them but the entrance to the property was surrounded by reporters and cameramen as well as several vans associated with the television news.

There was nothing for it but to wait until some political upheaval or new scandal drew them away; this didn't happen for several days.

Peter Mayhall was one of the first to get through when the Arkwrights recharged their mobile phones and the hounds of the media left to turn their attention to someone else. He invited Larissa to come and see him at his suite of offices in town. This was surprising, as he had always done his best to avoid her before. Stella wanted to accompany her but Peter said he preferred to see her alone.

'I don't like it.' Stella was miffed that he should make such a request. 'Just remember he's Miles's lawyer, not yours. You should be dealing with him through Roger rather than talking to him direct.'

'Why, Mom? Roger deals mainly with property — he's not that sort of lawyer. Peter Mayhall can run rings around him if he wants to.'

'Let Roger suggest someone, then.'

'What for? I don't want anything. It would be like dancing on Miles's grave.'

'Well, Miles deserves to have his grave danced upon. Don't agree to anything or sign any papers without talking it over with me.'

Larissa groaned.

She didn't dress up for the occasion, wearing her everyday jeans together with a black velour jacket and black silk scarf. Peter didn't keep her waiting and greeted her formally, shaking hands and saying what a tragedy it was and how sorry he felt for her loss. She responded with a wan smile, suspecting he trotted out the same platitudes to anyone who had suffered the death of a relative. She was struck again by how tidy and conventional Peter looked, sitting behind his tidy and conventional polished cedar desk; a picture-book solicitor, slender and athletic in a grey, pin-striped suit with a waistcoat to match. His fair hair was cropped short and parted on the side, probably in the same style he had worn since he was at school. He had always seemed to her to be a walking cliché: a successful, middle-aged man at the pinnacle of his career.

He had a large file in front of him, no doubt concerning Miles's affairs, and she hoped it didn't mean that Peter needed her to make any decisions about the estate. Her life was complicated enough without getting involved in Miles's dubious business dealings. He set her to rest on that score immediately, as if reading her mind.

'I'll come straight to the point, Larissa. As I'm sure you know, Miles was a stubborn man who didn't like to be crossed. He was angered by your refusal to comply with his wishes — '

'Because I wouldn't accept his pink diamonds and give him an easy divorce?'

'That's a part of it, certainly. In modern parlance Miles was a control freak. He wanted everyone to fall in with his plans and accept his decisions without question. Ultimately that may be what cost him his life.'

'So, do the police have any idea who . . . ?'

'Not yet. But I believe they have several leads that they're following up.'

'The longer it takes, the less likely they are to come up with a result,' she said with a sigh. 'Miles wasn't easy to live with — I should know — but I can't think of anyone who would hate him enough to kill him and dispose of his body like that.'

'Well, somebody did.' The solicitor cleared his throat. 'But I didn't call you in to speculate on the cause of your husband's death.'

'So why am I here, Peter? I hope you're not going to tell me I'm Miles's heir? Because if you are, I don't want it — any of it. I'm not the gold-digger you think I am.'

For the moment he seemed at a loss for words and Larissa saw that she had read his mind correctly. He had been expecting a very different reaction from Miles's widow.

'No, Larissa.' He sat back at last, regarding her, shaking his head. 'You are not Miles's heir. Surely, you remember signing a prenuptial agreement?'

She smiled. 'Peter, I was sixteen years old. I was excited about getting married and I've no idea what I signed.'

'Well, I have it here, and it clearly states that if Miles were to die before you — all too likely considering the difference in age — you would claim nothing from his estate except the clothing and jewellery acquired during the course of your married life together — however long or short that might be.'

She frowned. 'Really? Is that entirely legal? If I'd still been living with Miles as his wife — '

'Contest it, if you like. I don't think you'll win.'

'As I told you — I don't want anything — not now he's dead. But, out of curiosity, who *is* to inherit his fortune?'

'His sister. He never changed his original will — not even to add any legacies for loyal employees. In spite of the rift between them, Miles believed blood was thicker than water and so the only beneficiary is Morgan Barton who is his twin. She's a screenwriter in Los Angeles.'

'Nothing like Miles, then. I don't think he

had a creative bone in his body. I knew there was a sister living in America but he never told me she was his twin.'

'She was in touch with me from the moment she heard he was missing. Later she called again to say she was sure he was dead. I told her not to be fanciful and melodramatic but, of course, she was right. Twins have this form of telepathy, sometimes.'

'He never talked about her at all. I had the impression they didn't get on.'

'They didn't. Their relationship was nothing if not eccentric.'

'Well, thank you for giving me this news in person, Peter.' Larissa smiled and stood up, ready to shake his hand and leave. 'It's a load off my mind to know that I'm off the hook and can get on with the rest of my life.'

'Not quite. Morgan is on her way to Australia. She's asking to meet you.'

Larissa slumped. 'Oh, no. That's not necessary, is it? What can we possibly have to say to each other now?'

'She says she needs closure. She's arranging a simple cremation now that Miles's body has been released — a private ceremony — but she wants you to help her arrange a memorial service for Miles.'

'A memorial service? Why? Miles never had any time for religion, anyway.'

'No?' Peter shrugged. 'Well, maybe she does.'

* * *

Several things were making Larissa unhappy, the first being that she had quarrelled with David. Although he insisted that he had been trying to contact her all the time her phone was shut down, she continued to feel neglected and refused to accept his excuses.

'You could have come here in person, David. We needed your support.'

'Really? And get mobbed by that crowd of media vultures on your doorstep?'

'Why not? You run back home fast enough when your mother needs your protection from the media or the police.'

'You are much tougher than my mother. For that matter so is Stella.'

'That's irrelevant, David. And I can't talk now. Miles's sister is here from America and I have to meet her in town. If I don't leave at once I'm going to be late.'

'Miles's sister? Are you sure that's a good idea?'

'No. I'm not sure of anything any more, David. Not even you.'

'Larissa! Don't say that. Look, you're upset

and vulnerable right now. Let me pick you up and I'll go with you.'

'No. You'd be like a red rag to a bull, only making things worse.'

'How can they be any worse?' But there he was forced to leave it because she was gone.

11

Later, when she had calmed down, she wished she had agreed to let David accompany her. She knew she had treated him unfairly. It wasn't his fault that he had been absent from Warrandyte when the police brought the news of her husband's death. She owed him an apology but she didn't know how to climb down from her high horse to give it. And would he accept it if she did? David was capable of being just as proud and stubborn as she was.

She wasn't looking forward to this meeting with Miles's sister. What if Morgan expected her to play the grieving widow, taking an active part in the memorial service for Miles? She would feel like a hypocrite. All the same, she was curious about her American sister-in-law, imagining a typical Californian matron with shoulder-length blonde hair, an expensive spray tan combined with botox, and a set of perfect white teeth. As it happened, she couldn't have been more wrong. Morgan was someone entirely different although Larissa recognized her at once because she was so much like Miles.

They were to meet at a well-known café in Southbank, overlooking the river, both preferring to meet for the first time on neutral ground. The only thing Larissa had right about this woman was her hair which was a skilfully coloured gold blonde, but Morgan wore it short as a boy, almost shaved at the sides and leaving it longer on top where it flopped across her brow. Walking briskly into the café and looking around, searching the tables for Larissa, Morgan appeared easily as tall as most men. She was dressed in a mannish, tailored grey trouser suit with a white shirt and tie. It was like meeting a healthier, younger version of Miles and, almost against her will, Larissa felt the instant pull of attraction towards this person. She stood up from the table, waving to catch her attention and when the woman arrived, she tried to shake hands. Instead, Morgan pulled her into an intimate embrace, holding her close as if they had known one another for years. She smelled of a musky, unusual and not quite feminine cologne.

'Larissa,' Morgan murmured the name almost like a caress and smiled warmly, showing a perfect set of teeth, far too good to belong to a woman of her age. 'Miles always did have good taste in women.' The accent was American but restrained, her voice low and pleasing.

Blushing and unsure how to respond to this opening gambit, Larissa at last broke free of the woman's embrace. 'I'm so pleased to meet you,' she said, relying on convention. 'Welcome to Melbourne.'

'Good old Melbourne. I haven't been here for years but it doesn't change much, does it? Apart from that awful square opposite Flinders Street station. Those new buildings look as if they've been camouflaged against an airborne invasion. Whoever thought *that* was a good idea?'

'Surely, it's better than those old office blocks that were there before? Now we have a meeting place in the city for outdoor events as well as art galleries and a specialist cinema.' Larissa felt bound to defend her home town against this stranger's criticism.

'A specialist cinema?' Morgan echoed her words, amused by this description. 'For educational films no one wants to see?' She sat down, looking across at the river, allowing Larissa to order coffee from the hovering waitress and holding up a hand, refusing the offer of food. 'The Yarra still looks as if it flows upside down.' She turned back to Larissa. 'I wouldn't have come back at all, you know, if this hadn't happened.'

'It must be awful for you. To come home after all this time to find Miles gone?'

241

'Not really.' Morgan smiled ruefully. 'And this isn't home to me. Not any more. I'm not one of those mawkish expats who still call Australia home.' She mocked the phrase, wiggling her fingers beside her ears to make quotation marks as she spoke.

'I suppose not.' Larissa found she had little to say to this prickly, forthright woman, although there was much that she wanted to ask.

'Of course, I'm sorry my brother died so suddenly and in this horrible way but I can't pretend I'm in grief. I woke up one day and just knew he wasn't alive any more. In spite of our differences — and our animosities — we still had that odd connection that sometimes happens between twins. But I hadn't seen him or even spoken to him for years. My life won't change in the slightest because Miles is gone.'

Larissa thought differently, although she didn't say so. As the sole heir to Miles's business interests and fortune, Morgan's life was about to change a great deal.

The strong café lattes arrived promptly and Morgan sweetened hers with three sticks of sugar.

'I suppose you're wondering what happened?' Morgan smiled directly into Larissa's eyes and lowered her voice for dramatic effect. 'You can't imagine what could have caused such a terrible rift between twins?'

'No, not really,' Larissa mumbled. She *had* been wanting to know exactly that, but all of a sudden, she didn't want to hear Morgan's darker secrets; she already knew enough about Miles's.

'Not very talkative, are you?' Morgan regarded her critically, head on one side. 'Pretty enough but you don't have much to say for yourself. Not exactly the soul of wit.'

Larissa frowned, not knowing how to answer this; the woman seemed to enjoy disconcerting her.

'You don't know what to make of me, do you?' Morgan sat back and laughed. 'It's all right, I can't help myself, dear. I'm just a sour old hack who makes a living inventing dialogue for the soaps. Feisty heroines in filmy dresses and handsome, promiscuous men.' Morgan sat back, searching in a large black satchel to find cigarettes and preparing to light one up. The manageress was at their table on the instant before she could do so.

'I'm sorry, sir.' She addressed Morgan. 'But if you want to smoke, you'll have to move to one of the tables outside.'

'We'll stay where we are, thanks.' Morgan returned the packet to her handbag, giving the woman a catlike smile. 'And it's not 'sir', it's 'madam'.' Clearly, she enjoyed catching people on the wrong foot. 'But since you're here, you can bring two more cups of strong latte.'

'I'll have them sent over — madam,' the manageress said through clenched teeth before retreating to her position behind the bar. She continued to watch Morgan through narrowed eyes.

Morgan continued to smile at the woman's discomfiture. 'That happens all the time. Sometimes I think it would have been easier if Miles and I had been twin boys.'

Larissa ignored the remark, deciding to change the subject instead. 'You've seen the lawyer, Peter Mayhall, then?'

'About the inheritance? Yes. Isn't he precious? Just the right balance of public-school pomposity and legal jargon to inspire confidence.'

'Miles thought a lot of Peter. He respected him.'

'Respect?' Morgan gave a snort of laughter. 'A vastly overrated commodity.'

'Do you always do this? Pour scorn on everyone?' Larissa decided it was time to fight back. She'd had enough of Morgan's brand of deprecating humour.

'Oho, that's better. A bit of spirit at last. I've poked you out of your brittle shell of politeness.'

244

'I am not brittle.'

'I never said that you were. Only that you were wearing a brittle shell. At last I'm beginning to see the real Larissa — what Miles must have seen in you.'

'I don't need your approval.'

'Of course you don't.' Morgan sat back and laughed again. 'Lighten up. You take yourself far too seriously.' She smiled and thanked the waitress who had brought two more cups of coffee.

'And you don't take anything seriously enough. You probably go through life kicking hornets' nests.'

'Ah, you read that book too.' Morgan grinned. 'Good, wasn't it?'

'Don't change the subject. I want to talk about *you*. I wasn't going to mention it but now I really do want to know. What happened between you and Miles to make you fall out?'

Morgan took her time answering, stirring her coffee and then licking the spoon. Somehow she made even that small gesture sensual. 'Oh, it wasn't just the one thing, there were many. The last one was the final straw that broke the camel's back.'

'Don't fob me off with clichés. You've teased me long enough.'

'You think?' Morgan showed perfect teeth again, biting her lower lip. 'All right. But don't say you haven't been warned. You're not going to like it.' She paused, as if hoping Larissa might let her off the hook. But the younger woman just sat there waiting expectantly.

'Although Miles and I grew up happily together, we were always competitive. Physically, he was always more heavily built and detested not being athletic like me. I was better than he was at swimming and all sports. I even beat him at cricket. And as we grew older, we discovered another unfortunate thing. We had the same taste in women.'

'I see.' Larissa nodded.

'Do you?' Morgan smiled, crinkling the corners of her eyes, enjoying her memories. It made her look charming and mischievous, less than trustworthy. 'Oh, it didn't matter so much when we were young — we were just experimenting with life really — no one took anything seriously and we always got past it. We were parted for the first time when I went to college to take my degree in English and Miles stayed home, taking a course in accounting and business studies or something equally boring.' She stood up. 'Perhaps we'll go outside after all. I really could do with that cigarette.'

'You'll kill yourself with those things.' Without meaning to, Larissa found herself saying the same thing she used to say to Miles when he smoked too many cigars.

'Who's to care if I do?' Morgan shrugged. Outside, although the breeze was cool, they occupied another table and the older woman lit up, closing her eyes as she relished the first long drag on her cigarette.

'Don't you have anyone who cares about you, Morgan? In California?'

'How does the song go? Something about being a pirate — two hundred years too late. Miles and I were like a couple of pirates — far too similar in every way. We took what we wanted and sucked the life out of it before moving on.' She spoke lightly as if mocking her own bad behaviour. 'And, in answer to your question — no, there is no significant other waiting for me in California.'

'Not even a best friend?'

'Do you want to hear the rest of this story or not?'

'Yes. Sorry.'

'I didn't see Miles again for some time. I graduated with a spectacular result and I was on top of the world. I came home for Christmas to see everyone before taking off for America — I'd promised myself I'd work in California and make a fortune writing screenplays for blockbuster movies. Miles was married to his first wife at that time — Janis, her name was. She was quite lovely, like a fragile Dresden figurine — everything he had always wanted, he said. But the cracks in the marriage were already there — disillusionment setting in. Quite simply, Janis wanted a baby and Miles didn't. He was quite emphatic about it and wouldn't be moved. He said he didn't want any children destroying his lifestyle.'

'I know. I went through that with him, too.'

'Then you'll be aware.' Morgan smiled. 'The leopard cannot change his spots. Janis said Miles had married her under false pretences and wanted to punish him for his selfishness. She was like a ripe plum, ready to plunge into an affair and who was there to catch her but me? Of course, I couldn't give her the babies she wanted but I did represent a more sympathetic version of Miles. How could she resist? As you can imagine, all hell broke loose when Miles found out. He said I had ruined his life on purpose — untrue — he was doing that all on his own long before I came on the scene. He and Janis divorced and I went to America just as I'd planned. She wanted to go with me but I'd had enough by then and was bored with her whining. Miles vowed never to trust a woman again and that no wife — present or future — was going to inherit his estate. He also promised to curse me by making a will in my favour, leaving his property and business interests to me. He knew very well how I valued my carefree lifestyle and wouldn't want to be chained to something like that.'

'That's odd,' Larissa smiled. 'I didn't want it, either. I was so relieved when Peter told me he'd left it to you. Look on the bright side, Morgan. You can always sell up, take the money and run.'

Morgan rolled her eyes. 'That'll take months if not years, the way Miles set it up.'

'Can't Peter deal with it for you?'

'Not entirely. Unless we can find a loophole, there are clauses insisting that I have to spend at least six months of the year in this country. Miles knew that to comply with his conditions, I'd have to give up my work in California.'

'That's not fair.'

Morgan laughed again. 'When did Miles ever play fair? But the last laugh is on him because I don't care any more. I went to the States with stars in my eyes, expecting to make pots of money writing screenplay for mainstream movies. Instead, I've been in a straitjacket for years, churning out half-hour scripts for one of the daily soaps. I'm not even the story editor. And last month the show I've been working on for the past twenty years was cancelled without any warning. They said the actors were getting too old and the writing too stale. So Miles's 'punishment' for my sins is going to backfire. I can stay here as long as it takes to get the estate wound up. I might even start my own production company when I get back to the States.' Gleefully, she punched the air. 'Morgan with money! They'd better watch out. I can think of quite a few heads that deserve to get kicked.'

Unsure what to make of these revelations, Larissa glanced at her watch. 'I should be getting back. I live quite a long way from town and — '

'You can't go yet. We haven't discussed what you came for. The memorial service for Miles.'

'I'm not sure that's a good idea. It would be a travesty, feeling as we do. Nobody kept the faith.'

'That is exactly why we have to do it, Larissa. So we can both close the book on Miles and get on with our lives.'

'Not quite. The police haven't caught up with his murderer yet.'

'Ah. You speak of the delectable DI Wintergreen.' The mischievous grin reappeared.

'Delectable, is he?' Larissa raised her

eyebrows. 'I thought you liked women?'

'Oh, I do. But why should I restrict myself to just half the population?'

★ ★ ★

Miles's memorial service was not at all as Larissa had imagined, she having visualized a sober affair to mirror his public persona. Although in his lifetime she had rarely seen him in church except to attend a wedding, Morgan had gone back to their roots to take over one of the larger Anglican churches on the outskirts of town, even asking the minister to conduct a service and say a few words. After that, all semblance of convention came to an end. There was a celebration of Miles's life, including the raucous popular music he loved and speeches by various 'friends', most of whom Larissa had never met. She suspected some of them were scarcely acquainted with him at all. William Willett also indulged himself with a lengthy speech, ending in an impassioned plea for the police to track down the person who had committed this terrible crime against 'dear Miles'. Stella, seated next to her daughter, sighed and rolled her eyes. Sally wasn't there, having refused to have anything to do with it.

'I don't like funerals, they're creepy,' she

251

had said, shuddering and pulling a face. 'All that *ashes to ashes* and stuff.'

'It isn't exactly a funeral. It's just a memorial service,' her mother reminded her. 'And your sister needs your support.'

'Really? That'll be a first. Count me out, Mom.'

Standing at the rear of the church, in a position where they could see everyone, stood DI Wintergreen and Sergeant Jensen in their dark suits. Their gaze roved over the whole congregation, missing no one. Beside them stood David Riordan, wearing the dark-blue suit he sometimes wore to the races. Becoming aware that someone was watching her, Larissa turned and recognized David but thereafter chose to ignore him. Really, she was desperate to make her peace with him but she didn't know how to begin and her feelings were mixed.

After the service, when the three of them: Stella, herself and Morgan came out, blinking in the early afternoon sunlight, reporters and cameramen rushed towards them, making them recoil. They should have expected it and gone out of a side door. Fortunately for them, at that moment the attention of the media was diverted by two young women emerging from the church to confront each other on the steps, screaming and making a scene.

'Miles loved *me*, you bitch!' one of them yelled, slapping the other woman with her purse. 'He'd never look at a brass-faced ho like you!'

'He was mine, you fat cow!' the other one answered, fury contorting what might once have been pretty features. 'You look like a pig on its hind legs in those heels!'

This was the signal for battle. Hats were torn off and trampled on the ground as they struggled, grasping at clothing and pulling each other's hair until they were separated by family and friends. Larissa watched, fascinated, concluding that these must be two of Miles's girlfriends, enraged to discover that they were rivals for his affections.

At this point Morgan nudged her, indicating they should take the opportunity to make their escape. They had been surprised to find the church filled to capacity and, with no arrangements made to entertain all these people, they needed to get away fast.

The chauffeur had opened the door of the limo and Stella was already inside, urging them to follow, when something prompted Larissa to turn round yet again. Sergeant Jensen, backed by a few uniformed police from a patrol car parked on the pavement outside the church, was cautioning William Willett and snapping a pair of handcuffs on his wrists before loading him neatly into the back seat of the car. Murphy, who had been strolling beside him, saw this happening and tried to make a run for it but the crowd was too tightly packed and he didn't get far. He was quickly seized, cuffed and pushed into another unmarked police car parked on the street. Having made this surprise attack on the two men, the police quickly left the scene.

Impatient to leave before the reporters came back, Morgan pushed Larissa into the waiting limousine, climbed in behind her and slammed the door, telling the driver to step on it.

Scarcely able to make sense of what she'd just seen, Larissa continued to look out of the rear window at the crowd. The last person she saw was David standing on the steps of the church, staring after them as the limousine pulled away from the kerb.

12

No one had much to say as the driver eased the limousine into the traffic, leaving the church behind. Not even Morgan ventured a caustic remark about the unexpected arrest of Willett and his foreman or the unseemly fight between the two women on the steps. If she had seen David watching Larissa with such brooding intensity, she thought better of mentioning it. Instead, the three women travelled in silence, lost in their own thoughts. Only Stella seemed at all buoyant when the vehicle came to a smooth stop outside the main door of the hotel where Morgan was staying.

'You must come and see us at Warrandyte.' On impulse, she threw out the invitation, ignoring her daughter's pained expression and quick shake of the head. 'Too depressing for you to be left in the city alone, especially at such a difficult time.'

'Why, thank you, Stella, I'd love to visit you. I don't know much about horses but I'm always willing to learn.' Morgan smiled back at her new friend. She didn't spare a glance for Larissa, all too aware of her negative reaction to her mother's generosity. 'Hotels are comfortable enough these days but it's nice to be invited to someone's home. Makes a place seem more real somehow.' She gave Stella a quick peck on the cheek before getting out. 'I'll be in touch in a day or so when I've got myself sorted.' Then she gave her driver instructions to take his remaining passengers to Warrandyte and, with a final mocking salute to Larissa, disappeared through the revolving door that led into the hotel.

'Oh, Mom, why did you have to do that?' Larissa groaned as soon as Morgan was out of earshot. 'I thought we were seeing the last of her. She'd have to be one of the most perverse and abrasive people I've ever met.'

'You don't get her sense of humour, that's all. I find her interesting. Unusual.'

'She's unusual all right. Sees the world through jaundiced spectacles, sneering at everything. Some of the things she said would make your hair curl.'

Stella laughed. 'She's just trying to shock you, that's all. And it worked.'

She fixed her daughter with a look. 'All that aside — what's going on with you and David? I saw him watching you with his soul in his eyes, hoping to have a word outside the church. But you sailed past, ignoring him. He might as well not have been there.'

'Didn't we have enough to worry about? The press having a field day with those two women and Morgan pushing us into the car.'

'Those are excuses.'

Larissa sighed. 'I don't know what to say to him, Mom. He goes running off to his mother the moment she needs him, but when we could do with support he's nowhere to be found.'

'That's not fair. He was there today for us, wasn't he? You know Mrs Riordan has a lot on her plate with Johnnie still in a wheelchair.'

Larissa stared out of the window, cringing from Stella as if she were the voice of her own conscience. She knew she had been selfish; too absorbed in her own feelings to spare a thought for anyone else.

Stella persisted. 'Remember, you were the one who always urged him to go and look after his people at home.'

'Yes, I know. But he didn't have to stay away, did he?' Larissa felt bruised by her mother's criticism. 'And you've changed your tune a bit, haven't you? You were always trying to keep us apart.'

'When Miles was alive, yes. I thought there would be repercussions — and there were. But there's no need for that kind of caution now.'

'I see things differently. After all that's happened maybe I'm not ready to let David back into my life.'

'Honestly, Rissa. If anyone is perverse, it's you.'

'Mom, our whole world was turned upside down when Miles was found dead. We were besieged by reporters and television news people beating a path to our door.'

'My point exactly. David couldn't have reached us if he'd tried. And we switched off our phones to stop being hounded.'

'I know, I know.' Larissa had her arms across herself, almost rocking in her misery.

'So why not cut him some slack? Unbend a little, won't you? I'll talk to him first, if you like. I'm still short-handed around the stables and I need his help.'

'You can get other help. It doesn't have to be David.'

'Is that what you want? To cut him out of your life and alienate him completely?'

'No, of course not.' Larissa stared miserably out of the window where the wind was now turning to rain. 'So many awful things have happened that I don't know what I want.'

'Well, I do. I want David back. I don't have the time or the energy to coach someone new.'

'All right.' Larissa sighed, tired of her mother's urging. 'I will speak to him but let me do it in my own time.'

'Just don't leave it too long or we'll lose him for good.'

The following day, when the doorbell rang shortly after lunch, Sally ran to answer it, expecting it to be one of her friends. Instead, she came back to the kitchen, looking sullen, leading DI Wintergreen and Sergeant Jensen. She sat down with her mother and sister at the kitchen table, hoping to hear what they had to say.

'Go to your room Sally, please,' her mother said softly.

'Aw no, Mom, why can't I . . . ?'

'That is an order, not a request.' Stella was firm. 'Go now. And no eavesdropping on the stairs or outside the door.'

Sally flounced out and, moments later, the driving sound of repetitive pop music could be heard coming from her room.

Stella offered tea to the policemen but this time it was politely refused.

'All right,' Larissa said, folding her arms. 'I gather this isn't a social visit and we know you have Willett and his foreman in custody. How can we help you now?'

DI Wintergreen sat back and looked at her, trying to decide whether she was a hostile witness or not. 'We need you to tell us all you know of William Willett's business dealings with your husband.'

'His business dealings? I don't know much at all. Certainly nothing definite like names or dates that you can confirm. Miles's study was the warmest room in our house; the sun shone in for most of the day. I used to sit in there reading, curled up in one of his big wing chairs. Sometimes, when he was at work on his laptop or talking business on the phone, he'd forget I was there.'

'And who did he speak to? Regularly, I mean.'

'I don't know.' Larissa shrugged. 'He made and received lots of calls and I heard only one side of the conversation. Unless things got heated, I didn't pay much attention. Then I'd creep out past the desk on all fours and get out of there fast.'

'You thought he'd be angry to see you there?'

'Maybe. I didn't wait to find out.'

'So he never confided in you? Or spoke of his plans?'

Larissa laughed shortly as if the inspector had made a joke. 'Not at all. I was his child bride, not his confidante.' She thought for a moment before going on. 'Inspector, my husband was a wealthy man who had enough money to last him a lifetime. He wasn't mean with it, either — well, not while I was living with him, anyway. But for Miles the money was never enough. He craved excitement and adventure, always looking for something new. He liked to sail near the wind, to take risks. More than anything, he loved to gamble and win. Not for the money, he just didn't need it — he wanted praise for his cleverness. He was never happier than when standing on a chair at some late-night party, champagne-fuelled idiots all around him, raising their glasses and roaring *'For he's a jolly good fellow'*. It was something he needed to feel good about himself.'

'I get the picture, Mrs Barton. But if there's anything you can remember, however trivial it might seem, we'd like to hear it now.'

'I heard snatches of conversation only. Willett was always his greatest ally — their minds seemed to work the same way. They were like a pair of mischievous crooks who'd get involved in anything shady that would make money if they thought they could pull it off.'

'What sort of things?' The detective was interested now.

'To begin with it was just the usual scams. A good horse fitted with extra-heavy shoes to wear in training to make it look like a plodder in front of the press. Jockeys paid to impede a favourite's progress during a race. Complicated schemes for placing a large bet on a roughie just before the horses jumped out of the gates.'

'Yes, but not all of this is illegal and it's not really — '

'What you're looking for. I know. You need a much bigger reason for someone to murder Miles and bury him in a shallow grave. I'm sorry. I don't have the answer to that. What led you to arrest those two, anyway?'

'Too helpful — wouldn't leave well alone — tempting us to investigate further. Jensen here has a suspicious nature and took an opportunity to look in the boot of Willett's car.'

Andy Jensen cleared his throat, giving his inspector a meaningful look.

'Don't worry, Jensen,' Wintergreen said. 'Can't keep secrets for long in our business — it'll be all over the media in five minutes. Willett didn't clear up too well as there were traces of blood in his car, matching Barton's. After that, we went back to the stables and found more matching traces of blood on the floor in his office. That's where we believe your husband met his death.'

'Oh!' Larissa felt herself going pale.

'Willett and Murphy aren't seasoned

criminals — not when it comes to violence, anyway. They're not used to being in custody and this is a big wake-up call for both of them. When we interviewed them separately, each tried to lay the blame on the other. That's how it goes when people have committed a crime and they're frightened. Willett had the sense to keep quiet and wait for his lawyer but Murphy was anxious to talk and direct suspicion away from himself. He kept insisting he was only a pawn in their game. He said Willett was angry when Barton went off on a trip to China without finalizing their business because it left him short of money. Very short. So he made a point of meeting him at the airport on his return and bringing him back to the stables. The idea was to force Mr Barton to complete a deal on a horse called Maximo's Curse.' He looked at Larissa, raising his eyebrows.

'Yes,' she said. 'I know of Maximo's Curse. Nothing but trouble. A young friend of mine was injured while riding him.'

'Yes.' Wintergreen smiled briefly. 'And that's what started the argument. Barton refused to part with any more money or honour his spoken agreement to pay for the horse. He also let slip that he wanted to get out of horseracing altogether and accused Willett of being unable to move with the

263

times. Then, having roused the man's temper, he made matters worse by laughing at him. In the end, Murphy said, the situation deteriorated so far that they came to blows although he insists that he did his best to separate them and make them stop. During the scuffle, Barton collapsed and fell heavily to the floor. It should have ended there but Willett was too enraged to give up and he fell on Barton, continuing to thump his head on the stone floor. He didn't stop until there was a spreading stain of blood around Barton's shoulders and they knew it had all gone too far. Murphy wanted to call for an ambulance and say it was an accident but Willett wouldn't let him. Eventually, they decided to hide the body, burying it at Barton's deserted property in North Ringwood until they could think of a better way to dispose of it permanently.'

'Miles was murdered then?' Stella said.

'So Murphy says. Had Willett allowed him to call an ambulance, Barton might have been saved and they wouldn't be facing such serious charges now. Instead, they preferred to conceal the body, turning it into a major crime. Murphy was even stupid enough to be wearing a Rolex watch with Barton's initials engraved on the back.'

'I gave him that watch for our first

anniversary,' Larissa said, sighing. 'We were happy then — or so I thought at the time.'

'And there you have it.' Wintergreen looked at her expectantly. 'Unless you have something to add?'

Larissa shook her head slowly. 'Inspector, I've been gone from my husband's home for some time now. I saw him only once after that and it wasn't a happy experience for either of us.'

Concluding that the Arkwrights had nothing to add to what they already knew, the policemen took their leave.

★ ★ ★

Once more the story was the lead item on the early evening television news and the following morning all the newspapers carried it on the front page. Although it wasn't directly connected with horseracing, it was one of the greatest scandals to hit the industry for some time. Willett and Murphy, both with coats over their heads, were shown leaving the court, remanded in custody and without bail, to stand trial in a few months' time. Various reporters speculated on what might happen to Willett's stables and other business operations now. Apart from the few horses he owned himself, the rest had quickly been removed and given to the care of other trainers.

Stella arranged for David to come back to Warrandyte the following day but, expecting him to keep a low profile until things settled down, she neglected to mention this to her daughter. So, when Larissa went out to help tidy up the stables and hose down the horses after their morning exercise, she was surprised to find David already at work as usual, walking Golden Czarina. He gave her a tentative smile.

'Your mother called and said she needed me,' he said simply. 'I hope you don't mind?'

'Well, of course I mind.' Larissa stared at him, blurting the words without thinking. 'I asked her not to do that.'

'Why, Rissa?' he asked softly. 'I thought we had something special between us? What happened to change all that?'

'Do you really have to ask?'

'Look, I do understand how you feel. It's horrible what happened to Miles but it was nothing to do with us and it wasn't our fault. He was on a path to destruction long before we got involved.'

'We're not involved, David.' Sadly, she turned away from him. 'Not any more. Too much has happened.'

David hitched Czarina to a nearby rail and

rushed after her, catching her by the upper arms and forcing her to turn and face him. 'I understand how you feel but we have to get past all that. What was that night we spent in the hills, then? Lust, culminating in a one-night stand? And that other night in the cottage — just casual sex? An itch you needed to scratch?'

She winced at the harshness of his words, hanging her head so that she wouldn't have to meet his piercing gaze. 'Don't tear it all down, David. Just say we were caught up in a romance that shouldn't have happened at all.'

'But you can't have forgotten what you said — that you were happy for maybe the first time in your life. What we had was real and can be so again. It might be convenient for you to step aside from it now but I know how it felt at the time. I was there, remember?'

'Yes, but look at the fall-out now. Your career in tatters and Miles killed. When he was alive and strong, I could think of him as the enemy — the person who hurt me, the person I needed to fight for my rights and my freedom. But then he was dead and, even if I had nothing to do with it, I couldn't help feeling I was partly to blame.'

'What nonsense. You can't possibly blame yourself. Miles was a dinosaur. A controlling, old-fashioned husband who treated you like a possession, just like you said. A greedy man who betrayed you not once but many times throughout the course of your married life. And when he'd taken all that you had to offer, he wanted to bribe you into giving him an easy divorce. What kind of man does that?' He held on to her, forcing her to listen to him. 'But now — now he's dead, you want to turn him into a plaster saint. Well, I'm not going to let you because he's not worth it.'

'David, stop. You have to let me go.' She tried to wriggle free of his grasp.

'No. Not until I can make you see sense.' He kissed her, not fiercely but tenderly and with passion, hoping to revive the spark that had once been between them. Instead she remained limp and passive in his arms. At last he had to release her, standing aside and shaking his head. 'I see. I'm beginning to understand you now. After all, you were married to that man for ten years — it must be hard to set aside a decade of marriage just like that.' He snapped his fingers to illustrate it. 'What a fool I've been. My mother was right. She tried to warn me but I didn't want to hear it.'

He had all of Larissa's attention then. 'Why? What did she say?'

'That when people go through a divorce, they're emotionally unbalanced, not really themselves. They find a new love, very quickly sometimes. Someone to bolster their ego, to make them feel better about what's happening in their lives. But this new happiness is just an idea, an illusion — it isn't real.'

'No, David. It wasn't like that with us. It isn't the same.'

He ignored her, continuing as if she hadn't spoken. 'And later, when the divorce is finalized, that comforting, reliable shoulder isn't needed any more.' He was speaking softly, lost in his own thoughts. 'Finally, the poor fool is cut loose and is supposed to get over it. Pretend it never happened and move on with his life.'

She held up her hands as if to ward off his anger. 'Stop it, David. Stop saying these things. I can't bear it.'

'Well, maybe you'll have to.' He threw up his hands in a gesture of despair. 'Because that's how it seems to me. I love you, Rissa, but I can't do this any more. I've lost too much for you. I have no love, no career and my whole life is a mess. I'll have to go inter-state and find a way to make a new start.'

'No, David, don't do that.' Too late, she realized what she had set in motion and now she didn't know how to stop it. 'We need time, that's all. Time to find a way around this. Please don't leave.'

'Why not? You don't need me. You don't even want me to work here. You've made that abundantly clear. Apologize to your mother and say once again that I'm sorry to leave her short-handed. I'll call her later and explain.' He paused before looking her directly in the eye as he delivered his parting shot. 'Goodbye, Larissa. Maybe one day you'll find what you're looking for but somehow I doubt it. And me? I'll probably miss Czarina more than I'll miss any of you.' Then abruptly he turned away, almost stumbling in his haste to get into his car and put as much distance between them as possible.

At first the engine refused to start, giving Larissa time to catch up with him, banging the palm of her hand on the driver's side window to get his attention. He didn't even turn to look at her. With his jaw set and holding back the storm of emotion that threatened to unman him, he muttered curses under his breath until the engine caught and started as if by the force of his own willpower. As he accelerated away she had to leap aside to avoid a back wheel running over her foot. She watched him drive away, disappearing up the drive in a cloud of blue fumes from the exhaust.

She stared after him, wondering how things

could have gone so wrong and knowing it was all her own fault. So much had happened over the past few days that she needed time to absorb it before she could make sense of her life. Time that David couldn't or wouldn't let her have. She knew that he loved her; hadn't he proved it, time and time again? So why did she have to treat him so badly, forcing him to pick a quarrel over nothing? She didn't need to look far. The spectre of Miles stood between them more solid and threatening in death than he had ever been when he was alive.

Czarina, too, was watching David drive away, puzzled at being deserted in the middle of her walk. Meekly, she allowed Larissa to lead her back to her stall and see to her needs.

Then, as if things couldn't get any worse, just as Larissa was making her way to the house, hoping to gain the sanctuary of her bedroom and give way to the incipient tears that she had been suppressing until now, Morgan arrived, driving up in a small but nifty-looking four-wheel drive. They arrived at the back door simultaneously, giving Larissa no chance to slip inside first and escape. She tried to return Morgan's smile, but it faltered and the woman wasn't fooled.

'Well, don't look so pleased to see me,' she

said, believing herself to be the cause of Larissa's glum expression. 'Your mother did invite me, remember?' She gazed around her, taking a deep breath of fresh, country air. 'What a beautiful place you have here. You might be in the depths of the country, yet it's no more than an hour's drive from the city. So peaceful and near to the river as well.'

'It used to be a well-kept secret before the new freeways.' Larissa trotted out the same old platitudes she gave all new visitors to their home. 'People enjoy the convenience of the new roads but still resent having to pay. D'you want to come in?'

'Thanks. I thought you'd never ask.'

Still as abrasive as ever, Larissa thought.

'Mom?' she called, as she led the way to the kitchen. 'We have a guest.' She swallowed the sudden lump in her throat. 'No need to set another place for lunch. David's not staying — he's gone.'

'Where to now?' Her mother greeted this news with a less than happy expression. 'I saw him taking off up the drive as if the devil were at his heels.' She embraced Morgan, appearing genuinely pleased to see her. 'Hello Morgan. Welcome to our mess!' Without embarrassment, she pushed aside their breakfast dishes still on the table and in need of washing up. It was her habit to clear away everything after lunch.

'No. To me this is homey.' The American smiled. 'My father used to say an untidy house meant busy people, working on something more productive than housework.'

'And he was right. But it's kind of you to say so.' Stella seemed unusually pleased with her visitor. She even opened a tin of smoked oysters to go with their toasted sandwiches. Over lunch, Stella and Morgan did most of the talking, airing their theories on Willett and his foreman and speculating upon the outcome of their trial.

Larissa scarcely listened, picking at her sandwich with little enthusiasm for food. She was going over and over those last words with David, hoping that when he calmed down he would give her at least one more chance to put things right. Only now did she realize how selfish she had been, thinking only of herself, her own hurt. She had overestimated his capacity for forgiveness and injured his pride as well. Surely, he couldn't believe she had used him just as a prop to get through her divorce?

After serving them coffee Stella mumbled an excuse about seeing to the horses, leaving Morgan and her daughter alone to talk. The two women sat for a moment, sipping their coffee and regarding each other in awkward silence. Without Stella to keep the ball of conversation rolling, there seemed to be nothing to say. Morgan spoke at last, subjecting her brother's young widow to a piercing gaze.

'You need to snap out of it, Larissa,' she said. 'You're going to make yourself ill if you go on brooding like this.'

'Why should you care how I feel?' Larissa was in no mood to be lectured, scowling at her coffee, stirring it sulkily. 'What's it to you?'

'You must stop feeling guilty over what happened to Miles. He brought about his own destruction. It wasn't your fault.'

She was echoing David's words but Larissa refused to meet her gaze, unwilling to discuss these raw feelings with Miles's sister, a woman she disliked. 'I know that,' she muttered.

'That's what you say but you don't really believe it. Miles's influence can be insidious, even in death. He was my twin, remember and I knew him better than anyone. Selfish to the core, he was, just like me. And don't think it costs me nothing to say so.'

Against her will, Larissa found herself smiling, encouraging Morgan to go on.

'Look at it another way. What if you were the one who was dead and Miles was alive?

How much time d'you think he'd spend grieving for you?' Morgan waited for an answer although none came. 'He'd scarcely disrupt his schedule to go to your funeral.'

When Larissa spoke it was barely a whisper. 'Even if that were true, I can't help it. I can't help how I feel.'

'Yes, you can. If you won't see sense I'll have to make you. Before you lose that fine young man who's breaking his heart over you.'

'David?' Morgan had her attention then. 'What can you possibly know about him?'

'Only what your mother told me over the phone. She's been watching you disappear into this downward spiral, wondering how to stop it before it turns into full blown depression. Luckily, I'm here to help.'

'You can't help me. Nobody can.'

'My, but you're a hard nut to crack.' Morgan sighed. 'Larissa, look at yourself. A lovely young woman with most of your life still in front of you. Miles stole ten years from you, yes, but there's plenty of prime time left. So, tell me what you want out of life? If you don't think about it soon and make plans, you'll end up with nothing.'

'I don't know what you mean.'

'Clearly not. Right now, if you could have anything in the world that you wanted, anything at all regardless of money or effort, what would it be? What would satisfy you and please you the most?'

'I've never thought about it.' Larissa shrugged, unsure where this line of questioning was leading. 'While I was with Miles I had all the material things and wanted for nothing. I was happy enough while I was acquiring them, but they brought me no lasting pleasure.'

'Of course not.' Morgan made a dismissive gesture. 'That's not what I meant. Larissa, what are you going to achieve in life? Look at your mother — she's a successful racehorse trainer. Even your younger sister knows what she wants from college. Some people aspire to be very good actors or else succeed in a sport.'

'I was good at tennis once. But I'm not really a sports person. I don't have that kind of dedication.'

'Fine,' Morgan said with exaggerated patience. 'I'm not saying you should do any of those things. They're just examples to stimulate some ideas. Now, I want you to think about this carefully. If money were no object, what would you like to do with your life? What is most dear to your heart?'

'Oh, that's easy.' Larissa began to look animated for the first time. 'I'd breed horses, of course. It's what I've always wanted to do.

But Miles wouldn't take me seriously — he wouldn't believe I could do it. So I never had the opportunity.'

'Finally!' Morgan punched the air. 'An answer at long last. And do you know enough about breeding horses to get yourself started, or would you need to go somewhere to learn?'

'I was only a kid but I learned quite a lot from my father. He used to say the best horse wasn't always the obvious one, the expensive one that cost all the money. There were other things to look for, as well. Once, in my school holidays, I went with him to New Zealand to their sales. I had a great time. It was the best holiday we ever spent together as he was relaxed for once, even letting me choose a horse for him on my own. Mostly, he was a strict disciplinarian, not a comfortable parent at all, but there was nothing he didn't know about thoroughbreds and I think he enjoyed teaching me.'

'Go on then. Tell me how you'd go about it?'

'For a start, I'd buy good horses from all over the world and bring them back here to Australia. There's plenty of room to build another stable block here — another house even — without interfering with Mom's own schedules.'

'That's great. It's good to know you have a plan.'

'Oh, it isn't a plan.' Larissa shrugged. 'More like a pipe dream.'

'No, it's possible, Larissa. It could be real,' Morgan, reached for her shoulder bag. 'Before coming to visit you here, I saw Peter Mayhall. He's been holding something that belongs to you and wasn't quite sure what to do with it. I said I'd deliver it to you in person.' She took a small, soft leather pouch from her bag and placed it on the table between them.

Looking at it, Larissa shivered, thinking she had seen that little pouch before. Cautiously, she opened it, allowing the pink diamond bracelet to fall out into her hand. Quickly, she thrust it back inside as if the diamonds were burning her.

'No. I don't want them.' Her throat felt so dry she could scarcely speak. 'I didn't want them when Miles tried to give them to me and I don't want them now. They're part of his estate so they must belong to you.'

'No. Miles left very clear instructions in writing. Peter Mayhall is quite insistent that they're meant for you. Only you.'

'I shouldn't take them.' Larissa tossed the pouch from one hand to the other as if she was trying not to let them rest in her hands for too long. 'I'm sure they'd bring me no luck. It would be like sipping from the poisoned chalice.'

Morgan laughed. 'What an imagination you have. The one good thing that Miles ever did for the women he left was to provide them with a small portion of his wealth — something that he'd never miss. He didn't have much of a conscience but he tried to give them the means to move on without him.'

Larissa thought for a moment. 'And I'm his third wife. Two other women must have been given pink diamonds before.'

'Did it never occur to you to find out what they did with them?'

Larissa shook her head. 'It was no business of mine. They were gone from his life and I never knew them.'

'Well, you're a lot less inquisitive than I am. Janis, his first wife, wasn't all that imaginative. She sold her diamonds and used the money to dress herself well and go on long-distance cruises until she landed herself another rich husband. Still married today. Very happily, I believe.'

'And the second?' Now her curiosity had been aroused, Larissa wanted to hear more.

'She started a hairdressing and beauty salon in a department store. Now she has salons in every capital city and she's a wealthy woman in her own right. In your case, if you follow through with the horses, I'd say you have the potential to do better than either of them.'

13

David burst into his mother's home like a whirlwind. Patsy was washing up after lunch and Johnnie was in the adjoining family room watching an American soap opera. He'd become strangely addicted to these during his convalescence. Scarcely troubling to greet them, David ran to his bedroom, grabbed the big canvas holdall from under his bed and started hurling clothes randomly inside it. Arms folded, his mother leaned in the doorway, watching him.

'Where on earth are you going now?' she asked. 'And don't throw all your clothes in, higgledy-piggledy like that. I spent some time ironing those T-shirts.'

'They're just T-shirts, Mum. It doesn't matter whether they're ironed or not.'

'I'll remember that next time,' Patsy said with a sniff.

'And I'll need the cards for my savings accounts, Mum. I know I asked you to put them away for safe keeping but — '

'And that's where they're staying. In safe keeping. I won't have you dashing all over the place wasting your savings just because you've fallen out with that woman. She was using you up, just as I said. Good job you woke up before it was too late.'

David closed his eyes, trying to hold his temper in check. 'Do stop rattling, Mum. I can't think straight.'

'You haven't been thinking straight for some time. Letting that woman pull you around by the nose.'

'Mum, just stop it. And stop calling Larissa *that woman*.' David was losing it and his voice rose. 'And give me my cards right now or I'll ransack your room till I find them.'

'All right. All right. You don't have to snap my head off.' Patsy took a step backwards, shocked, and realizing too late that she might have deserved it. She expected fire and temper from Johnnie but it was rare for her gentle, elder son to raise his voice to her.

'And give me my passport as well because you never know — '

'Your passport?' Patsy was stunned now, scarcely able to speak above a whisper. 'What can you possibly want with that?'

'I'll take it with me — just in case. Good job I had it renewed when I was thinking of going to England to ride last year.'

'You're not going there now, Son?'

'I dunno, Mum. I have to keep all my options open. If I can't find a stable and

282

someone willing to give me some rides inter-state, I'll have to try my luck overseas. Maybe I'll go to Hong Kong or Macao. They pay good money there and I'll make enough to send something home to help you and John.'

'The money isn't important, David, but — '

'Yeah? That's what everyone says until they have empty pockets.'

'Our pockets aren't empty now. Thanks to you, our Johnnie has his insurance. I'm sure I'm speaking for both of us when I say I'd much rather you stayed here in Melbourne with us.'

'Mum, I can't. The racing world is too small. Everywhere I went, I might bump into Rissa. I really do need to make a clean break.'

'I can't believe how that woman got under your skin. The trouble she's caused.'

'Mum!' He raised a hand as if to push away the flow of her words.

'This isn't like you. You used to be such a happy, carefree lad who went out with lots of girls. It's as if that — as if she's bewitched you.'

'Take a good look at me, Mum. I'm twenty-five years old, not a lad any more. I had to fall in love properly some time.'

'I know. But why did it have to be her?' Patsy shook her head, knowing they would never see eye to eye on this subject.

'Look. Finish packing for me, will you. You'll make a much better job of it than I will. And I'm sorry I snapped, but please find my passport and cards.'

'Flattery will get you everywhere.' Patsy offered her cheek for the kiss of peace.

'And while you do that, I'll bring in some Thai take-away for a little celebratory dinner before I go.'

'It won't feel like a celebration. You're leaving and I don't know when we're going to see you again.'

'Call it a wake, then, if you must. But I'm setting off right after dinner tonight before . . . ' He hesitated, having been about to say *before Larissa comes looking for me*. Instead he said: 'before I change my mind.'

* * *

The spicy Thai food didn't bring the atmosphere of lighthearted celebration that he'd hoped for. Johnnie was the only one who ate his meal with any real gusto. Too emotional to enjoy any food, Patsy prodded it around her plate while David ate just to feed himself and without any relish.

Dreading his mother's scarcely withheld tears, he didn't prolong the moment of parting. Having decided to leave the truck at

284

home in the garage, he was taking the train into town and then an airport bus or a taxi to the airport. Unsure where his quest for employment might take him, he didn't want to dispose of the vehicle and lose money if he needed to go overseas.

Arriving at the airport shortly before the last domestic flights were due to leave, he went up to the Qantas desk and asked if there were any vacancies left on the last flight to Sydney. The blonde, middle-aged clerk, weary at the end of a long shift, looked down her nose at his untidy clothes and lack of substantial luggage.

'You didn't book?' she asked, consulting her list.

David shrugged.

'No-o,' she drawled after scanning several lists. 'Can't give you anything till early tomorrow morning. You could stay at the airport hotel — they have vacancies there.'

'Thanks, but I want to leave town tonight. What about Brisbane, then? Or Adelaide? Any seats available there?'

She gave him a suspicious glance before returning to her computer screen, absent-mindedly tapping a few keys. He wondered how she could type at all with those long, false nails. 'You don't care where you go, then?'

'Not really. Long as I can get out of Melbourne tonight.'

'Excuse me for just a moment,' she said, leaving her desk and ignoring the groans of the queue of people lining up behind David, hoping to be checked in. 'Wait here. I won't be long.'

Everyone watched, scowling, as she caught up with two security guards, pointing back to her desk while engaging them in earnest conversation. The two men returned with her and took up positions on either side of David.

'If you'd be good enough to step away from the counter, for a moment, sir,' one of them said. 'And quietly, please. We don't want to make a fuss now, do we?'

David stared at them in astonishment. 'Why? What's this about? Search me and look in my bag, if you must. I'm not carrying any dangerous weapons or drugs.'

'That's as may be. But you want to leave town in a hurry and don't seem to mind where you go. How do we know you're not on the run, having committed some crime?'

'You don't. Except if I were a criminal, I might use a little more guile?'

'That isn't for us to say, sir. But we'll need to detain you until we have you checked out by the police.'

'The police? Oh for God's sake. Now it's a

crime to want to go inter-state!'

It must have been a busy night for the police because it took them some time to arrive and establish that David was no sort of criminal or wanted for any offence. By then, all the flights within Australia had left and he didn't have the heart to try his luck with the internationals, who would be equally, if not more suspicious of his motives.

Swearing quietly under his breath, he picked up his bag and marched out of the terminal, preparing to take the clerk's first suggestion of booking into the airport hotel. When a tall, mannish-looking woman of middle years moved into his space, accosting him outside the door, he sighed and closed his eyes, thinking: *What now?*

'David Riordan! By all that's wonderful. You're still here.'

'So I am,' he snapped back, in no mood to be gracious. 'What's it to you?' The woman did seem vaguely familiar although he couldn't place her right away.

'Touchy, aren't we? That's not nice when I've come all this way to do you a favour.'

'Why should you do me a favour? Look, lady, I've just had the worst day of my life and you're not making it any better. You might think you know me but you don't. I need you to let me pass and get out of here.'

'And so you shall. I'm about to play fairy godmother here. Just be grateful I caught you before you left.'

David gave her a sideways glance as if he thought she might be insane.

'No, not mad. Just quirky,' she said, and smiled, holding out her hand to introduce herself. 'Morgan Barton. Come on, let's get you out of here.'

'I'm not going anywhere with you. I don't even know you.'

'Yes, you do. I've just introduced myself. Morgan — Miles Barton's twin sister. Here at your service — and Larissa's, of course.'

'So Larissa sent you, did she? Well, you can tell her from me — we have no more to say to each other.'

'That's as may be.' She gave a quick glance around. 'Look. I need to leave before someone gives me a ticket.' Morgan indicated the small car she had parked illegally outside Departures. 'I'm not supposed to be here.'

'Feel free to leave any time,' he said with a shrug. 'I won't stop you.'

'Wretched man,' she muttered to herself. 'Can't think what Larissa sees in you. Thin as a rail and a face like a claw hammer with that pointed chin. I suppose she fell for those big, brown, puppy-dog eyes.' Before he realized what she would do, she grabbed his bag and threw it into the back seat of her car, giving him no option but to follow.

'Are you always this rude?' In spite of himself, he was beginning to be entertained by her.

'Probably.' She grinned back at him. 'As well as being intolerant, I call a spade a spade. I'm too old to bother with any pretence.' She almost pushed him into the front passenger seat before getting into the car herself and driving off at speed. She had spotted an official with a notepad, headed their way.

'Where are you taking me?' he asked, realizing he had just been abducted by Miles Barton's crazy sister. 'I don't want to go home.'

'Fine.' Morgan drove at speed, changing lanes often and weaving in and out of the traffic when they reached the motorway, making him nervous. 'Relax. I'm a very good driver.' She grinned, sensing his apprehension.

'And I'm not going back to Warrandyte, either.'

'I know. You and the lovely Rissa had words.'

'What happened between Larissa and me is our business — not yours.'

'Now, David, how can I play fairy godmother if you won't confide in me?'

'I never asked you to interfere.' He scowled at her. 'I'll bet Larissa didn't either.'

'Oh, but interfering is what I do best.' Morgan patted his knee, irritating him further. 'How about neutral ground, then? My hotel? I have a suite with two separate bedrooms so you won't have to sleep with me.'

David stared at her, appalled. 'I have no intention of sleeping with — !'

'Good,' Morgan said. 'I'm glad that's settled. Because you're not really my type.'

David resisted the urge to laugh.

As he followed Morgan into her hotel at the prestigious end of town, he realized he was entering a world of luxury of which he had little previous experience. And, although it was late — well after midnight — the lower floors were a hive of activity still. Without speaking to anyone, Morgan marched across the foyer as if she owned the place, heading for the bank of lifts. The doors of one opened as soon as they stood in front of it. As it carried them swiftly upwards, David was reminded of his dishevelled appearance by the sight of his reflection in the surrounding mirrors, and he felt embarrassed to be carrying the battered canvas bag he took to the track and which had seen better days.

He had come straight from the stables and,

although he had taken a moment to put on a clean shirt and jacket before leaving home, he was still wearing the same pair of jeans and dirty riding boots. He could only hope he wasn't leaving a trail of dried mud behind him. But the lift doors opened at last, expelling them into a thickly carpeted corridor with subdued reproduction art deco lighting along the walls. David looked all around, whistling appreciatively.

'You can thank Peter Mayhall for this — Miles's lawyer.' Once again Morgan seemed able to read his thoughts. 'I'm not used to this kind of pampering either. I live in a one room studio in LA.' She paused as they reached the door of her suite. 'Have you eaten? It's late but I can persuade them to send up a plate of sandwiches if you haven't.'

'No, I'll be fine,' David said. 'Just point me in the direction of a shower and bed and I'll be out like a light. People who look after horses aren't really used to late nights.'

'I'm so sorry, David.' Morgan was smiling and didn't look in the least bit sorrowful, he thought. 'But I have another surprise before I can let you do that. I did say I was going to play fairy godmother tonight.' She flung open the door to the suite, practically shoving him inside.

Almost before he saw her he sensed she

was there. Larissa was seated on a couch in front of a flat screen TV. She sprang to her feet as soon as they came in and switched it off, seeming just as tense and uncomfortable with the situation as he was. Her jeans and sweatshirt were crumpled, her hair tangled and on end as if she'd been scrubbing her hands through it in frustration for most of the night. If she had been wearing any make-up it had worn off.

'Don't blame me for this, David,' she said. 'Morgan hijacked me. Said she had something she wanted to discuss away from Sally and Mom. I thought we'd go to a café but she brought me up here instead. Then she took off without explanation, saying she wouldn't be long. That was over two hours ago. I haven't even had dinner yet.'

'You were comfortable enough, weren't you?' Morgan waved away the criticism. 'I told you to get room service to send up some food. As you see, I have your defecting boyfriend here, safe and sound. I hope it will be worth the wait.'

'And I hope you don't think this was my idea,' David said. 'I expected to be on my way to Sydney or Hong Kong by now. Instead, thanks to our *fairy godmother* . . . ' he gave Morgan a murderous leer, 'I find myself also hijacked and brought up here.'

'Well.' Morgan smiled brightly. 'I'll leave you two to iron out your differences while I see if I can find congenial company in the lounge room downstairs. Help yourselves to the mini-bar — I won't mind.'

'No! Don't you dare leave me again,' Larissa spoke through clenched teeth. 'You've wasted your time, Morgan, bringing me here under false pretences. I want to go home — now!'

But Morgan ignored her and with a twiddle of her fingers in farewell, she left them alone.

'Can you believe it.' Exasperated, Larissa flung herself down on the couch while David seemed more amused than annoyed that they had been thrust into each other's company yet again.

'It isn't funny, David. She's an interfering old bag.'

'I know,' he said, unable to stop himself laughing. 'Isn't she priceless?' He turned on the television again, pretending to scan the channels. 'I know you don't want to talk so we might as well entertain ourselves until she comes back. Oh look, there's a horror movie — that might be fun. Or do you prefer reality? A bit of *Dancing With the Stars?*'

'No. I'd have gone home already but I don't have enough for a cab. They won't take anyone at night without payment up front.'

'Oh, I know,' he said without offering to give her the fare.

'I'm not staying here with you.'

'Fine. You can always go downstairs and find Morgan. Bully her into taking you home.' David smiled.

It seemed to Larissa that he was being deliberately unhelpful. 'You are as exasperating as she is. Are you sure you didn't plan this whole thing together?'

He looked at her directly then, giving her the impression that he didn't like what he saw.

'To be honest, Rissa, after the way we parted this morning, you're the last person I wanted to see tonight.'

'Oh.' She sat down heavily, the wind taken out of her sails.

'Oh, indeed.' He crossed the room to sit in another armchair, as far away from her as he could. There was silence as they both sat, lost in their thoughts, reliving the events of the day.

'It didn't happen the way you said.' She was speaking so softly that he had trouble hearing her. 'Not at all.'

'What didn't?' Battered and exhausted by the day's events, he found it painful to sit here with Larissa, forced to be in the same room, yet emotionally miles apart. He needed a hot shower followed by a long sleep in a comfortable bed. Only then would he feel able to deal with the situation rationally.

'Your mother has always thought the worst of me and there's nothing I can do about that.' She too sounded worn out and defeated. 'But I never used you as a prop to get through my divorce. And I've thought and thought about it and I still don't know what went so wrong and why you're so angry with me now.'

'And I wonder if we ever understood one another at all? I thought we were in this together, ready to stand up to Miles and whatever he threw at us. Then, when he died, everything changed and you turned on me, shutting me out. It seemed as if you were behind reinforced glass and I couldn't make you hear me, no matter how hard I tried.'

'But you left me to face all that misery on my own.'

'You weren't alone. You had Stella there to support you. She's a strong one, your mother.'

'And you came back to us only because you needed the work.'

'Is that what you think?' He shrugged. 'Whatever I do I can't win, can I?'

'I don't know, David.' Although her voice had softened, she couldn't look at him but sat staring at her hands, unable to meet his piercing gaze. 'I'm just so confused, so tired of thinking about it all.'

He crossed the room, coming to sit beside her. 'For a start, you have to stop feeling guilty about Miles. He was a spoilt, rich idiot who made a mess of his life. A lot of them do.'

'He left me some money, you know.'

'And that changed the way you felt about him? I thought you said he left everything to Morgan?'

'All except this.' She found her handbag and pulled out a little suede pouch. Inside was a bracelet of brilliant pink stones that sparkled in the lamplight as she dangled it from one finger.

'That's a pretty thing,' he said. 'Why don't you wear it?'

'I can't possibly. Those are pink diamonds — worth a small fortune.'

He peered at them more closely. 'Really? They don't look all that — '

'Oh, that's what I said at first. But, trust me. When I sell them, I'll have enough money to build a new set of stables at Warrandyte, apart from my mother's. There are several paddocks that we're not using right now.' As she thought about these ambitions, her enthusiasm rose and the feelings of animosity she had harboured towards him started to melt away. 'And when it's all ready, I'll go to New Zealand and buy a few mares to start off my breeding programme.'

'But that's a great idea.' Although nothing had yet been resolved, David found himself caught up in her enthusiasm. 'I have friends there — some people who breed horses near Wanganui and I'm sure they'd be delighted to share their knowledge and give you some tips.'

'Good. After that, I'll go to England — to Berkshire. My father was always talking about the thoroughbreds he saw there.'

'Oh yes. And I know what to look for — I could go with you, too.' Carried away with the possibility of realizing a dream, the words were out before it dawned on him what he was saying, and he pulled himself up. 'But wait a minute. That won't be possible, will it? I can't be part of such an unequal partnership. I have no money to invest in your venture and I'd only be holding you back. I'm sorry, Rissa. It's no good talking about all this because it's not going anywhere. And now I really do have to go.'

He took a deep breath and, as if he couldn't stand to be in the same room with her any more, stood up and collected his shabby bag from where he'd dropped it beside the door. He couldn't look at that face any more, bright with anticipation of what she hoped to achieve and the wonderful future that might now be within her grasp.

He halted for a moment at the door, trying to think of something to say. ''Bye, Rissa. I wish you well — please believe that. And I'm sure that whatever you do, you'll be a success.'

She ran to the door and stood in front of it, refusing to let him pass.

'You can't leave me now, I won't let you.' She was almost breathless, wondering what she would do if he left her. He could go anywhere in the world and she wouldn't know where to find him. 'David, you can't do this to me,' she said. 'Not now. Raising my hopes by offering your help and taking it back moments later. It's cruel.'

'We have to be realistic. It isn't to be. I can't attach myself to your good fortune like a hired hand. We've been down that path already. It didn't work out.'

'But we can make it work — I know we can. I'll need help. But my mother's time is committed and stretched to the limits already. I can't take on something of this magnitude on my own.'

'You won't be alone for long,' he murmured. Beyond weary now, he decided to

take a taxi home and make proper arrangements to leave when he'd had a good night's
sleep in his own bed. He looked into her face
for the last time; the face he had once hoped
to spend the rest of his life with and saw that
she too was so choked with emotion she
could think of nothing to say. Wordlessly,
she stood aside to let him pass and he left,
closing the door very quietly behind him.

Larissa sat down, waiting for the tears to
come but they didn't. When Morgan returned
five minutes later, she was sitting on the couch,
looking stunned and staring at the blank television screen.

'I saw David leave and he didn't look
happy,' Morgan said. 'It didn't work out,
then?'

Slowly, Larissa shook her head.

14

'You're back!' Patsy was at the front door almost as soon as she heard David's key in the lock. 'I knew you'd think better of it.'

'Don't get your hopes up, Mum.' He slumped in the doorway. 'I was just too late to get on a plane tonight.'

'So where have you been until this hour? You look exhausted. Johnnie went to bed hours ago and I've been watching the tennis on television. Very good match it was, too.'

'Mum, I'm completely bushed. Let's talk in the morning.'

'But what have you . . . ?'

'In the morning, Mum — please.'

'Let me make up your bed for you, then. I stripped it and put the sheets in the washing machine right after you left.'

'Leave it, Mum. I'm tired enough to sleep in a blanket on the floor.'

'You'll do no such thing.' She pushed him in front of her into the small lounge. David had the feeling that people had been pushing and pulling him to go everywhere all night. 'And you can drink that cup of tea while I do it.' She pointed to a full cup sitting on the coffee table. 'I've only just made it.'

Of course, when she came back just ten minutes later, the cup of tea was untouched and David fast asleep on the couch. Patsy clicked her tongue, knowing it would be useless to try and wake him now. Instead she pulled off his boots, covered him with a warm blanket, switched off the television and went to bed.

In the morning, she didn't raise any issues with him until Johnnie had been sent off in a taxi to spend the morning in hydrotherapy at the hospital. With his thoughts centred on his own activities, he seemed neither surprised nor concerned that his brother was home again.

Patsy said nothing to David until she had made a fresh pot of coffee and taken it into the lounge, where he was lying exactly where she had left him the night before.

'So what happened?' she asked, sitting down beside him. 'Why didn't that harpy bring you back home?'

'What harpy?' He squinted at her. 'Surely, you can't mean Larissa?'

'Madame Barton, of course. Came burning over here in that hire car of hers, looking for you and giving me no peace till I said where you'd gone. I'm telling you, that poor little car will be no use to anyone by the time she gives it back.'

'Mum, please. It doesn't matter about the car.'

'She told me your leaving was a mistake and I had to agree with her. So she went after you, saying you were unlikely to catch a flight at that time of night. Obviously, you missed her. She would have brought you home and you wouldn't have had to take a cab.'

'Mum, stop it. I can't get a word in edgeways.' Leaving out most of the details, he gave his mother a shortened version of all that had taken place that night, including meeting up with Larissa in Morgan's suite. How it had so nearly been all right until he realized that if they were to join forces in buying and breeding horses, the partnership could never be equal. Not unless he had some money of his own to put into her ambitious scheme.

'And there you have it.' He let out a long sigh. 'So near and yet so far.'

'Ah, well. Maybe it's for the best.'

'Trust you to say that.' He pulled the blanket around him again and turned his back on her, expecting her to leave and let him try to get back to sleep. 'You never really liked her, did you, Mum? Married before and older than me, if only by a couple of years. Which did you think was the greater sin?'

Instead of responding to the taunt, Patsy

just sat there, silent and lost in thought. This surprised him. Usually, when challenged, she opened her mouth and let all her thoughts tumble out, tactful or not.

'David,' she said at last, after clearing her throat. 'There's something I have to tell you. Maybe I was wrong not to say something before, but you know how I feel about money. I was scared it might change things between us. We've always got on so well, fighting hardships together — I liked to think of us as we three against the rest of the world.'

'There's nothing noble about fighting hardship, Mum. Most of the time it's just bloody miserable,' he said, growing impatient with her simplistic viewpoint. 'Come on then, tell me. What is this great secret of yours?'

'I'm not sure I should say anything, even now. But the fact is that you do have money, David. And so does Johnnie. Money that's been held in trust in savings accounts for some time.'

He stared at her for a moment, unable to take it in. 'We have money? But where does it come from?'

Patsy twisted her hands in her lap, looking uncomfortable. 'From your father, of course. He died some time ago when you were still a minor or the solicitor would have contacted you directly.'

'So it's true, then. Our father really is dead?'

'Yes, but as we hadn't heard from him for such a long time, I saw no point in causing an upset by mentioning it.'

'Only you could think like that, Mum. It wouldn't have upset Johnnie; he scarcely remembers him. So how did he die?'

For a moment Patsy seemed unwilling to say, then it came out in a rush. 'Fool that he was, he went camping beside a crocodile-infested river. Some other people saw the croc take him but it all happened so quickly there was nothing they could do. Nothing was left but the remains of his camp. His body was never found.'

Before he could stop himself, David laughed. 'I'm sorry, Mum. But that's the story I made up to tell people when I was a kid.'

'I know. That's why I didn't want to say. You might think you'd wished it on him somehow.'

'I don't feel anything, Mum. I was upset when he left us but I can't even remember what he looked like now. Photographs are so frozen — they don't tell you anything.' David thought for a moment. 'But how did he come to have money? If he was homeless and destitute, as you say, camping out by a river — '

'No, you don't understand. That was a

leisure pursuit — entertainment. Mostly, he lived in some posh hotel — never bothered to cater for himself. And that's all I knew until this solicitor from Darwin contacted me to say he had left a substantial sum of money for you two boys. Of course, your father didn't leave me anything. Our parting was too bitter for that.'

'Mum, just tell me. Where did his money come from? Horses?'

'Good heavens, no. Your father was hopeless at the punt. In his latter years he discovered a new obsession — precious stones. He went searching for them in all those god-forsaken hot places in the interior, frying his brains if he had any left. The solicitor said that he travelled all over from Anakie in Central Queensland to Lightning Ridge. When he did strike it lucky with opals, he sold out to one of the big companies. Didn't want to be real miner or a jeweller himself. That's so like your father. He always preferred the thrill of the chase.'

'Mum, whoa! Let's back up a minute here. So how much money are we talking about? Twenty or thirty grand? What?'

Once again Patsy looked uncomfortable, refusing to meet his gaze as if she was unwilling to say.

'I'm not entirely sure. But with interest,

you and John should have roughly two hundred thousand dollars, give or take a bit.'

'Half of two hundred thousand dollars?' David clasped his hands to his head, staring at her in astonishment. 'You don't say.'

'Not half.' Patsy cleared her throat. 'Two hundred thousand each. And with interest, now it's probably quite a lot more.'

'But Mum, that's a life-altering sum of money! Why on earth didn't you tell us before?'

'And have you running off all over the world with it? Squandering it until it was all gone?'

'I'm well over age, Mum. I should have been told.'

'Well, I'm telling you now, aren't I?' Patsy glared at him.

'And what about John? That sort of money would buy him the best of care. He could have — '

'Nothing wrong with the care that he's having now. You'll see. He'll be back to his old self before too long.'

David said nothing more. Much as he loved his mother, he knew that she could be a stubborn and difficult woman. Having old-fashioned ideas that money corrupted, she could easily have kept the matter of their inheritance a secret until she died. But this legacy from his father changed everything. He could join Larissa as an equal partner — provided she would still have him — and hold his head high. He couldn't wait to see her.

★ ★ ★

When he drove up to the Arkwright property at Warrandyte, having valet-cleaned the truck, polishing the purple duco paintwork until it looked new, it was Stella who came out of the house to meet him, arms folded and ready to head him off before he reached the front door. Unsmiling and dressed for the stables, she looked both businesslike and implacable.

'So,' she said, tilting her chin at him and fixing him with a stern look. 'If you think you can come and go as you please here, you're mistaken. Not after leaving me in the lurch and breaking my poor daughter's heart.'

He gave her a sheepish smile. 'I'm sorry, Stella. I know I should have said I was leaving. Things got a bit out of hand.'

'Things got more than a bit out of hand from the moment you came here.' Stella's voice rose, along with her temper. 'So you can turn around, start up that purple monster of yours and get the hell out of here.'

'Not until I've seen Larissa. I have

something important to tell her — some really good news. If, after hearing it, she still wants me to go, then I will.'

'No. You've done enough damage already. She's been through too much. Pilloried by the press, Miles dying in that terrible way and finally, after everything, rejected by you.'

'But I haven't rejected her. I never meant — '

'People who do harm never do. Anyway, you can't see her now. She's sedated and sleeping.'

'Then I'll stay here and wait until she wakes up.' David also folded his arms and leaned back against his car.

Before Stella could renew her arguments, Sally came running out of the house towards him, hurling herself into his arms and planting a smacking kiss on his cheek.

'David Riordan! And about time, too. Come on in. Larissa's been sleeping for twelve hours straight. She'll have to wake up soon.'

Stella gave an exasperated snort, sounding just like one of her horses, while David grinned at her cheerfully over Sally's head.

'I'd love to, Sally. Thanks,' he said.

'She isn't herself,' Stella called after him. 'And if you upset her again, you'll answer to me.'

David resisted the urge to give a mocking

impression of terror before following Sally into the house.

★ ★ ★

But Larissa didn't appear for some time, making him wonder whether she intended to see him at all. If Stella returned first, she would certainly throw him out. He sat in the kitchen with Sally for the best part of an hour, listening with only half an ear to her chatter concerning her latest boyfriends, the music she had on her iPod and the results she was hoping for from her recent exams.

Refusing to join them, Stella had gone to the stables, not just to stay out of David's way but to keep an eye on the new girl she had just employed. From Ireland originally and bearing the name of Brigid, after the martyred saint, the girl seemed almost too good to be true. Stella was determined to find out if there was any way she could fault her.

At last Larissa appeared, looking pale and ethereal, wearing a silk kimono that was almost as pale as her skin. Her eyes were made up to conceal the dark circles beneath them and she had used rouge on her cheekbones to give herself colour; instead it only accentuated her pallor. Such sleep as she had received from the pills appeared to have done her no good at all.

'David,' she said without preamble. 'I don't know why you're here but, whatever it is, I'm not interested. I can't live on this emotional see-saw any more. I need some peace and quiet.'

'I can't go before you hear what I have to say.' He glanced at Sally. 'Thanks for everything, Sal, and I love you but I need to speak to your sister alone.'

For once Sally left without argument, but not before she'd given him a lingering kiss on the cheek and a meaningful glance at her sister, who sat down at the table looking listless, waiting for him to speak. He tried to smile but it wavered when he saw she wasn't about to give him any help.

'Can I have a shot of that whiskey your mother keeps by for emergencies?'

Larissa shrugged, pointing to the cupboard and glasses, indicating that he should serve himself. 'If you think it'll help.'

He went to the cupboard and found a bottle of the good Irish whiskey he loved and which he had given to Stella some time ago. He found two tumblers and some ice and then sloshed a good measure into both of them.

'You know I don't like to drink spirits . . . ' Larissa began.

'Bad luck. Today you do.'

She took a small sip and pulled a face, making David smile. 'It'll take a long time to make an alcoholic out of you,' he said.

'Get on with it, then. You didn't come here to talk about whiskey.'

'No. I came to discuss that partnership we were talking about the other day.'

'Oh that?' She was determined not to let him off the hook. 'As I remember it, you walked out, saying it wasn't going to work.'

'And that's what I thought. But I know it'll work now because I can match your investment.'

She stared at him for a long moment, looking stricken, all her defences and barriers suddenly swept aside. 'Oh David, no! Even if it means we can be real partners, I can't let you go into debt. It wouldn't be right.'

'In debt?' He almost laughed at the suggestion. 'How can I possibly get into debt? Who in their right mind would lend money to a horseman who can't find work? Not even Stella wants to employ me now. No. My mother just did the right thing and told me the truth. I've inherited a substantial sum of money from my father. Johnnie is getting the same. It seems our dad was a successful prospector and fossicker — '

'And he found gold? They do say there's as much and more than there was in the last century if people would only roll up their sleeves, pick up a metal detector and look.'

'No. He made his money from sapphires and also black opal. Apparently, he went all over the place in Queensland and New South Wales. Went a bit crazy in the end. His solicitor told Mum he was quite obsessed.'

'But why on earth didn't she tell you before? Instead of letting you — '

'She has some strange ideas sometimes. Thinks it's character-building for people to struggle and suffer hardship.'

'Inverted snobbery.'

'Is that what they call it? I thought it was something peculiar to my mother.'

'Our mothers. Wonderful, aren't they? Between the pair of them they've nearly managed to wreck things between us.'

'But not quite.' Suddenly, he felt shy with her and held out his hand to shake on the deal, scarcely daring to hope for anything more. 'You'll accept my offer, Larissa? We can be business partners after all?'

She took his hand and pulled it around her, moving into his space and winding her arms about his neck.

'Oh David,' she whispered. 'I've been such a fool, wasting all this time. If you'll have me, I'd like us to be partners in every sense of the word.'

He kissed her then. It was a long and passionate one and when they eventually came up for air and looked into each other's eyes, he could see that the life and colour had returned to her face and her eyes were sparkling again.

Suddenly, they realized they weren't alone. Sally bounded into the room, cheering. 'Good-oh! Does this mean I can be a bridesmaid again? I can hardly remember the first time when you got married to Miles — I wouldn't have been much more than five.'

'Sally!' Too happy to be cross with her sister, Larissa suppressed a giggle. 'Have you been listening at keyholes again?'

15

They were soon to discover that although they were together now and sure that the problems between them were over, their mothers remained clinging to their disapproval. Unalike in so many other ways, Stella and Patsy maintained a united front, still nurturing the hope that the couple would come to their senses and part. Aside from Morgan, whom they regarded as a loose cannon, the only person who seemed happy about their rediscovered romance was Sally.

David had come to the house at Warrandyte on a Sunday, at a time when he expected the family to be gathered in the kitchen right after lunch. But even after listening to their plans, Stella remained implacable, leaving him sighing and shaking his head.

'Why can't you trust me?' he asked, exasperated at last. 'We used to be the best of friends.'

'So we were,' replied Stella, rising from her seat at the table and standing with her hands on the back of the chair. 'Before you became so unreliable.'

'Oh, Mom, how can you say that?' Larissa

broke in. 'When David has done so much with Czarina and worked so hard for you . . . '

'Of course. When it suited him.' Stella turned on her. 'You can't see the truth with those stars in your eyes. Your man here has no land of his own so he's setting his sights on mine.' She gave David a hard stare. 'And if you think you can waltz in here and take over my paddocks to build whatever you like, you've got another think coming.'

'You're so wrong, Mom.' Larissa sighed. 'It wasn't David's idea to take over some land here, it was mine. You haven't made proper use of those back paddocks for years. Surely we can come to a happy arrangement that benefits all of us? We can cross over and help one another. But if we have to use all our resources to *buy* a new place of our own — even supposing we could find one that ticks all the boxes — we won't have any money left to purchase our horses.'

'Never mind.' Stella said, eyes bright with malice. 'David came up with miraculous money before. Perhaps he can do so again.' She glanced at her watch, muttering half to herself, 'I must go and see what Brigid is doing. I can't trust that girl to do anything properly on her own.'

'Mom, please don't leave,' Larissa said. 'We

315

need to thrash this out now.'

'You don't understand.' Her mother was determined to have the last word. 'I don't need to do anything. I'm perfectly happy with things the way they are.'

'No, you're not.' Larissa was getting angry now. 'You know Brigid only works when she thinks you're looking. Basically, she's lazy and she'll have to go. But if David and I are close by, you'll have back-up all the time.'

'Larissa, I managed perfectly well without you for almost ten years. I can easily do so again. There are plenty of good girls and boys who like working with horses.' She went to leave the room, pausing to speak to David before she went out. 'And I don't expect to see you here when I come back.'

Larissa blew out a long breath when her mother had gone, wondering what could have gone so wrong.

'What's the matter with her?' she said to David at last. 'She used to think the world of you.'

'The menopause,' Sally ventured in ominous tones, having watched the escalating drama without saying anything so far. 'She's been foul to me lately. My friends say the same. Some of their mothers go quite bananas at this time of life.'

'OK. I can see no alternative, Rissa,' David

said. 'We'll have to elope. Present our mothers with a fait accompli and hope to bring them round later.'

'No-o,' Sally wailed. She had been following the conversation with mounting dismay. 'I did so want to be a bridesmaid. A proper one this time.'

'Sally,' Larissa said gently, 'I can't have a great big wedding like last time — I don't even want one. And it wouldn't be quite the thing as Miles has just died.'

'Miles!' Sally wasn't to be appeased. 'He made you miserable when he was alive and he's still casting a shadow now that he's dead.'

David was looking thoughtful. 'There could be an alternative. A compromise that will suit everyone.'

'Even our mothers?' Larissa put in eagerly.

'Oh now, don't let's get carried away.' He gave her a wry smile. 'I was thinking of Conor, up in the hills.'

'After what happened the last time? You have to be joking.'

'That wasn't his fault. And he owes us, doesn't he? We can have a discreet wedding up there with a marriage celebrant. And, if Sally still wants to be your attendant, she can.'

'I don't like the sound of 'discreet'.' Sally

317

pulled a face. 'I was hoping for music and dancing.'

'You can have music and dancing any time,' Larissa said. 'I think it has to be this way or nothing.'

'And you're not going to tell Mrs Riordan — or Mom? Won't they be twice as mad when they find out later on?'

Larissa shrugged. 'That's a risk we'll have to take. You can be my attendant and David will bring Johnnie.'

'But if you remember, we fell out. I don't think he likes me any more.'

Larissa put an arm round her sister's shoulders and gave her a shake. 'This occasion isn't about you, Sal, it's about David and me. Having said that, I'm sure Johnnie would like to forget the past and meet you halfway. But not a word to Mom about any of this.'

★ ★ ★

The only other person to whom she confided her plans was Morgan. Strangely, in spite of her initial dislike of the American woman, they had become firm friends. With the help of Miles's solicitor, Peter Mayhall, she was making good progress in the disposal of her brother's business interests and assets and she

318

was hoping to return to Los Angeles and set up her own film production company before too long. They met at what was becoming their favourite café at Southbank and Rissa lost no time in voicing her concerns.

'I can't think what's got into Mom,' she said. 'It's as if a different person is living inside her skin. This isn't like her at all.'

'Well, for one thing, she's probably disappointed,' Morgan said. 'She'd only just got used to having you home and you're talking of getting married and leaving again.'

'That's just it. I wasn't. David and I hoped to settle there with her and build a new stables of our own.'

'And did you ask her if she would like this, or just assume it?'

'She's my mother, Morgan. I thought she'd be pleased.'

'Pleased to turn over half of her land to you? And then later, when your husband has forgotten who owns it, have him telling her what to do?'

'David's not like that. He wouldn't.'

'Not *now* he wouldn't. Because he's young. What about further down the track when he's forty-five and she's pushing seventy? He'll want to take over her part of the business as well as his own.'

'I see.' Larissa sighed. 'I suppose you're

319

right. I never thought of it in exactly that way.'

'There could be another solution, you know. But it'll take quite a lot of planning on your part — as well as back-breaking hard work.'

'Tell me. Because if we don't make this deal with Mom, we'll have to shelve our plans for the moment. Maybe they're too ambitious in any case.'

'Nonsense. Nothing is ever achieved without stretching yourself — reaching out for what you want.'

'Yes, but . . . '

'I hate that word. Do you want to hear my solution or not?'

'Yes, please.'

'I'm thinking about that wreck of a place in Ringwood. The one Miles bought from his friend. I don't want it. I can't do anything with it. But I think you could. There's enough land around it for you to fence some paddocks and build a decent stables. So I'd like you and David to have it. Unless it troubles you that Miles was buried there?'

'Not at all. Because he isn't there now. You had him safely cremated and scattered the ashes in the sea.'

'Well, then? What do you think?'

'Morgan, it's so generous, but it's too

much. I'm grateful but I can't let you do this. Even without the old homestead, in today's market the land alone would be worth a fortune.'

'Larissa, I don't care. Miles left me more money than I'll ever use, even if I waste it on two production companies. Peter Mayhall has already sold the mansion in Brighton even in these tough economic times.' She laughed shortly. 'You and David should have the old wreck knocked down, get a mortgage and build whatever you want. There's an old gatekeeper's cottage you can move into short term. From memory it's in better condition than the house.'

'I can't believe you're doing this for me when I was so awful to you.'

'Not really. You were just transferring some of your anger at Miles. If it makes you feel any better, I misjudged you, too, expecting you to be the 'pretty face with no brains' that Miles usually went for.'

Morgan stood up, glancing at her watch. 'Have to go visit the lovely Mayhall. Every time I see him, he's made me more money. You get in touch with him soon. I've already asked him to set the wheels in motion to transfer the title of that old place in Ringwood to David and you.'

'Morgan, it means the world to us. I just

don't know what to say.'

'Then say nothing. Think of it as a wedding present. I shall expect an invite to the wedding, of course.'

'But there's not really going to be one. Just a simple ceremony with my sister and David's brother, Johnnie.'

'And me. Or the deal is off.'

Larissa could see that she meant it, too.

Later, she and David went to look at the property in North Ringwood and fell in love with the cottage, surrounded by native bushes and trees and alive with bird life. Surprisingly, the sweeping views from the cottage across the suburbs to the Dandenongs were even more spectacular than those from the house.

'I like the cottage just as it is,' Rissa said. 'It's made of the same solid red brick as the house and even the roof is sound. It probably needs new wiring and I'd like a new kitchen and bathroom. And when the main house is knocked down, that could be the site for our stables.'

David nodded but she could see she didn't have his full attention. He was watching an old man in a wheelchair coming slowly towards them, negotiating the potholes in the path. 'Who's that?' he asked.

'Mr Dennison!' Larissa recognized the old man when he drew close enough. She bent to kiss his cheek. 'Should you be out in this cold wind?' He already looked pale and chilled although he was warmly wrapped in scarves and with a rug across his knees.

'Larissa, my dear,' he responded warmly. 'I got someone to drive me out as I wanted one last look at the old place. I hope you don't mind.'

'Of course not.' She clasped his gloved hands. 'It was your home for so many years.' She turned to introduce David. 'This is David Riordan. We're going into partnership here.' As Dennison had been Miles's friend, she thought it more tactful not to mention their marriage plans.

'Full partnership, I hope.' The old man was quick to perceive the rapport between them. 'I always thought Miles was too old for you. Everyone did. Disgraceful of your father to marry you off to his friend.'

Larissa changed the subject, not wanting to buy into criticism of Miles and her father. 'I was so sorry to hear about Luke,' she said, watching the old man's expression falter at the mention of his son.

'It pains me to think about it and sometimes I find it hard to believe that he's gone while I'm still here. Luke had the whole of his life in front of him. I told him the house was gone and to leave well alone but he never listened to me. He should never gone to take issue with Miles.'

'I saw him at Miles's office that day,' Larissa said. 'The same day as the accident.'

'If it *was* an accident.' The old man's lips twisted with bitterness.

Larissa stared at him. This was a thought she had done her best to suppress. 'You're not saying Miles had something to do with . . . ?'

'Take no notice of me, Larissa. I shouldn't have said anything at all. Miles is gone now and so is my son. I'm getting old and fearful, with far too much imagination.' He shivered. 'I don't think I can go any further today. I should be leaving now.'

'We'll help you get back to the car,' David said, taking charge of the wheelchair so that Mr Dennison didn't have to roll the wheels himself. The old man had given them a lot to think about.

On the way back to the front gate, Mr Dennison made small talk about the various unusual shrubs in the garden, telling them which ones attracted the prettiest birds.

'I was just coming to look for you.' His driver met them, taking over the wheelchair from David. 'I was starting to worry. You've been a long time and it's getting cold.'

'I'm all right.' Mr Dennison suppressed the need to cough. 'Don't fuss so.'

'I'm not. But I know what Matron will say if I let you get pneumonia.'

Dennison waved his objections away, speaking to Rissa who had leaned forward, hugging him to say goodbye. 'I'm so glad I've seen you and your young man,' he said. 'You'll bring life and energy to the old place again. Yarraview House, like me, is too old to be saved but I know you'll make good use of the land.'

As Larissa watched his driver settle him into the back seat of the car, once more tucking his rug around his knees, her eyes pricked with unexpected tears. Mr Dennison, who had seemed so vital and full of energy during her years with Miles, seemed suddenly to have grown old and frail. The heart had gone out of him after losing his son. Somehow she knew she wouldn't be seeing him again.

'Rissa? You're upset. What is it?' David was shaking her out of her reverie. 'I thought you were happy with Yarraview Cottage, but if it's all too much, you have only to say.'

'No, David, it's fine.' She gripped his hands to reassure him. 'I was thinking that maybe William Willett and Murphy deserve what they'll get. But look at that nice old man — his son was a wastrel but he didn't deserve to lose him.'

'And you think Miles had him killed for trying to get in his way?' David voiced her thoughts.

'Who knows?' Larissa sighed. 'As Mr Dennison said, they're both dead and gone. So it doesn't matter any more.'

16

The wedding ceremony was to take place on a Wednesday evening, usually a quiet night at Conor's restaurant. Having sworn Sally to secrecy, Larissa took her to Chadstone shopping centre to choose a dress. Although Larissa herself was quickly satisfied with a simple, cream silk gown and a matching wrap from one of the department stores, Sally insisted on going to every one of the trendy shops that catered for teenagers and testing her sister's patience by trying on everything. At last Larissa insisted that it was time to choose and Sally went back to the first store they had visited and bought the very first dress she had seen — a frothy creation in blue chiffon.

'That's settled then!' Sally said brightly. 'Now we have to think about shoes.'

Larissa groaned, thinking of the many pairs of shoes she had left behind in the mansion at Brighton and which Joan Hudson had sold. Eventually she persuaded her sister that they were too tired and footsore to try on shoes that day, promising herself that next time Sally went shopping for clothes, she should do so alone.

★ ★ ★

On the night of the wedding Conor had provided a pathway of fairy lights along the drive to make it look extra festive. The room set aside for the ceremony and subsequent celebration was small and, although Larissa had assured Conor they wouldn't need many seats, ten had been provided and the room was fragrant with bouquets of freesias and white lilies in tall vases, together with trails of fresh green ivy.

Larissa and Sally were changing in the room that was later to be the couple's honeymoon suite. Morgan agreed to stay sober in order to drive Sally and John back home. Since the ceremony was to be so small and poorly attended, Larissa didn't think it mattered that there was no one to give her away. Conor phoned through to tell them that the wedding celebrant, David and Johnnie were already in place. All it needed now was for Morgan to arrive. Another half hour was to pass before she did and Conor rang again, sounding tense, telling them everyone was now present and correct.

Sally took a deep breath, fanning herself and making her sister smile.

'Look at you, Sal,' she said. 'I'm the one who should be nervous, not you.'

328

'I don't know.' Sally refused to be teased out of her mood. 'There's a funny atmosphere in the air this evening. I can't help feeling that something might go wrong.'

'Why? Everyone's here who needs to be here — even Morgan. What can possibly go wrong now?' Larissa adjusted the little white hat she had chosen to wear instead of a veil, straightened her shoulders and set off on the small woodland path leading back to the restaurant where the ceremony was due to take place. Sally followed, carrying a small posy of flowers and shaking her head. In addition to David's car and her own, Morgan's little hired car also stood waiting outside the restaurant.

'You look quite lovely, Larissa,' Conor said with a smile as he met her outside the room where the ceremony was to take place. Since they had decided to keep it simple and dispense with any traditional music, it was left to Conor to announce the arrival of the bride.

'Ladies and gentlemen!' he called out in ringing tones as he flung open the door, holding it open for Larissa to pass. 'I give you the bride!'

The room was lit only by candlelight and the first person she saw was the imposing figure of the white-haired celebrant, smiling and waiting to greet her. Then her gaze turned towards David with Johnnie beside him, supported rather perilously on two sticks. Only then did she register that there were two more women besides Morgan, standing to one side and, with a sinking feeling in her stomach, she knew immediately that Miles's twin had betrayed her. Sally's premonition was correct.

Both Stella and Patsy were standing there, straight-backed, their indignation visible even from the rear. They were still wearing their everyday clothes. Neither of them had troubled to dress for a wedding. Only Morgan, looking as if she were off to the races in a pink tweed suit, together with a huge picture hat, turned to smile at her, appearing completely relaxed.

Larissa didn't return her smile and would have backed out of the room at once had Sally not been right behind her. She closed her eyes, waiting for the storm to break over their heads in the form of angry words from her mother. Unexpectedly, it was Patsy who turned and was first to speak.

'Did you really think I would let my son get married without me? I knew something was going on — I felt it in my bones — and I knew that meddlesome woman had something to do with it.' She jerked her head towards Morgan. 'I compared notes with Stella and it didn't take long for us to get to the bottom of it — Sally dancing around the house in that fancy dress and a florist ringing up to confirm an order for flowers.'

Stella seemed unable to say anything for a moment, lips trembling and eyes swimming with tears. 'Oh, Rissa.' She spoke in a whisper at last. 'How could I let things go so wrong between us? So badly that you needed to get married to David in secret when I wasn't there?'

'Oh, Mom.' Larissa went into her mother's embrace, her own eyes filling with tears.

'Come on now, you mustn't cry.' Stella wiped away her daughter's spilled tears with her fingers and provided a tissue from her handbag. 'A bride is supposed to look radiant on her wedding day.'

Larissa took the tissue and blew her nose, too full of emotion to speak.

A tall man in his sixties and with a shock of white hair, the wedding celebrant cleared his throat to get their attention. 'Are we ready to proceed then?' he asked. 'We're already running half an hour late.'

With an anxious glance at Patsy, Larissa took her place at David's side. Her future mother-in-law might never like her but, hopefully, they could achieve some sort of truce.

It didn't take long for the bride and groom to exchange their simple vows, the wedding celebrant dashed off to another appointment and the small wedding party sat down at the round table provided.

Morgan was first to break the awkward silence that, for the moment, surrounded them.

'If this night hasn't gone according to plan, it's my fault,' she said simply. 'But I know a lot about human nature and about feuds. Miles and I endured a love-hate relationship for years. I know Larissa and David thought they would cause far less drama if they were married quietly but I had to disagree.' She shrugged. 'I acted only out of goodwill and in the best interests of all of you. A rift caused by a secret wedding would surely take much longer to heal than the little awkwardness you are feeling tonight.' She glanced around at the unsmiling faces turned towards her. 'And if I was wrong and I've made things worse than they already were, then I'm sorry.' She raised one of the glasses of champagne that Conor had been discreetly filling. 'But I hope you can open your hearts and join me in a toast to the bride and groom!'

For a moment there was silence around the table as they absorbed Morgan's sentiments. Patsy and Stella glanced at one another and stood up, raising their glasses and echoing Morgan's words in unison. 'To the bride and groom!'

After that, everyone relaxed and had a good time, enjoying the delicious paella Conor had provided for the wedding feast. Clearly, Morgan had informed him of the two extra guests as there was more than enough for everyone.

At the end of the evening, although it might have been due to the champagne, Stella and Patsy fell into each other's arms, vowing eternal friendship. Stella even invited Patsy to come to Warrandyte to help care for the horses as Brigid had taken herself off in a huff, unable to meet her employer's exacting standards.

'Sure'n I'd love to an' I'll do what I can. I've missed being around horses,' Patsy said. Then, exhibiting her arthritic fingers, 'But there's nothing I can do about this.'

'It's your brain I need, not your brawn,' Stella told her. 'You're of the old school and you know how racing stables need to be run. I want someone I can rely upon; someone who knows what they're doing around feed and who can keep an eye on the youngsters and make them toe the line.'

'Oh, I can do that all right.' Patsy grinned. 'I love bossin' people around.'

David and Johnnie exchanged glances with raised eyebrows.

At last it was time for the small wedding

party to leave. Sally had made her peace with Johnnie, who appeared just as smitten as he had been once before, although his brother quietly warned him not to let things get out of hand.

Morgan started gathering together the three women and Johnnie, ready to leave. She alone had taken very little to drink and was able to drive.

'I do hope I did right?' She took Larissa and David aside to speak to them before leaving. 'I just can't help meddling — it's in my nature.'

'You did exactly right,' said Larissa, embracing her. 'You've been the best friend anyone could wish for. And we can't thank you enough for that place at Ringwood. The demolition has already started and we're saving one or two of the old doors with stained glass to use for the office of our new stables.'

'I hope it won't hold too many bad memories for some people,' Morgan said, glancing at Johnnie.

'Don't worry.' David smiled. 'We won't take him there until everything's all shiny and new. I hope everything goes well with your new production company in the States.'

'I'm sure it will.' Morgan's smile became wicked. 'I'm looking forward to settling one or two scores with old enemies when I get back.'

'Ooh!' David said, shivering slightly as he watched the tall woman leave, shepherding her rather tipsy charges ahead of her. 'She's a wonderful friend but she could be an implacable enemy. I wouldn't care to be on the wrong side of *her*.'

'No, indeed.' Larissa said, thinking of Miles as she smiled and waved them on their way. There were times when Morgan had reminded her all too vividly of her dead brother.

While she was doing this, David collected the key to Conor's most luxurious cabin, which included a jacuzzi as well as other luxurious bath fittings.

Half an hour later, they were lying there, revelling in the warm water, fizzing up all around them.

'Don't go to sleep and drown,' David warned her as Larissa sank into the seductive bubbles.

'Why not?' she murmured. 'I'll never be happier than I am right now.'

'Are you sure?' He roused her with a bruising, passionate kiss that brought her back to full wakefulness. 'You're not sorry we're having just a few days here when we could have had a honeymoon up North in the Whitsundays, or gone to Bali?'

'No. I can't think of anything but our new venture and seeing it come to life. The thought of building new stables exactly the way we want them. Then, in the new year, we'll go to New Zealand to choose some mares to start our breeding programme . . . '

'You've thought of everything, haven't you?'

'Not entirely. After that, we have to plan our attack on England and Europe.' She eased herself into his arms, suddenly more than ready to make love again. 'It's all ahead of us, David. I can't wait for the rest of our lives to begin.'

We do hope that you have enjoyed reading this large print book.

Did you know that all of our titles are available for purchase?

We publish a wide range of high quality large print books including:
Romances, Mysteries, Classics
General Fiction
Non Fiction and Westerns

Special interest titles available in large print are:
The Little Oxford Dictionary
Music Book
Song Book
Hymn Book
Service Book

Also available from us courtesy of Oxford University Press:
Young Readers' Dictionary
(large print edition)
Young Readers' Thesaurus
(large print edition)

For further information or a free brochure, please contact us at:
Ulverscroft Large Print Books Ltd.,
The Green, Bradgate Road, Anstey,
Leicester, LE7 7FU, England.
Tel: (00 44) 0116 236 4325
Fax: (00 44) 0116 234 0205

Other titles published by
The House of Ulverscroft:

INDIGO NIGHTS

Heather Graves

Having both suffered loss, Paige McHugh and Luke Sandford are wary of trusting again. They have a comfortable working relationship as jockey and trainer; Paige knows they've no business falling in love, particularly as Luke's fiancée isn't quite his ex. However, after winning the prestigious Golden Slipper in Sydney, their emotions overtake them. But is their relationship doomed? And who is causing trouble for Paige and her grandmother? Who's behind the frightening nocturnal visits to their isolated home? Then the safety of Paige's little son, Marc, is also threatened — can the mystery be solved before tragedy strikes?